Y0-BGH-349

ANCHOR
in the WIND

BY GRETA HEMSTROM

Greta Hemstrom 2019

The front cover is an oil painting of the house the author grew up in during the 1930s and '40s, located at that time about ten miles northeast of Colby, Kansas.

© Copyright 2015 Greta Hemstrom
All rights reserved in whole or in part.
ISBN 978-0-9965828-0-3
Library of Congress Control Number: 2015946702

First Edition
Printed in the United States of America
Cover and text design by Laurie Goralka Design

For more information contact: gmhemstrom@centurylink.net

Dedication

This novel is dedicated to my mother, Kathleen Stella Sharp, a pioneer of the far-reaching prairies of northwestern Kansas in the 1930s during the Great Depression and Dust Bowl days. Out in that open expanse, there were very few amenities available to the women on those dryland farms; hard work from dawn until long after sunset was their way of life.

I hope to honor my mother by giving a peek at what her life was like. This is a work of fiction and only the name of the main character is hers. Many of the things that happen are made up by me and do not reflect upon anyone else. The story is also about my growing up on those Kansas prairies and includes some of my own feelings and experiences, as I lived in circumstances much similar to my mother's most of my life.

My mother was an example of how to keep going—even when it seemed impossible to do so—to make the best of circumstances and tough out the hard times. I see this same strength in my grown children—my sons and daughters—as they have struggled to give their children the best that they can give.

My mother died when she was forty-six and I was twenty-two. I miss her every day; I wish deeply that my children had known her and that she had known them.

This story is for you, Mom, from me, and I'll see you again in heaven.

The windmill was a device that pumped water.

Author's Note

The reader should be aware that there are no real people in this book. It is a work of fiction; the characters portrayed are entirely imaginary. I have, however, used my mother's first name and her personality for the main character. Many of the events and settings are genuine, such as the northwest Kansas area, the Dust Bowl days, the weather, and the hardships of the times—all described as best as I can recall them and from the research I conducted.

Acknowledgements

I am overwhelmed by those who encouraged me to keep writing and rewriting this story, to polish it so I would not be embarrassed to get it published. The foremost of these people is Carole London, my former publisher now retired, who read it through several times and insisted that I go forward. Even when I grew exceedingly tired of it, she constantly pushed me to finish.

A thanks to Tina McNew for the title, *Anchor in the Wind*, when I could come up with nothing suitable.

My husband has always given me space to work on this book. He listened when I grumbled, gritched, and griped, and continually assured me the book would be a good one. I thank him for that and I hope that he's right.

I appreciate my sons—Miles for saving parts of the story from a disastrous demise with his unlimited computer know-how and Van for teaching my computer a thing or two.

I thank my friends for standing by me in the death of our son, Clay. Though I went into the pits of grief, these friends did not veer away but stayed within my peripheral vision, steady and true. I also wish to thank our and Clay's musician friends, especially Jerry Hawthorne for his timely message of hope. I thank my family for standing by and being strong during the dreadful time of deep sorrow that grieved all of us. I thank Bonnie Beach for the excellent and extensive job she did editing the manuscript and Carole London for her perfect job of proofreading it.

Thanks to the Montrose County Historical Museum for allowing photographs of antiques to serve as references for illustrations in the book.

Introduction

Wheat prices were good during the 1920s, so the government encouraged farmers to grow it. It was a crop that did well in the arid environment of western Kansas and eastern Colorado. Eventually, though, farmers were so successful that there was too much wheat. Elevators couldn't handle it all, and much of it was piled on the ground where it rotted and then was no good for anything. The weather, too, was an enemy, with hailstorms and heavy rains occurring just before harvest. It wasn't uncommon for the grain to be pounded into the ground where it would mold.

The Dust Bowl days came about on the heels of the Great Depression of the 1930s. Together, these two disasters set the farmers up for a very tough time. The Dust Bowl was caused by the government's ill-advised farming practices of plowing up the buffalo grass that had kept the soil anchored for thousands of years.

Buffalo grass was resistant to drought and fed sixty thousand-plus buffalo long before the pioneers arrived. Plowed up, it left the fine, sand-like soil at the mercy of the constant prevailing west wind blowing through the prairie states. Those plowing practices, combined with the extensive drought that occurred during that time, created so much dust that it became a killer, not only to livestock but to any crop, be it a garden or field, and to humans when it clogged their lungs, resulting in dust pneumonia.

The government offered to subsidize the farmers, paying them to leave their fields fallow to lower the excess wheat supplies. The only work done was the regular discing of the fields to keep them weed-free. The subsidized money allowed the farmers to keep their farms and plant crops other than wheat. Under President Franklin Roosevelt's administration, the federal government created several agencies to educate farmers about soil conservation and antierosion techniques, which greatly improved farming practices. By 1939, after nearly a decade of dirt and dust, the drought ended when regular rainfall returned to the region.

For more detailed information, see *The Worst Hard Time* by Timothy Egan, *Rainwater* by Sandra Brown, and *Out of the Dust* by Karen Hesse.

1932

With a sigh, Kate walked out of the kitchen onto the porch and pulled herself tall, her hands on the small of her back. As she rubbed the tiredness there, she looked to the west across the flat, dry land that seemed hostile to most, but it looked beautiful to her: rich, strong, and vibrant with a free spirit that moved across it like the heat waves in the summertime. This was a lovely April morning with the small creatures in full chorus and active in the buffalo grass and weeds. The birds were in tune with the fineness of the day, and the air was warm and silky against her arms. She walked the length of the porch and back then eased herself into the comfort of her old rocker. She pulled a handkerchief from her smock pocket to pat her forehead and neck, then tucked it between her swollen breasts to absorb the pooling sweat. Leaning over her rounded stomach, she smiled at the protesting kick of the baby within, as she grabbed a handful of new peas that Billy had just picked. Placing them on the newspaper spread across her lap, she began popping the pods open and letting the glistening green peas drop with a *ping* into the bowl placed on the floor beside her rocker. The peas had come on early this year, and it would be a treat for the family to have new potatoes and peas for their noon meal.

As she sat, she made a mental note to again ask Jim to sharpen her kitchen knives, her scissors, and the garden hoe. She had almost cut her finger this morning with a dull paring knife as she peeled potatoes and chopped hash browns for breakfast. Her mind wandered now: There was something else she wanted her husband to fix, but she just couldn't remember what it was. As she pondered what that could be, she stopped her rocker in mid-motion, pea pod poised in her hand, and listened. She heard something...what was it?

With eyes closed, she sat still, her mind sorting through the sounds around her, and she heard only the everyday family noises. From the garden came the *scritch scritch scritch* of sixteen-year-old Billy hoeing the new onions, pea vines, potatoes, radishes, and other freshening vegetables, his efforts accompanied by Brownie's barking. Though Billy repeatedly ordered him to stop, the silly dog only barked louder with each scolding. In the kitchen, fourteen-year-old Evvie clanked the lids of the cast-iron kitchen range and shoved in more wood to keep the oven heat just right to evenly bake the bread. As Evvie went about her work, she made up a nonsense song for baby brother, Timothy, who pounded his highchair tray with a spoon, one of his favorite pastimes. When he did that, it always gave Kate such a headache, so she was glad it was Evvie in there with Timothy and not herself.

Opening her eyes, Kate ducked her head to look beyond the porch eave to where Jim stood—looking small on the windmill platform about thirty-five feet up—repairing gears. Between the blows of the hammer on the gears in the center of the ten-foot-diameter fan, he carried on an argument with twins Leah and Leslie on the ground below, who wanted to climb up. "Because you're only five," he told them. "Billy's sixteen. *That's* why he can climb up here." Kate knew that her chubby twin daughters would soon come complaining to her, as indignant and fiery as their red hair gave them permission to be.

Sure enough, when they realized they had lost the argument, they came fussing. She said, "If your dad told you no, then it's no. I don't want another word from either of you about it. Now, you can either pull weeds in the garden while Billy hoes or you can find something else to do." Rather than pull weeds, they skittered toward the huge oak tree and the swing that Jim had created from an old tire.

She shook her head and smiled at their retreating backs but, in their absence, the eerie uneasiness returned to her. Tuning her senses to her surroundings, she again heard nothing out of the ordinary. "Just my imagination," she said to herself, dropping more shelled peas into the bowl. When she grabbed the next handful, she received another kick of protest from her unborn child, due in a couple of months. Tired, she leaned back, closed her eyes again, and inhaled the heady fragrance of the sweet peas that climbed the porch trellis. She placed the pods onto the newspaper in her lap and gently rocked, content in the scent of prairie soil and the green wheat warming under the spring sun. She heard the prairie softly singing the eternal song of the ages—of times long gone, of living things through thousands of eons: of a history so far back and vital that it was difficult for her to comprehend how it could possibly be. She took another deep breath; it was all so beautiful and peaceful. She was drifting into a light doze when she heard Billy's horse, Cotton, whinny in the corral, and then the cattle began to low in the pasture. She sat up. A strange shifting of the breeze rippled a deep sense of unrest through her once again. She heaved herself up, laid the newspaper full of unshelled peas in the rocker seat, and walked to the porch step to call to Jim. "Do you feel that?"

"Feel what?" he yelled over his shoulder as he tightened a bolt on the windmill fan.

"Well, I don't know exactly, but there's a strange change in the breeze just now."

"Probably something you ate," he replied, smiling as he teased her a little. But then he turned and looked down at her. "Unless it's the baby. Is it? If it is, I'd better get down and get the car cranked up."

"No. Not that," she assured him, "but something."

"Well, I'll be down in a bit and have a look around. It's likely some blankety-blank livestock breaking through the fence, or a coyote howling, or skunk threatening the chickens," he shrugged his shoulders. "I'll be down to see as soon as I tighten a couple more bolts." As he turned back to his work, she heard him mutter, "Who knows what it could be. It's always something. There's *always* something going on or something to fix." He pounded the stubborn bolt home with a savage whack and secured the nut.

The sight of him stretched up like that—tall and manly, striped blue-and-gray overalls pulled tight against his body, engineer hat cocked off-center—created a pulsing heat through her. Smiling, she ran her hand over her protruding stomach to remind herself that his magnetism was why she was pregnant again. Though he was in his late forties, and had become a little heavier, and wasn't quite as agile in his middle age, to her he was still that tall, lean, dark-haired handsome man with steady blue eyes and a wide, ready smile—tough, but gentle and fair. Nodding, she walked back to the rocker but didn't sit down, for the uneasy feeling was growing. Slowly, she walked around the rocker and back to the porch railing. She looked up at him again and told herself that if Jim felt nothing in the atmosphere, then it seemed silly for her to be nervous and jumpy. But that something that he didn't feel still nagged at her. When she scanned the northwest skyline, her heart stuttered a little. She squinted at a strip of discoloration, low and sketchy along the horizon.

"Did you want me, Mama?" Evvie asked, poking her head out the screen door.

"I was talking to your dad," Kate replied absently, her eye on the brown swipe. "I wonder what that is over there," she pointed.

"I don't know, Mama," Evvie answered impatiently, "but I do know that the heat in the kitchen is awful." She stepped out, puffing out her cheeks. Timothy, fourteen months old, was astride her hip, a bottle of formula for him in her hand.

"I know," Kate replied, nodding as she continued to stare. "Stay out here and cool off a while. I'll feed Timothy." She took the baby and, with another look at the sky, noticed that the smudge had thinned. Relieved, she returned to her rocker and sat down, adjusted Timothy around her stomach, and tipped the bottle into his mouth. "Must've been a farmer burning something over there; it seems to be dying down now. Something just doesn't feel quite right, though," she puzzled, rocking in rhythm to Timmy's gulps.

"Maybe it's because you're…uh…well, you know…" Evvie stammered and, with a flush, glanced at Kate's stomach. She was embarrassed because she wasn't yet comfortable with woman-talk, but she was trying to be. "I heard Anna say that some women get fanciful during…" She paused and blushed, then said, "I better check on the bread, make sure it's not burning." She ducked back into the kitchen where she worked with a loud clanging and banging of pans.

"Maybe I *am* fanciful," Kate whispered to Timothy, smiling down at him and tweaking him under the chin. He smiled back, his teeth holding tight to the nipple of the bottle, milk seeping from the corners of his mouth. She shifted him again to a more comfortable position across her belly, though she knew that no position was going to be really comfortable. With her eyes on the horizon, she rocked and crooned an old lullaby that her mother had sung: "Too-ra-loo-ra-loo-ral, Too-ra-loo-ra-li/Too-ra-loo-ra-loo-ral, Hush, now don't you cry!" She couldn't remember if there was more to the song, so she repeated that part then ended with, "That's an Irish lul-la-by."

As she finished the song, a slither of fear rippled up her spine. Far away, so low she could barely hear it, came a hissing. Holding fast to Timothy, she lurched to her feet, ignoring the thump and rattle of his bottle as it bounced across the rough porch boards. With him squalling at her shoulder, she scurried to the north end of the porch, shielded her eyes against the sun, and gasped. Across the far-reaching fields of wheat, a smutty cloud rolled straight for their farm. The cerulean-blue sky darkened as the apparition spun closer.

"Dust storm!" she cried out to Jim, Timothy screaming in her ear. Jim glanced down at her and looked to where she pointed. He ordered the twins off the swings and to the house, yelled at Billy, and reached down for his tools. The twins squalled in terror, their plump legs pumping toward her. Billy came on the run and jumped onto the porch, Brownie at full stretch behind him. Evvie, her face stricken and white, pushed open the screen door.

"Dust storm, Mama?"

"Yes! Dust storm! Do exactly as I say and do it now," Kate ordered in a no-nonsense voice. She handed the squealing Timothy to Evvie. "Get him inside. Wet enough of your dad's kerchiefs for our faces. In the rag bag are old shirts, washcloths, and other rags to stuff around the windows. In my bedroom closet are old sheets: shake them out and hang them over the windows."

"I know, Mama," Evvie replied. "I've done it before!" She whirled and hurried inside.

"Get this stuff in the house, Billy." Kate indicated the rocker, peas, and miscellaneous items on the porch. "Leah, you and Leslie stop crying this instant, get inside, and help Evvie. I mean it! No arguing. Go!" She opened the screen door and pushed them through, oblivious to their protests. "Now stay in there and help." She grabbed the knob to the heavy inside door and snapped it shut behind them.

Kate let the screen door slam behind her and ran to the porch edge to see what was keeping Jim. When she looked up, she couldn't believe her eyes: He was still up there on the windmill platform! That he would be reaching up to secure another bolt was beyond comprehension. What in the world was he doing?!

"Get down from there, Jim! Get down!" she shouted over the increasing noise of the wind. He waved, securing the hammer in the loop on the side of his overalls and settling his hat.

In an instant the sky filled with chattering birds. They fluttered nervously in the locust tree and on the ground. The dark cloud now blotted the brassy sun. A gritty breeze kicked up little dust devils, scattering the birds like dry leaves. The yard gate swung back and forth, sounding out a nerve-racking squeal on its hinges. Tumbleweeds spooled across the yard and clung tightly to the woven-wire fence. The birds flew off in a frenzy to escape.

Through grit in her eyes, she squinted up at Jim. "Jim! What are you doing?!" As he stepped across the wooden platform to the ladder and placed his foot on the top rung, a sudden gust spun the windmill fan around, and the whipping tail slammed him across his back. He teetered, missed the first rung, and toppled over.

"No!" Kate screamed, watching in horror as he flung out his arms, clawing for something to grasp. The wind caught him, twisted him about, and snapped his legs over his head. He fell head over heels, his cry trailing him like a spiraling banner. In slow motion, Kate clearly saw him look at her. There was fear in his eyes, but there was also a knowing in his face. She felt paralyzed as she saw him twist and turn like a puppet on tangled strings.

He landed with a soft thud, puffs of dust billowing around him— dust that the wind swept away as though it were nothing. He moved once and then lay still. She wanted to run to him but couldn't. Billy tore by her calling, "Dad! Dad!" She grabbed at his shirt, but he ripped loose, leaning into the wind until his image grew dim in the thickening dust. Realizing that he would get lost, she took one step after him, and another, and then ran down the steps. Evvie pushed by her, hauling Timothy on her hip, her long hair a dark wind-tangle around her and the baby. Kate seized her arm and hung on. The twins tugged at her skirt, then hid their faces against her legs. "Mommy, Mommy! Daddy fell!"

"Get back in the house, Evvie," she ordered sternly, "and take these children with you. I'll see to your dad. Do not come out, do you hear me?" She pointed them to the door. When she saw that Evvie was doing as she was told, she turned, her heart thudding, and started to run.

Driving dust pellets stung her arms and legs. The wind whipped and twisted her smock up around her breasts. She couldn't move fast enough. Her feet felt heavy, as if she were in a nightmare and running through a gummy quagmire. As she ran, holding her stomach with both hands, she wondered if they could find their way back, or if she and Billy could carry Jim to the house where she could tend his injuries. She stumbled blindly on until she ran smack into Billy, where he squatted next to his dad. She pushed him aside and knelt down. "Get to the house, Billy! Get to the house and call Grant."

"I think Dad is dead, Mom." His face screwed up in terror, Billy hunkered back on his haunches. "Dad's dead, Mom. He's dead. My dad is dead," Billy repeated over and over, trembling.

"Billy! I said go call Grant! Your dad is *not* dead, but we need to get him into the house. Go call Grant! Now! Follow the fence so you won't get lost."

When Billy didn't move, she shook him. As if hypnotized, he looked at her vacantly. "My dad is dead, Mom. He's dead." She slapped him. That she had done that shocked her as much as it did him, for she had never done so, but the thought that Billy might be right was one she couldn't face.

"He is *not* dead, I tell you! Now *go!*" Billy glared at her, his face dark with pain. Rivulets of tears mixed with dirt ran to the corners of his mouth. Slowly he stood, turned, and then ran for the house, ignoring her instructions to follow the fence line. She was relieved to hear that Evvie was ringing the dinner bell, a sound he could follow.

Kate turned back to Jim. He lay like a crumpled and discarded rag doll that had been pitched in a fit of temper. With one blue eye open, he stared up. The other eye was closed. His face was contorted, surprised. His dark hair sprung out like railroad spikes; his fingers, hooked like talons.

"Jim, can you hear me?" Tentatively, afraid she might add to his injuries, she touched his shoulder. When he didn't respond, she gently laid her hand on his chest to feel for a heartbeat, then jerked back in horror when his bones grated under her fingers. Not believing what she knew to be true, she put her ear over his heart. She heard nothing but death.

A scream welled up from deep inside. When his hand flopped into her lap, the scream ripped from her throat and tore through the top of her head. It twisted and turned on the wind like dark blood streaming onto the prairie, staining it red. She stood up. She shrieked at the windmill and then at the wind. In her anguish, Kate's screaming grew and fed upon itself. She began to tear her smock into shreds, throwing the tatters into the howling, gaping, sucking mouth of the wind. She tore at her hair and watched as the wind twisted its strands into stringy snakes, slithering and gone.

She could follow. She could be gone. The wind could fly her away from where Jim lay…fly her to a place where he waited, out there in the stinging dust. She could call his name; he would answer. Was that him calling her? "Don't move! I'm coming!" she shouted. The wind swirled her words around and back into her mouth, filling it with powdery dust. "I'm coming!" she cried out, her voice raspy. She ran clumsily toward him, stumbling in the furrows of the fallow field. On and on she ran until she could run no more. Gasping for air, dust filling her mouth, she dropped to the ground, hoping the wind would blow until she was completely covered and buried forever. Forever.

Beyond the wind, she heard Brownie barking and voices close at hand. Someone turned her over, lifted her head. Grant's voice came to her through the fog. "Here's some water, Kate." He put the canteen to her lips and let water dribble in. She sputtered, choked, and gagged on the mud in her mouth. Grant sat her up so she could spit it out. He wiped her chin and gently dribbled another bit of water past her lips. This time she swallowed and let more and more water slide down her parched throat.

Though her eyes refused to open, her mind saw Grant Sloan, a six-foot tall cowboy from Wyoming who had come to work for her father one summer and had fallen for her sister, Betty. He was gentle but physically tough and strong, hardworking, soft spoken, honest, kind, and preferred to ride his horse instead of a tractor. As he lifted her, he said, "We'll get you home, Kate. Don't worry. We'll get you home."

"Wet this kerchief, Billy, and I'll wipe her face," Kate heard him say. Gratefully, she breathed in the cool dampness of the cloth as he carefully cleaned her face and tied a wet cloth over her mouth and nose to breathe through. "Is she all right, Uncle Grant?" Billy asked. "She's not gonna die, is she?" She heard the catch in his voice. Her heart went out to him, but she couldn't summon the strength to open her eyes or move at all; the wind blew too heavily against her soul.

"She's not going die, no, but I reckon she's not good either," Grant said. "Get back, Brownie," he ordered the dog. "We've got to get her into my saddle, so help me with that." Grant's voice echoed in her head as though in a rain barrel. While Brownie barked and barked, they hefted her sideways behind the saddle horn. Grant's horse stepped around nervously, bridle jingling. "Whoa, Badger," Grant soothed. "It's okay, old boy. It's just another passenger for you to carry." Badger nickered in answer and quieted down.

"While I get aboard, Billy, you just hold her there," Grant said. He swung on behind her and placed his arm around her to steady her weight. "Okay, Billy," he raised his voice against the wind. With his mouth too close to her ear, the sound reverberated behind her eyes. "Get on your mare and we'll let these horses and Brownie find their way back to the barn. Pull that kerchief back up around your nose and mouth," he instructed. "I'll do the same." She felt Grant adjust the damp cloth around her nose and mouth, then he murmured to her, "Don't want you breathing anymore dust than you already have, Kate. You shore don't need dust pneumonia on top of everything else that's happened." But she wasn't too concerned about pneumonia: She just wanted to go home and crawl into bed with Jim and sleep. With a grunt, Grant adjusted his hold on her and urged his horse forward with a soft, "Find the way, Badger." The saddle horn jabbed her in the ribs and, when she groaned with each step, Grant shifted her and stuffed something soft between her and the saddle horn.

🐎 🐎 🐎

In the pitch-dark of night, Kate woke in the softness of their bed. She wondered how she got there, but then she heard the wind rattling the shingles of the roof. *Jim must get those nailed down before they blow off*, she thought. Through the closed windows, dust sifted in like the skittering of tiny mouse feet. She felt awful, like she had the flu or something. She reached back for Jim but found no comforting warmth from his body or an imprint in his pillow. *He's just gone out to the toilet, that's all,* she told herself; *he'll soon come in and snuggle up against me. In just a little while, he'll be right here.* She drifted off, stirred, and felt for him again. *Why would he be gone this long?* She raised her head, listened, but heard nothing except the wind and the flapping of the shingles, her head pounding in rhythm with them.

Supporting her stomach with her hands, she sat up and thought she caught the sound of him mouthing his tuneless rendition of "My Bonnie Lies over the Ocean," which he always annoyingly repeated over and over on his way back from the outhouse. She held her breath and cocked her head; nothing—nothing but the eternal wind. Even if he were singing, the wind would blow the words away and she wouldn't hear him. He had been gone too long; she'd better get up to check on him.

She slid off the bed but when her tingling, unsteady feet touched the floor, her legs buckled and she staggered to a chair, which toppled and hit the floor with a loud clatter. She grabbed the edge of the dresser and heard bare feet slapping across the kitchen linoleum. Her older sister, Betty, came scurrying through the door carrying a kerosene lamp, her blonde hair braided into a waist-length plait that swung to and fro across her broad back. Betty was two years older and three inches taller than Kate, somewhat heavy—not fat—but definitely carrying a few extra pounds. It was Betty's nature to take charge of situations in a no-nonsense manner. As sisters growing up together, they had always been close. Even when Kate's refusal to yield to Betty's bossiness caused friction at times, they had remained the best of friends, in spite of it.

Betty's flannel nightgown swished against her legs as she hurried toward her. "Kate, what are you doing? You're not supposed to be up, you know," Betty scolded as she set the flickering lamp on the dresser. She righted the chair and took Kate's arm. "I've never seen the likes of this wind and it's getting on my nerves, to say the least! Come on, now, let's get you back to bed. With all this noisy rummaging around, you'll

wake everybody up. It's the middle of the night," she chided, and then
hesitated. "Oh, maybe you need to use the pot. Here, I'll help you."

"No, I don't need the chamber pot, Betty," Kate declared in a
raspy voice. She pulled her arm away, then leaned shakily against the
dresser. "What're you doing here?"

"Well, I'm staying over for a day or two until you get back on
your feet," Betty answered, tugging the bedcovers straight then turning them back. "Now back to bed with you." She reached out for
Kate.

Outhouses preceded indoor plumbing on farms in the 1930s.

"Back on my feet? I'm not sick," Kate protested. "I feel groggy but otherwise, just fine. I got up to go out and check on Jim. He went to the outhouse and has been out there too long. Maybe he fell or something." With a stunned expression, the blood drained from Betty's face, and seeing that, Kate felt her insides twist and turn cold. "What's wrong?" she asked, but deep inside she knew, and a terrible trembling started at her very core. She pushed back the memory of Jim falling, of her running in the dust storm, of Grant and Billy finding her. She tried to bury it, but she saw it all in Betty's face.

"Kate…" Betty said softly, "you were lost in the dust storm yesterday. Grant and Billie found you and brought you back here in bad shape, and I put you to bed. We'll talk more about this tomorrow but for now, just go back to bed," she urged. Her blue eyes filled with deep compassion as she gently eased Kate under the quilt and patted her cheek. "You need to rest," she said. "Doctor Jensen said to give you this to help you sleep, if necessary. And I think it is necessary. So—here now. Swallow." Betty spooned a vile-tasting liquid into Kate's mouth, and though she sputtered and gagged, she took it willingly. She wanted sleep—she wanted to blot out what she knew and what Betty had said. The darkness of the medicine invaded her brain. She wanted forever not to wake in the light of tomorrow, but she knew it would all be there when the next day came.

"Rest, Kate. Call me if you need me." Betty smoothed the covers again. She picked up the lamp and went out, closing the door softly behind her.

The wind and dust slithered into the inky corners of Kate's mind, then the dream came in on the moaning of the wind—the haunting dream of Jim falling, falling, falling; the screaming wind, the sky wild and dark, the world spinning like a top. She shrieked and Betty came running. "It's all right, Kate. Shh, shh, shh, it's all right." She crawled in beside Kate, holding her close, whispering soothingly. With Betty's arms around her, Kate drifted into sleep, sobbing.

Kate stirred. Squinting one eye against the morning light that streamed through her east window, she sat up then fell back, eyes closed. The *thwack thwack thwack* of hammering coming from some-where close outside sent orange flashes of piercing pain against her eyelids. "Oh, please. Stop," she mewed, holding her throbbing head in her hands. Added to that outside noise was the clang and bang of stove lids, pots, and pans, mixed with the aroma of coffee, bacon, and the soft talk of several women in the kitchen. *What are a bunch of women doing in my kitchen this early in the day?* she wondered. And her, still in bed! She sat up, but when her head exploded with excru-ciating pain, she eased herself back down and reached for Jim's pil-low to clap it over her head. But all the racket seemed to intensify: the pounding from outside and the kitchen clatter—chatter, clatter, chatter.

Finally, she flung aside the pillow and covers, edged over to the bedside, and carefully sat up, her feet dangling. Waiting for the room to stop spinning, she slid off, grasped the iron bedstead—its chipped, white paint rough under her hand—and stood up. When she thought her legs would hold her, she took a tentative step, and then another. Her stomach lurched. She grabbed the chamber pot from under the bed and threw up, the baby inside her kicking in protest. When the gagging eased, she sat back down on the bed, chamber pot close at hand. As she sat, blinded by her headache and her stomach whirling, Betty bustled through the door.

"Oh, my! Oh, good land! I *thought* I heard you!" Betty exclaimed. "You shouldn't be up, Kate. Here, let me hold that for you." She reached for the slop jar as Kate vomited again. "Now, see? You've made yourself sick," Betty accused as she tucked a hairpin back into her blonde braid, which today encircled her head like a crown. Her voice and blue eyes turned stern as she helped Kate stand. "Doctor Jensen said for you to stay in bed for a day or two so the baby wouldn't come early." She returned Kate to the bed and patted the covers smooth once again.

By that time, there was a palpable roaring in Kate's ears. "This baby is going to come right now if you don't stop that noise from outside and from the kitchen!" she said through her teeth. "Stop the noises. Please!"

"Oh, my goodness," Betty repeated, scowling. "I told Grant to have those men build that coffin in the barn or shop, away from the house. I can't believe they would do that right outside your window. Men just have no sense," she huffed. "I'll be right back." Kate heard the screen door slam as Betty went out. Though she couldn't hear the words, she could discern Betty's higher-pitched voice and the low murmuring of the men as they gradually moved away from the house. In a few minutes, when Betty entered the bedroom with a glass of water, the noise from outside had stopped.

"Oh, yes, the quiet is wonderful," Kate sighed and relaxed a little. But after a brief pause, she sat up and took the offered glass of water. "And now," she took a drink and looked at Betty, "just who are those people in my kitchen making all *that* noise?" She took another sip.

"Why, it's the women from our Ladies' Aid Club. They've come to prepare the meal for after the funeral," Betty replied. "That's their husbands out there working on the coffin."

Kate choked and spilled the water. Betty took the glass and started mopping up the mess with a rag. Though she had heard it earlier, Kate had let the word "coffin" slide by, but now that both "funeral" and "coffin" had been uttered, the whole impact of what was going on came roaring back to her. The rippling tremors started again, and with them came a dreadful pain in the left side of her heart. She suddenly asked, "When is the funeral?"

"At eleven today," Betty replied softly.

Kate glanced at her alarm clock. "It's ten o'clock now!" she exclaimed. She hurriedly moved to swing her legs over the edge of the bed. When she stood, the awful pain in her heart traveled down and across her back, and her knees almost buckled.

"I'm so sorry," Betty murmured, clutching Kate's arm to ease her back into bed.

"No," Kate said firmly and jerked her arm loose from Betty's grip. Standing her ground, shaky though she was, she said, "You weren't going to tell me?"

"The doctor gave strict orders for you to stay in bed to prevent a premature birth," Betty replied. "After all, you still have a couple of months before this baby is due, you know."

"I don't care what the doctor said. I am going to my husband's funeral today. Just get me some aspirin and find my black maternity skirt and smock in the closet." She bent over in intense pain, her hand pressing against the soft side of her back. She hoped that the baby wasn't really coming today.

Betty left and came back with two aspirin and more water. As she handed them to Kate, a gentle knock came at the door. When Betty opened it a crack, one of the women—Elmira Johnson—wanted to know if everything was all right and could the women come in. Kate could hear them murmuring in the background, and when Betty looked back at her, she shook her head. Betty assured Elmira that all was well and that Kate was getting dressed for the funeral. "You can see her then," she said, gently closing the door. She found Kate's black skirt and smock in the closet and laid them on the bed.

"You go on out, Betty," Kate said. "I'll get ready by myself. Thank you for not letting them in. I don't want to see anyone right now."

"Well…all right," Betty sighed. She slipped out the door and, as she was closing it, said, "Ladies, everything's fine. Kate wants to be alone for now. Let's get back to the meal and finish it up."

Slowly, Kate slid the slip down over her shoulders and stomach and then buttoned the smock over it. Grabbing the bedstead, she stepped into her maternity skirt and tied the strings across the circular cut-out in front, fashioned to accommodate her bulging stomach. While she dressed, she tried to remember being rescued by Grant and Billy from the dust storm, but couldn't recall any of it. Trying to ignore the quiet discussion she heard through the closed door about her "delicate condition" and "at this terribly trying time," she bent over with a grunt to tie her shoes. Then she heard Roberta Reese say, "What will the poor thing do? She'll be all by herself with those five children—and expecting another! How will she manage?"

Kate heard several subdued replies, none of which she really wanted to know. She wished everyone would just go away and leave her alone without all the hovering, watching, whispering. She wasn't a weak, simpering, helpless woman; she and the children would go on. But then she thought of Jim not being around, and that reduced her to silent, rolling tears…tears she tried desperately to control, because she didn't want anyone feeling sorry for her or saying, "Jim is in a better place, you know" or "God has a plan for you and everything is going to be all right." Jim was in a better place than right here with her and his family? God had a plan for her? What kind of plan would be possible without Jim? How dare anyone say that to her! How utterly insensitive!

When she finished dressing, Kate combed her hair and looked at her image in the mirror. She was appalled at the pale agony reflected there. *Maybe a little rouge would help,* she thought, so she scrounged in the top drawer of the old dresser to find the small round container, swiped the red color with the pad, and dabbed some of it high on her cheekbones, which made her resemble a circus clown. She grabbed one of her hankies and rubbed vigorously until most of it was gone. She looked at her reflection again and shook her head in resignation, then muttered, "I am what I am," and turned away.

Straightening her spine, she took a deep breath, opened the door, and walked into the kitchen full of women, who immediately hushed their gossip and looked at her. Some wore pity, which she didn't like, and some showed deep concern, which she shunned because it turned her heart to liquid, and she didn't want to cry. Out of duty, she felt, they all approached her with condolences, which Kate acknowledged through a stiff smile. She turned to Betty.

"Is Jim in the spare room?"

"Yes," Betty nodded, "I'll go with you."

"No, thank you. But send in the children." As she walked toward the room, the distance to the closed door seemed miles away and her legs felt like sticks. The women remained quiet, but an uncertain rustling revealed their restless curiosity. She wondered if she could make it inside the door without crumbling, but she stiffened her knees and took step after step until she turned the knob and pushed the door open.

The spare room, which was used mostly for storage and infrequent guests, was stuffy and smelled strongly of furniture polish and floor wax. The double bed where Jim lay took up most of the space. The bed and the large dresser against the wall left just a narrow path in which to walk. The chintz curtains were tied back, cobwebs knocked down, and the linoleum clean. Light from the room's one window fell across Jim's body.

She closed the door behind her and walked to where he lay in his best suit, his hair combed back and his face pale and still. When she rested her hand on his chest, he felt cold and stiff, as hard and lifeless as a rock. To keep from fainting, she grabbed the bedstead and slid to her knees, crying in great gulping sobs. As she gradually began to feel calm, she heard activity outside the room; when the door opened, Betty ushered in the children.

"Here they are, Kate. Do you want me to stay?"

"No, just close the door behind you." Kate straightened her back, adjusted her hair, and wiped at the tears.

With the excitement of finally seeing their mother, the twins ran in but stopped at the sight of their dad on the bed. They edged up and stood silently beside her, then clung to her legs. Though her heart ached for them, she could only put her arms around them, saying nothing. With great resolution, Kate turned to face her children. Evvie, holding wide-eyed Timothy, stepped timidly to her and leaned against her, tears flowing. But Billy stood alone, staring dry-eyed out the window, his face set and stony. "Billy," she said, untangling herself enough to motion him into the family circle. He turned and shook his head, cold eyes defiant.

"Don't shut me out, Billy," she pleaded quietly.

"My dad's gone," he said, "and you can't do anything about it. I'll never see him again."

She nodded but couldn't form an answer. Her scrambled thoughts were interrupted by a knock on the door. "See who it is, Evvie," Kate said, but it opened just then.

"It's time to go," Betty said as she poked her head in.

The rest of the day was a blur of scenes: walking through the kitchen with the children while the women stood back and murmured; climbing the hill to the family graveyard, which held her and Jim's parents, two infant children, as well as Jim's five-year-old brother—and now it waited for Jim. The lowering of Jim's casket into the newly turned earth, taking up the shovel for the first soil upon his coffin, the walk back down the hill, the large potluck meal for relatives and friends, where everyone laughed and joked as if it were a party while she sat in the bedroom with Betty and close neighbors, Maxine and Dorothy, listening to the festivities, unable to eat—it was all a huge blur. At the end of the day, it was a relief when everyone finally said their goodbyes except Grant, Betty, and their children.

Grant and his son, Jack, age fourteen, helped Billy with the chores that evening, after which it was decided that Grant and Jack would go home to do their chores while Betty and the children—Emma, sixteen, and Kenneth, six—would stay the night. Grant would return the next morning to help Billy with the outside chores while Jack stayed behind to tend to theirs. Kate agreed with the plan, though she really didn't want the noise of the children and busyness of Betty. All she really wanted was to be left alone, to climb into a hole and pull it in after her, but she realized that the children needed relief from the sorrow and grief. She knew, too, that she was still in a weakened condition from being lost in the dust storm and the funeral, and it would be good to have Betty and her daughter around to help Evvie with the household.

The part of the day that she would remember best and cherish forever happened while the service was going on. As the crowd of friends and neighbors stood in the burial plot, the stiff breeze sweeping her lacey black smock to and fro, she heard the contented gurgling of her two infants who had died just ten months apart between the births of Evvie and the twins. As the men lowered Jim's casket into the dark hole, Kate heard his infectious laughter close at hand. When she looked up, she saw him as real as life. He was just beyond the fence, a baby held close in each arm: together and happy. He waved to her, nodded, and then carried their babies, James William and Ina Glenyce, across the top of the wheat, as though he was walking on water, then they faded away. Knowing that they waited for her caused a warmth to flush throughout her body, easing the piercing agony. Someday they would be together again in that land far away.

At noon the next day, Betty and the girls warmed up some of the food brought in by neighbors. Though Betty's bunch ate with savor and much chattering, Kate and her children ate in relative silence. Nauseous at the sight of all the food, Kate took up a small plate for Timothy. She mashed green beans and scalloped potatoes with her fork, placed a tiny portion of red Jell-O on it, and set the plate on Timothy's highchair tray, where he spooned it into his mouth as best as he could. From Evvie's green-tinged face, Kate knew that her stomach was rebelling, too. Though Billy's appetite was not as ravenous as usual, he kept his head down and focused on eating his food. He seemed to enjoy the variety of casseroles and desserts, a change from their usual fare of meat, potatoes, and gravy. The twins, of course, were as picky as always, but they would be hungry by suppertime, and then they would eat.

By the third day of Betty and her children being around all the time and Grant most of the time, Kate was finished with it all. She wanted only to be alone with her family; she needed time to think. So, over the noisy breakfast table, she gently told Grant and Betty that she felt it was enough. "I've really appreciated your help and I'm beholden to you, but the children and I should begin to take care of things by ourselves."

When Betty started to protest, Grant interrupted. "Kate's right. We need to go home and see to our things. Billy is strong and able do the chores; Evvie is a wonder at housework. Kate needs time to figure out what she's going to do. But," he added, "I'll come over every day or so to check on how you're doing." Kate nodded her gratitude. He nodded back.

"I think Kate needs more help," Betty objected. "She's been through a lot in the last couple of weeks."

"We're only a phone call away if she needs us," Grant said. "She needs some space and time."

"Well…all right," Betty relented reluctantly. "But me and the children would like to come over with Grant on occasion, if that's all right with you, Kate. We'll have a cup of coffee and the children can have some fun together."

"Of course," Kate nodded, "please, do come when you can. I'll need your suggestions and ideas." She knew that Betty wouldn't make it too often because she carried a heavy load of work in her own house. "Thank you for taking the time to help me with the funeral, chores, and all."

"Well," Grant said as he finished the last sip of his coffee, "we'll leave right after we get done outside." He stood, laid a hand on Kate's shoulder as he walked by, and motioned for Billy and Jack to come with him.

There was very little talk as Kate, Betty, Evvie, and Emma cleaned up the kitchen, swept the floors, straightened the house, and made the beds, while the younger ones entertained themselves in the living room. Kate could tell that Betty was sad and miffed, because she usually kept up a running conversation about any and every little thing that popped into her head. This morning, though, Betty went about quietly, keeping her own counsel. After the house was straightened and the two of them began dividing up the bounty of food brought in by friends and neighbors, Kate said, "I hope you're not upset with me, Betty, but it's time for us to begin on our own routine. You're only six or seven miles away and, like Grant said, I can call if I need you. You're worried about us, I know, but we'll be fine."

"Yes, I hope you will, but's it's all so sad that I can hardly bear to think about it. How will you handle it all?"

"Well…somehow, someway, I'll succeed in keeping this place and this family together," Kate responded, halfway wondering just who she was trying to convince. "Now, let's load up this food while Grant and the boys are finishing the chores. The children can help us, and then you can get back to your home and your life."

After the food was loaded, Grant, Betty, and family left for home, much to the relief of Kate and the kids, who jumped around, hollered, and did the dance of joy. They were glad to have their own beds and rooms back to normal.

When the supper dishes and the chores were done and the full moon was just rising, Kate picked up Timothy and started up the hill to the graveyard: The twins, somewhat subdued by Kate's somber mood, soon caught up with her, and Evvie and Billy followed along behind. As they walked, Evvie quietly shared her thoughts and feelings with Billy. "All those people," she said, "they laughed like the dinner was a party. With our dad gone, I thought it was shameful and disgusting. I didn't feel like laughing, for sure. Did you?" she asked.

"Huh," was the only thing Billy said. It was a sullen response.

When they reached the graveyard, Evvie went ahead and held open the sagging iron gate. The twins, forgetting to be subdued, skipped through first, hand in hand. After Evvie and Kate had passed through, Kate handed Timothy to Evvie and waited for Billy to catch up with her. Ignoring her, he walked through, latched the gate, and went on. Puzzled, she caught up with him and asked what was troubling him. With eyes on the ground, he mumbled, "Nothing," and walked on ahead. She looked at his back, shook her head, and considered what the problem might be.

"Billy," she said as she followed him. He turned and glared at her, then walked on and plopped down on the old rusted iron bench.

"Leave me alone, Mom. Just leave me alone," he muttered as she placed her hand on his shoulder.

"All right," she said, then walked to the gravesite.

Seeing the newly turned soil atop Jim's grave cut viciously through her; she reached out for the back of the other iron bench, eased her awkward body onto it, and took Timothy from Evvie. He wanted down, so she steadied him on his uncertain legs. Billy sat across from her and Evvie leaned against her, sobbing. The twins gathered close and wailed, though they didn't really understand what was going on. Timothy tottered back to her, his arms raised to be picked up. He cried because Evvie and the twins were crying.

"Hush, now," Kate said quietly. "Look up. Do you see the man in the moon? Do you see him smiling at us? He's happy because we can see his happy face. He likes us."

Evvie wiped her eyes, looked up, and nodded. Billy sat, head down, brooding.

"I see him," Leah sniffled. "Do you, Leslie?"

"Me, too," she responded with a smile in her voice.

Timothy pointed up and jabbered something that pertained to the moon and then giggled.

With the children quieted, Kate began to tell them stories of their father…stories of how—long before he knew Kate—he had proved up the 160-acre homestead between his parent's place, who had migrated from Nebraska years before, and the homestead of Kate's parent's, who had arrived from Missouri shortly after Jim's parents. She went on with how she had met him at a barn dance, when she was at the end of her senior year at Gem High School. A month later he had asked her to marry him, and she was just nineteen that June when the Justice of the Peace in Goodland, Kansas, performed the wedding ceremony. Her parents had opposed the marriage because Jim was

ten years her senior, which they felt was too much of an age difference. He was quite a rounder, too, they said, but against their wishes,
she had said yes. She and Jim began their life together on the stark
Kansas prairie, where the unbroken horizon reached forever across
acres and acres of buffalo grass, wheat fields, and pastures. This expanse
was interrupted only by sparsely scattered homesteader's houses, a few
trees, and windmills that stood gaunt against the open sky.

As she remembered aloud to the children, the locusts began their
nightly whirring. Kate listened for a while, and then continued by
telling them about the two babies born between Evvie and the twins.
There was sickly Ina Glenyce, who lived only three months before
dying, and then ten months later, feeble little premature William, who
had struggled for a week before dying in her arms one night. Both had
been born with the same fair skin and thick, coppery-colored hair as
Billy and the twins.

As Kate talked softly into the night, the children dozed off until
only she was awake with Timothy on her lap: The twins leaned against
her, Billy was on the ground, and Evvie had curled up on the other
bench. Looking at the first stars, she recalled that long-ago quiet evening under the moon when Jim had brought her to this half section of
land to show her his holdings. Tall, with dark-brown hair and piercing
blue eyes, he had swept her up in his dream of dryland farming, of
growing wheat that produced ten bushels to the acre—even as much
as thirty in a good year. It was then he had asked her to marry him.
When she immediately said yes, he picked her up and swung her
around until she was giddy. He had kissed her soundly and set her on
her feet, then said, "We'll have a big family and be rich, Kate. It'll be
a great life." He had laughed that full laugh of his and had kissed her
again.

She had been beautiful back then at about five feet tall with black
curly hair and dark eyes. She barely reached Jim's shoulder. Many
times he had said that she was no bigger than a bar of soap after a hard
day's washing. But, oh, the work she had done. She had loved the life
they had: the work, work, and work they did together to make the
farm pay. Every year, year-and-a-half, or two years she had birthed a
child and did what it took to keep them healthy and growing. Now,
at thirty-eight, she was no longer that youthful, beautiful woman. She

ran her work-worn hands over her bulging stomach, thinking how her small figure had grown more pear-shaped with each child. The ceaseless Kansas wind had whipped the curl from her hair, which had faded to gray with the passing years and now required a permanent wave to replace that natural curl. Looking at the sleeping children, she wondered if she could make it alone.

The big, full moon cast a brilliance across the land's lonely openness, and though many people felt lost in all that space, she felt at home in it. It was beautiful to her—rich, strong, and glorious, full of a wild spirit that seemed to move across it. She and Jim had both felt that unalterable sense of freedom. Now, here she was without him, alone with the children and without his foresight. She sighed and looked up again, remembering their years together as they created a life for themselves and these beautiful children—and one more coming! "Oh, Jim, I miss you so. Why couldn't you have gotten down from the windmill when I first warned you? Why?" There was no answer. She looked at the man in the moon, but there was no answer there, either. It soon ducked behind an errant cloud, and the stars winked at her with the secret answer

With another sigh, she wiped the tears from her cheeks. She gently shook Evvie awake and called softly to Billy. With Evvie carrying Leslie, Billy carrying Leah, and Kate carrying Timothy, they trudged home in the moon's shadows. As she put Timothy to bed, Evvie and Billy saw to the twins, and then the three of them said goodnight. Gratefully, she climbed into her own bed, the family secure in theirs.

She was restless—tossing, turning, legs jerking. When she finally fell asleep, she dreamed of Jim spinning and grasping for something to hang onto, of him hitting the ground in a cloud of dust. She sat up, heart racing. When her whirling senses settled, she realized it was just a terrible dream, but a true one that would haunt her for the rest of her life. Knowing she wouldn't get back to sleep, she made her way to the kitchen, perked coffee, and paced the floor, holding the hot cup in her cold hands against her chest. Her mind was a mess of black thoughts: anger at his carelessness, terrified at what had happened, feeling that she wasn't going to make it and that she was going crazy, and fearful that she couldn't manage the farm and the children alone. She swallowed an aspirin, fixed some hot milk with toast, and went back to bed, hoping she could sleep until the morning light beamed in her window.

About three o'clock, she woke in a drenching sweat, heart pounding and the covers twisted tightly around her. She struggled out of them and got up again, threw Jim's old shirt around her shoulders, and went to check on the sleeping children. Striking a match to the lantern that hung by the back door, she went out to the toilet and came back, entered the house, and walked around—looking out the windows at the disappearing moon—and finally crawled into bed again, only to toss and turn for what seemed like hours. When she finally dozed off, the same dream haunted her. Realizing that sleep was impossible, she got up, tiptoed to the kitchen, and added kindling to the embers in the range. As the stale coffee heated, she kept thinking about how to start this day without Jim. The silent weeping began again and, from past experiences, she knew it wouldn't stop for hours; tears would just seep out and run down her face with no sound. Because she would be crying, she knew the twins and Evvie would cry, too. But for them, she would get through this one day, and then the next day and the next, and someday she'd wake one morning and maybe—just maybe—the pain would be manageable. But right now, it just didn't seem possible. She wiped at her eyes, took a deep breath, straightened her spine, and whispered to herself, "I can do it. I can do it. I *must do it*, for me and the children."

Billy soon came out of his bedroom dressed for chores. As he grabbed the milk bucket, he didn't speak at all but headed for the barn to milk before it was time to catch the bus. She heard Evvie fussing at the twins to get dressed and stop squabbling with each other. Timothy, for some reason, hadn't yet awakened. Wiping her eyes for the hundredth time, Kate stuffed the wet handkerchief into her smock pocket, poured herself another cup of coffee, and placed the large skillet on the hot stove. She arranged the bacon in it, cracked the eggs and beat them with a fork, and took a look at the biscuits browning in the oven. By the time the school bus stopped for Evvie and Billy at a little past seven thirty, breakfast was over and Kate had cleared the table.

After she combed the twins' hair, she picked Timothy up, strad-dled him across her hip, and went out to look at her garden, the twins skipping along beside her. Though covered with dust, the rad-ishes, carrots, beets, onions, potatoes, and green beans were doing well. Grant, Jack, and Billy had watered a couple of times in the last week, but everything needed water again. She would remind Billy to do that today. In her mind's eye, she clearly saw Jim hauling buckets of water to the garden the day he had died, and that picture brought on a fresh seepage of tears.

"Why are you crying, Mommy?" Leah asked.

"Oh, I'm crying because your daddy isn't here and I miss him." She wiped the tears with the hem of her smock.

"I miss him, too," Leslie wailed, and then Leah and Timothy started in.

"Oh, girls, I know you miss him, but I can't stand the noise you're making. You'll feel better if you go swing a while or help Timothy dig in the dirt," Kate urged. She was suddenly so tired that she walked to the porch and eased into her rocker. As she watched the twins and Timothy dig in the loose soil, talking and giggling, she wondered about Billy and his surliness. She knew the girls mourned because Evvie cried frequently and the twins begged for their daddy, but Billy said nothing. He went around in a sullen mood all the time. She had been so caught up in her own grief that she had neglected him. When he returned from school today, she must try to talk to him.

She did try. That evening, after he had watered the garden, she walked with him to the barn and stood behind him as he sat on the milk stool. Hesitantly, she approached the subject by asking how school was—the lessons, his friends, and Janice, the girl he liked. She received only a grunt or shrug of his shoulders to each inquiry. She heaved a big sigh and asked him outright if he missed his dad. He jumped up, the three-legged milk stool toppling and milk spilling. He shoved past her and stomped out the door, leaving the cow in the stanchion with the kickers on. Kate looked after him with astonishment as he headed toward the house with a half pail of milk. She wondered if he would

strain and separate it or just pour it into a jar. Exasperated at his rude-
ness and miffed that he hadn't finished milking, she shook her head,
took off the kickers and released the stanchion bar, and then shooed
Bessie out of the barn and into the pasture.

Making her way back to the house, she felt angry with him, but
if she told him so, would that make the situation worse? What could
she do to help him? Torn by his alienation from her, she decided for
now to let it go and see if the problem would run its course. Maybe
soon, if she didn't ask him directly, he would tell her why he was so
ill-tempered. But time went by, and Billy continued to go about in
silence—crabby, hateful, and disagreeable. His attitude was so awful
that Evvie and the twins avoided him completely, which didn't seem
to bother him at all.

Pondering this, she remembered then that Jim had always insisted
that only sissies cry, not men. Was Billy holding all that ache inside
because he felt he was now the *man* of the family? If so, how could
she convince him that, when their hearts are broken, men *did* cry?
She could see that she wasn't much better than Billy, though, for Jim's
death had held so much heartache that she could barely be civil to
the children or anyone else. She worked as hard as she could every
day, hoping that nighttime would hurry along so she would slip into a
totally oblivious sleep devoid of all haunting dreams. But the bed was
so empty, so cold, and so lonely that she lay there with her heart aching
and tears dripping until, toward morning, she fell into an exhausted,
dream-riddled, agitated sleep. The days dragged on, and though she
noticed the wheat turning color, the garden growing, and her little
ones running around, there was no joy in any of it.

Grant, Betty, and their children were frequent visitors. Grant spent
time helping Billy do the repairs around the farm, showing him and
Jack how to mend, patch, or rebuild that which Billy didn't know
how to do or couldn't do alone. Betty and Emma pitched in with the
household cleaning and sewing and helped to weed the garden, while
Kenneth and Timothy played nearby. It all seemed tiresome to Kate,
but she kept going because it had to be done.

One June morning several weeks later, after school was dismissed for the summer and the mulberries were ripening, Kate heard the rooster crow and swung her feet over the bedside. When she reached back to tickle Jim awake and felt the empty spot on his side of the bed, the scene of him falling began running through her mind again. Determined not to let that picture play out, she stood and shook herself loose from it, then dressed hurriedly and went outside while the children slept.

When she stepped off the porch and the heat hit her in the face like a hot pillow and daybreak fractured a brassy horizon, she knew it was going to be a scorcher of a day. She stood for a moment, taking in the stillness of the scene, then went back in and shook Billy awake to milk the cow. When he growled at her, she went out to feed and water the chickens and then did the same for Cotton, Billy's white mare, leaving Billy to his attitude. When she finished and came back into the house, she stepped into Evvie's room to wake her to start breakfast and see to the twins and Timothy.

When she was sure that Evvie was up and moving around, Kate went back outside and carried water to the garden, which was a mighty strain on her huge belly. After pouring it onto the strawberries, she straightened, rubbed her back, and noticed ominous clouds darkening the western sky. She hoped they would bring a cooling rain, but it would probably be a gullywasher, from the looks of it.

The gentle morning breeze that usually accompanied the dawn hadn't sprung up yet, and that was strange for this time of year. She went to the well house to dip two buckets into the holding tank, returned to the garden, and poured the water on the peas and then the radish and onion rows. She straightened again and thought how much easier it would be if Jim had piped the water from the windmill to the garden and into the house, as planned. There always seemed to be something more pressing that was earmarked for their money than piped water, though. She shook her head and wondered if she would someday have enough money to do that. The thought flashed through her mind that she should buy a hose the next time she was in town, and maybe Grant could rig up a fitting to attach it to the pipe in the well house and out to the garden. That shouldn't be too difficult to do, and it would certainly save the strain on her. *Why hadn't Jim thought of that?* she wondered. Why hadn't *she?*

Taking up the hem of her smock, she dampened it with the wetness in the bottom of the bucket, swiped at her face, and then breathed through the wet fabric for welcome moisture. Looking west again, she noticed the clouds had advanced some. "Probably no rain here, though," she said aloud as she shooed a robin from the strawberries. Moisture always seemed to go around their place. She shooed another robin away. "I must have Evvie pick the strawberries today or the birds will have them all before we have any," she muttered.

Standing in the garden, she listened to a nearby meadowlark burst into its song of brightly tumbled notes. Across the width of the north wheat field, two cock pheasants squawked challenges at each other and sparrows twittered in the locust tree, from the top of which a mockingbird teased Spook, the black cat, by imitating a tom threatening her kittens. *Such a fine day*, Kate thought, *very hot, though, and close, but nevertheless fine.*

As the morning progressed, the heat grew thicker and, in her advanced pregnancy, Kate suffered terribly with it. While they ate their noon meal, Timothy whined incessantly, the twins bickered endlessly, and all three picked at their food. When she could no longer stand it, Kate put Timothy to bed for his nap and, after repeated, unheeded warnings, she sat the twins in opposite corners with orders to stay put until they had her permission to move. They howled in protest and then took to making faces at each other, twittering and giggling. Tired of scolding them, Kate turned their chairs to the wall and walked outside to escape their bawling. Unable to tolerate the noise, Billy and Evvie soon joined her on the porch with their full plates. The twins howled the louder for being left alone, so Kate shut the door and let them howl. With a heavy sigh, she strolled to the railing of the porch and leaned on it.

"It's the heat, Mama. That's why they're so fussy," Evvie explained. "I'm so hot and itchy myself that I could scream."

"I know," Kate replied with another deep sigh. "It really *is* hot. And so close."

She stepped off the porch, fanning herself with the hem of her smock. Looking up, she saw with a tingle of alarm that the clouds overhead roiled in a sickly green fury. Then she noticed a strange, metallic odor that swirled in the slight breeze, which had suddenly turned cold. She shivered. When she smoothed the goose bumps on her arms, the fine hairs crackled with electricity. As she watched the sky Billy joined her, his red hair standing on end and willowing to and fro in the stiffening breeze. When he attempted to smooth it down, it popped and crackled like fire in a stove. He looked at her and said in a low voice, his belligerence temporarily on hold, "Mom, what is it?"

"Electricity in the air. A bad storm is headed our way," she replied, searching the clouds again. Toward the southwest, she saw a cloud tail dip daintily to the earth, then lift, gather strength, and dip again. Like a snake, it coiled in upon itself as the funnel grew and moved toward them. Fear struck through her then.

"A cyclone, Billy!" she gasped, pointing. "Hurry! Go open the cellar door!" Billy took off. Brownie, thinking it was some kind of game, bounded alongside him, barking hysterically while nipping at Billy's heels. Kate rushed up the steps and onto the porch where Evvie, her eyes wide with alarm, held Timothy.

"What is it, Mama?"

"Cyclone! Get Timothy to the cellar. I'll grab the twins." When Evvie didn't move, Kate commanded, "*Go!* We need to get into the cellar!" She gave her a push. With Timothy on her hip, Evvie raced for the cellar in an awkward, lopsided stride that jostled him into laughing with every jolting step.

Inside the house, Kate grabbed the surprised twins, whipped a bottle of baby formula from the icebox, and sprinted across the yard, her belly joggling painfully. As they ran, the twins yelped and bellered in protest. When they stumbled, Kate jerked them to their feet and kept going.

She saw the cyclone touch down at the neighbors a half-mile west. As it spun closer, the roar became deafening, and the wind buffeted them about. Though Kate tightened her grip and fought to stay upright, the twins' protests turned to howls of terror as the wind snatched them off their feet. By the time they reached the cellar, the wind had turned icy. She herded the twins in to Billy and he pushed them on to Evvie, who crouched on the lower steps of the cellar, holding Timothy. Then Billy held out his hand to her.

But she heard the windmill chugging desperately, and when she looked, the fan was spinning and howling like a dervish. She knew she had to turn it off before it was torn to smithereens. No windmill, no water; no water, no anything. The windmill was an anchor on this parched land, the only thing making it possible to survive here. When he realized what she planned to do, Billy lunged for her and grabbed her arm. "No, Mom!" he yelled.

She jerked loose from his hold and dashed for the windmill, every step a battle against the cold blast. When she reached it, it took all her strength to release the tie-down rope and let the shut-off lever flip up. Immediately, the fan whirled sideways to the wind and stopped spinning, halting the mad pumping of water. By that time, the holding tank had overflowed and water was pouring down a slope, flooding the driveway.

As she turned back toward the cellar, hail began pelting her with stinging pain. The pieces grew in size and felt like marbles shot from a slingshot, and they were just as deadly. Flinching, she darted for the cellar, arms over her head to ward off the smarting bits of ice. The chickens squawked by her, their feathers flying loose around them; the corral fence ripped loose and went spiraling up within the vortex. A fierce gust threw her forward and she felt herself being lifted up. Fighting desperately to stay earthbound and upright, she scrabbled forward. Just as she came abreast of the cellar door, a gust blew her beyond it. She knew then that she wouldn't have the strength to fight her way back to it and safety.

"Mom!" she heard Billy yell. Then she felt him grab her arm, tugging until the socket felt as though it would tear loose from her shoulder. With one last mighty heave, he pulled her onto the first step. Evvie reached up and helped her stumble to the bottom, where she eased her mother onto the step. Shaking with exhaustion, Kate gasped for air. She gathered the twins close to her, then picked up Timothy, who had crawled across the dirt floor, crying.

She looked up and noticed that Billy was straining to close the cellar door. When she saw that he wasn't going to succeed, she stood to help him, but Evvie pushed by her. "No, Mama, I'll help him." And with that, she sprang up the steps. Gratefully, Kate snuggled the warm bodies of the little ones against her, anxiously watching as Billy and Evvie stretched over, grabbed the iron handle, and grappled with the heavy, cumbersome door. Exerting every ounce of their combined strength, they managed to power it over, ducking as the door banged shut on the overhead frame.

Knowing that the heavy door protected them, Kate sighed and buried her face in Timothy's soft baby hair, which smelled of Ivory soap. *We're all safe for now,* she thought, her heart gradually slowing to a normal beat.

White and shaken, Evvie panted, "I didn't think we could do it." She plopped down beside Kate.

"But you did! You and Billy closed the door against that storm out there," Kate replied. She reached over and smoothed Evvie's long tangled hair.

At the top of the stairs, Billy sat under the door, his face set. He fiddled angrily with the rope around his waist, trying to untie it. She hadn't noticed before, but the other end was tied to the cellar door handle to anchor him to it—just in case. She thought that was very clever of him and opened her mouth to tell him so, but shut it when she noticed that his efforts were jerky and contorted. She wondered why, but when he avoided looking at her, she suspected it had something to do with her, as usual. She quietly said to Evvie, "Get that other rope hanging over there to tie the door down before it's sucked open."

"Mama, I'll get the rope, but I'm not going up there while he's having such a fit. I'll just hand it to him." Kate looked up at Billy and nodded in agreement.

Overhearing them, Billy snarled, "Yeah, hand it here and I'll do it!" Agitated, he grabbed the rope and tied it to an anchoring iron attached to the side wall of the steps. Then, red-faced, he gave up on loosening the knot at his waist and jerked savagely on the other end that was tied to the door handle until that knot tore loose. Kate knew from the stiffness of his stance that he would only balk at anything she said to him, so she kept quiet and watched him secure the rope to the door. She was too exhausted to pursue the issue, anyway. Instead, she carried the worry with her as she handed Timothy to Evvie, moved the twins aside, and retrieved candles and matches, which were wrapped in wax pouches on a shelf behind the empty canning jars. She set the candles on old jar lids that were kept for that purpose. Lighting two of them, she listened to the wind howl as her legs and belly ached from the strain of running. Though a dim light came through the boards of the cellar door, it was nice to have the candlelight to relieve more of the cellar's murkiness.

She pulled a lard can from under the bottom shelf and sat on it, took the whimpering Timothy on her lap, and pulled the twins close, shushing their fears. All the while, she watched Billy take his pocket knife from his overall pocket and slash recklessly at the frayed rope around his waist. In spite of her weariness and her hesitation to say anything to him, she cautioned above the howl of the wind, "Billy, you're going to cut yourself if you keep on. Why are you so mad at that rope? It held you. And frankly, I'm surprised that it did. It's so old and used up it could easily have snapped. You saved my life and kept yourself secure by tying that rope around you and to the door. It held us. So why are you so mad?"

He glared narrowly at her. "Yeah, it held all right." His insolent attitude stung her. Talking back to her or Jim had never ever been allowed, and she wouldn't allow it now. She started to reprimand him but stopped when he flung the hacked-up rope into a dark corner, his every move furious and vicious. In the flickering candlelight, his green eyes flared like a feral cat's. Affronted by his behavior, she stood, set Timothy on the lard can, and looked a question at Evvie, who in turn raised her eyebrows and shrugged, then edged into the corner of the step. The twins stared at Billy with big eyes and puckered up, ready to bawl again. "Billy!" Kate snapped. "How dare you speak to me like that! Here we are, in this cellar, with a dangerous storm outside and you, young man, are behaving like a spoiled brat. So just stop it!"

He turned toward the cellar door as though he were going into the storm. "Billy!" Kate called out. He swung around, his face distorted with anger. Just then, the wind flung something against the door and he jumped. But his fright fueled more anger, and he turned back toward the door and slammed his fist against it, swearing a blue streak when his knuckles bled.

Shocked by his language, she marched up the steps, grabbed his shirt, and pulled him down into the cellar. She grabbed him by both arms and looked up into his mottled face, then shook him hard, but the effort barely moved his body. She knew he was strong enough to knock her down with one smack, but he didn't. She knew that *he* knew that he could knock her down, too, but he only gave her a quiz-zical look, as though she were slightly crazy.

With her grip still tight, all she could think to say was, "Billy Boyd Robinson, there has never been and never will be any swearing in this house, and you know it! Do you hear me? Stop this behavior right now! What in the world has gotten into you?"

"I'm not in the house, Mom!" he shouted.

"Well, you can't swear in the cellar, either! Or the barn, the chicken house, or the field!"

Looking at him, she realized that what she had just said was ridic-ulous. She stood facing him, wondering what to do, but then she gently released her hold and took his hand. Though she thought he would jerk it away, he instead followed her further into the cellar's dimness without a word.

"Now," she said, "talk to me. What's wrong?"

All the arguing and noise of the wind had frightened the twins, so they grabbed her legs and clung, hampering her. She unhooked them from her and sat them down beside Evvie, then pulled out another lard can and motioned for Billy to sit. He did, chin in hand and silent, his anger seemingly spent.

She sat down on the other lard can. "Billy," she said, "talk." With palms up and arms outstretched, she shrugged in puzzlement. "I don't know what's going on. Tell me."

He flared. "Dad died out there in the wind, so I guess you wanted to die, too, to be with him, and leave us here alone!" He swiped his hand around to indicate Timothy, the twins, and Evvie. "And just now, out there in the wind, leaving us alone . . . we're just too much bother for you, I guess," he snarled. Appalled, she gaped at him. "Go ahead, Mom. Admit it. You've done nothing but be sad since Dad died. You act like we're nothing but a terrible burden to you."

Kate gasped and heard Evvie do the same. Gathering her wits, Kate replied evenly but passionately, trying desperately to keep the situation level. "That is *not* true, Billy. You children are my sanity in all this sorrow and grief. I'm telling you that right now. You're my world, as I am yours. Yes, I miss your dad, but I have the five of you and another child coming. I'll be here for a long time, I promise you." She paused and then went on. "As for the windmill, it's the anchor that holds us to this farm. You must know that if we don't have water, we cannot stay on this place, which was your father's dream as well as mine. I had to turn it off before the wind mangled it. It would cost more money than we have to replace it or even fix it." She paused again. "Do you understand, Billy? Do you?"

He nodded and muttered, looking at the floor. "I just didn't want *you* to die, too."

"Billy, look at me." She put her fingers to his chin and turned his face toward her. "I don't want to die, and I don't plan to do so for a long time." With a stunning clarity, she now saw just how closely she had come to death. Her children would be orphans and would have had to live in the care of some other family—hopefully with Grant and Betty—but it wouldn't be with her, she realized with a shudder.

When Billy's eyes met hers, she saw unshed tears well up and watched as he struggled to contain them. Her heart went out to him. "It's okay to cry, Billy," she said softly.

He shook his head and replied, "Guys don't cry. Dad said that guys don't cry."

"Yes, I heard him tell you that, and I scolded him for it each time. But your dad could be as stubborn as a mule, and he held to that idea no matter what I said." She reached for him, but he shoved her hand away, so she sat, tears sliding down her face. Evvie wiped her eyes and looked at her brother with empathy. For once, the twins and Timothy were quiet, with questioning eyes on their mother. "It's all right for men to cry, Billy," she repeated, and with those words, the dam broke and Billy cried in huge, gulping sobs. The minutes passed and he slowly collected himself. Though tears still trickled down all their faces, they hunkered close together in the cellar, the wind howling.

Suddenly, the noise stopped and they were surrounded by silence. "It's over, Mama!" cried Evvie. "We can get out of here now." Brownie tore up the stairs and whined at the top, but Kate hesitated, her arm out as a barrier to her children.

"No," she said, shaking her head. "No, just wait for a bit. I'm not sure it's over yet." She had no more than mouthed the words when a powerful gust slammed another heavy object against the door. They all jumped and looked up. The object banged and spun, banged and spun, each time increasing in intensity. Brownie yipped and slunk back down the stairs to crawl under the shelves as far back as he could get.

"Mommy, Mommy! It's a monster! He's trying to get in and eat us!" Leslie cried out. The twins buried their faces in Kate's lap as Timothy held out his arms to be picked up.

"Shush," Kate said, "it's only a tree limb or a piece of metal." But something even heavier and bigger started a weird thumping on the door.

Evvie shrieked, "It *is* a monster, Mama, and it *is* trying to get in!"

"It ain't a monster!" Billy stood up and, feigning bravery, glanced at his siblings, curled his lip, and rolled his eyes. He laughed evilly, as if *he* were the monster, and the little ones screamed.

"Hush, all of you," Kate ordered. Shaking her head at Billy, she said, "he's just being silly, but he's right. It's not a monster. It's the cyclone. It's touched ground again and it's right close by. But we're safe in here. And don't say 'ain't,' Billy," she corrected, immediately realizing again the absurdity of it all. A cyclone was just outside the door, scouring the farm of their possessions, and here she was, correcting Billy's grammar.

Billy, looking up at the door and the noise, replied automatically, "Yes, Ma'am." Then he turned and looked at her, grinning.

She shrugged her shoulders, as if to apologize for herself, and Billy, understanding, nodded to accept her apology. She knew then that things were all right between them, at least for the time being.

Then there was dead silence outside once again.

"Listen," Kate whispered. "No wind." They looked at each other, a thick hush surrounding them.

"What's happening now?" Evvie quietly asked. "Does a cyclone have more than one eye?"

Billy scoffed. "No," he said, "a cyclone only has one eye, like a cyclops."

Evvie frowned a query at him, "Cyclops?"

"Yeah," he challenged, arms akimbo and chin out. "Cyclops. You don't know about Cyclops, the one-eyed monster in literature? Well, I guess you just aren't old enough yet and haven't learned that in school," he smirked.

Before Evvie could voice a retort, Kate interrupted, sending a warning glare at him. "Since there's no wind, I think we can get out of this cellar. Let's just peek out first."

Billy brushed by as Evvie took the twins' hands. Kate followed, carrying Timothy. But Brownie scooted past all of them and waited just under the door, panting and grinning. When Billy lifted the heavy door and eased it back on its prop, Brownie charged out and, like four gophers, the children poked their heads out. Kate blew out the candles and followed, Timothy against her shoulder.

"The sun is shining, Mom," Billy announced, and they all clambered into the brightness.

When Kate reached the top of the stairs and could see out, what she saw made her smile: the twins skipping around, Brownie chasing his tail, Evvie staring around in silence, and Billy walking and looking around, assessing the damage. She took the last step out and gasped at the destruction. The whole scene looked as if an angry giant had used an eggbeater to whip everything up and up, and then had flicked each item off to land where it might.

Turning slowly, fearful of what she might find, she looked beyond the immediate destruction and found that the house, barn, privy, and the windmill had escaped major damage with only a few shingles and boards blown off the buildings. The chicken house, however, had been lifted off its foundation, spun around, and tossed upside down over the pasture fence; its roof, nests, and roosts were smashed beyond repair. Her immediate thought was that she and Billy could build makeshift roosts in the granary for tonight and herd the silly hens in each evening to keep them safe from preying varmints. Her thoughts were interrupted by the twins' exclamations.

"Look at the chickens, Mommy!" Leah shrieked. "They don't got no feathers!"

"Neither does that old rooster!" Leslie piped up. Forgetting their recent terror in the cellar, they ran about laughing and chasing the hapless, featherless things. Brownie helped them out as much as he could until Kate shouted at them all to stop or the hens would never lay an egg again. Ever.

They stopped, but she heard Leah mutter, "Oh, phooey. We can't chase 'em no more." Leslie sighed, and they walked off in a pout.

Kate's house on the prairie.

Brownie, however, just looked at Kate, his tongue hanging out in a guilty dog-grin. Then he ran playful circles around the twins until they began to run away from him, saying, "Catch us, Brownie. Catch us if you can!" They climbed up on the tractor, teasing the dog and crying, "Wolf! Wolf!" and pretending to be scared. He joyfully played the game by growling and jumping up, trying to catch them.

How wonderful, Kate thought, *to have the ability to forget troubles that quickly, and then go on as though nothing is wrong.* Timothy gurgled at their antics and squirmed until she put him down to try out his new walking ability. Though his bowed baby legs were unsteady, he nevertheless struggled on, delighted with his newfound freedom. Kate watched, amused. When Timothy came alongside the tractor, Brownie trotted over to him, licked his face, and walked docilely by him as if to protect him against harm. The twins let out a protest of jealousy and called sweetly to Brownie to coax him back to the game, but the dog ignored them and didn't leave his post beside Timothy.

Kate was taking all that in when Billy walked up and said, "It must have been the edge of the twister. Not much damage to the windmill, just a blade or two gone. The house and the barn are minus a few shingles and a board or two. Nothing that I can't fix." He tried to lower his changing voice into a more manly resonance. "The cow is standing at the pasture gate, looking puzzled—looking at me like 'What just happened?' I guess I should run her back out to the pasture until milking time." With that, he adopted his dad's stride and drove Bessie into the pasture. Brownie barked an apology to Timothy and ran ahead of Billy, biting at Bessie's heels to hurry her along. Bessie turned and faced Brownie, daring him to bite her again. With that challenge, Brownie retreated back to Billy, tail between his legs.

"Well, leave her alone," Billy said, "or she *will* do you damage."

Watching, Kate realized that Billy had grown stronger and become more grown up since Jim's death. But remembering his tears in the cellar, her heart went out to him: She knew that he would always miss his dad terribly. Billy was a handsome redhead, a strong, well-built young man, though he didn't acknowledge any of that. He wore a size thirteen shoe and, at sixteen, was already nearly six feet tall. Once he grew out of his teens, she knew that he would be a fine and honorable man. She proudly watched while he and

Brownie herded Bessie into the pasture, then she jerked herself back into the present situation.

She called after him. "I'm going to check the wheat crop north of the house." He nodded and waved without looking back. Kate asked Evvie to watch Timothy and the twins, but when they protested, she said, "Well, all right, come on along." Evvie picked up Timothy and came abreast of Kate with the twins following, jostling each other.

As they made their way to the field, which lay behind the chicken house and outbuildings, Kate stopped several times in amazement, pointing out how the storm had driven wheat straws like arrows— neither broken nor twisted—completely through posts. Evvie and the little ones examined the strange and weird phenomenon with awe. While they discussed the sight, Kate rounded the granary and gasped at the destruction of the field, which yesterday had been beautifully headed out, tall and just beginning to turn a pale yellow. With a fist to her mouth, tears splashed over her knuckles and onto her smock. That field, which had had the promise of producing close to fifteen bushels per acre, was now a twisted, sodden mass. Her first thought was how they would survive without the cash from it. She knew in her heart that the other fields had been hit, too, but how could she possibly pay the bills and keep the farm going now?

"What will we do, Mama?" Evvie asked.

"I just don't know," Kate answered, shaking her head, wiping her tears with the back of her hand.

Deep in their thoughts and staring at the field, they hadn't noticed Grant ride up. When he spoke, it startled them both. "Oh, I'm sorry, Kate, Evvie. Didn't mean to scare you," he apologized as he swung off his horse and came over to stand beside them. "I reckon it looks really bad, doesn't it?" His voice was full of sympathy, all of which nearly undid Kate. "But I figure it will stand back up and ripen and be a good crop."

She turned back to view the field, but mostly she needed to gain control of herself and steady her voice. She cleared her throat and asked, "Do you really think so?"

Turning to look up at him, she noticed that his color was off. He actually looked sick, but before she could say anything, he said, "I rode over to see if the twister did any damage here. I see it dumped the chicken house on the other side of the corral fence, but I didn't see much damage elsewhere. Your other fields escaped and look great. I came over as soon as I could. Are you faring all right?" he asked, making a point of not looking at her protruding belly. "Kids okay?"

She nodded. "We're fine, but we had to spend some time in the cellar with things banging the door. That was an adventure, just in itself."

"I imagine so," he replied. They both looked out over the wheat field.

"It was more than you would think. I'll tell you about it sometime."

He looked a question at her, but when she shook her head, he cleared his throat and stated in an off-handed manner, "The twister took the roof off our house."

She whirled. "What? The roof of your house is gone?" *It's no wonder he's pale*, she thought, and then she noticed that his hands were shaking as he held onto the reins.

"Well, not *all* the roof, just part of it."

"What about Betty and the children? Where are they? Are they all right?"

"They're safe," he said, "scared, but safe. They're cleaning debris out of the house so we can get around in it." He cleared his throat again and shifted from one foot to the other. "Didn't hear it comin'. We were inside, eating our noon meal, when all at once it started hailing big baseball-size chunks of ice. Windows started breaking, glass all over the floor of the living room, and then rain poured in. We ran for the hall and stayed there because of the fierce lightening popping and cracking close around." He cast a glance in the direction of his home. "And then, all of a sudden there was this loud whooshing sound. I felt my hair stand on end. Straight up! I looked around and everybody's hair was on end, too. Then I felt a vacuum pulling at us, like sucking us up, and my heart plumb quit beating." He flicked a chunk of mud from his trouser leg and straightened.

"The girls and Betty crouched down as low as they could, screaming and hollering and hiding their faces. Our little guy grabbed onto his mama's neck and hung on, bawling like a newborn calf." Grant heaved a huge sigh and went on as though once he had started talking, he couldn't stop. "Jack swore like an old salt. I never ever thought he knew such words." As she and Evvie stared openmouthed at him, he cocked a grin at Kate and speculated, "I reckon he'll be in big trouble for that, once his mama gets around to remembering." Kate nodded. She had never heard him say more than ten words at a time, and she could see that he wanted to tell her more, so she waited.

Sobering, he continued, "I heard hail and rain hitting the floor above us, and then another loud *whoosh*, like the end of the world: The roof went up and I figured for sure we were goners. I just knew we'd be sucked up along with it, so I wrapped my arms around everybody and yelled for them to hang on for dear life, and we did. The house got pounded on by rain and hail, but it held and nobody got hurt."

"Grant! That's wonderful!" Kate exclaimed. In her excitement, she grabbed his arm and held on until he drew back. He shifted his feet, embarrassed, so she released her grip, stepped back, and waited for him to go on. Evvie stood close to her.

"Yep," he answered, "just a scratch or two and minor cuts from busted-up glass and bruises from falling stuff. Powerful fright, though, and will be every time the wind blows from now on, I 'spect."

He ran his fingers through Badger's tangled forelock.

"But the house? Do Betty and the children need to come over here for a while?"

"It's just part of the roof. Coulda been worse." He paused, and then repeated softly, as though to himself. "Yep, it sure coulda been a lot worse."

"I'm so thankful you're all fine. Billy can help you with the roof, if you need him. And if Betty and the children need a place to sleep or stay, they certainly are welcome here," Kate assured him.

"I'll tell her that, though she'll probably want to see to our house and all," he hesitated, running his hand down Badger's neck. "And I think Billy has enough to do around here. I have help," he replied, and then said, "I stopped at the Jones place on my way over, and Henry will be helping me and Jack with our roof. We should have it fixed in three, maybe four days." Then he suggested, "Let's take a look around and see what kind of damage you have here." They walked about, Grant leading Badger by his reins, and inspected the house and the outbuildings. "Things look pretty good; with a board here and a nail there, it will be in good shape in no time." He clucked in sympathy at the tangled corral fence and chicken house. "Looks to me like Billy and me have some work to do around here," he stated dryly. "Don't worry about it right now, though. The two of us can fix up the granary so the chickens can roost in there tonight. We'll tend to the rest of it after I get our roof fixed."

"Well...Billy and I can get something in the granary for the chickens," Kate replied. "You fix your roof first before helping us."

"Are you sure?"

"Yes, I'm sure. You go home now and see to your family."

"The cattle in the east pasture behind the barn look good. Noticed them when I rode in," Grant said, taking up the reins.

"Oh, that's good news! Thank you, Grant, for coming over."

He nodded, swung aboard Badger, and tipped his hat to her. "No need to thank me, Kate—we're family. Once I get Jack and Henry to work on the roof, I'll be over so Billy and me can get the chicken house fixed. We'll see about the corral fence, too. They were working on the phone line when I came over, so the lines should be up again in a day or two, I 'spect. Meanwhile, if you need anything, send Billy over." He reined Badger around and rode off, tall and lean in the saddle. She watched until she couldn't see him any longer, then she walked to the house, feeling extremely, utterly tired and worried.

True to his word, Grant came over a few days later. Together, he and Billy set the chicken house upright and temporarily nailed it together, then moved the chickens back in. After lunch, they repaired the corral fence and replaced the missing house shingles and windmill blades. They hammered sheets of old metal, which Jim kept for such purposes, on the roof of the barn to cover holes. It took them all day but, by suppertime, things had been jerry-rigged until a later time when it could all be done properly.

"I'll be helping the fellas with my roof until it's done, so I'll see you in another three, four days, Kate," Grant called as he stuck his head in the door. "With neighbors coming again tomorrow, we should have our roof done by that time. Billy can take care of things around here until I get back. And don't worry—the wheat will straighten in a few days." Grant was right: In a short while, the wheat began to recover. In about ten days, it stood straight, with the heads upright and bending with the breezes.

Though her heart ached for Jim, she, Billy, and Evvie were kept busy with chores and repairs. They were so busy that she had very little time for grief. With Grant's help, a new chicken house was constructed by salvaging lumber from the old one and from pieces of scrap lumber that Jim had stored from other projects. In two weeks or so, things were pretty well fixed up. It was the daily chores and the coming harvest that kept Kate so busy that she flopped into bed at night and slept through until dawn.

On a calm Monday morning—Monday always being laundry day—Kate retrieved the oval copper boiler from a nail on the outside back porch wall and placed it atop the two burners of the blue-enameled kerosene stove, located in the southwest corner of the back room. She was so huge and bulky now that she asked Billy to move the washing machine into the middle of the room, place the bench with the two rinse tubs beside it and fill them with water. Kate placed a basket on a chair beside the last rinse tub where the clothes would fall after going through the wringer before being hung outside to dry. But first, Billy was to fill the copper kettle atop the stove so she could heat water for the washing machine.

Billy made several trips to and from the well house, where he dipped two buckets at a time into the large round galvanized holding tank, carried them back to the house, and dumped the water into the copper kettle. When he had it full, he filled the rinse tubs. Into the last tub, Kate added Mrs. Stewart's bluing to make the white clothes whiter. Evvie, meantime, gathered up dirty clothes throughout the house and sorted them by whites, light colors, dark colors, and then the overalls, all of which would take all day to wash and dry.

To light the burners under the copper kettle, Kate pulled the spring-hinged door on the front of the stove down, lifted the first of the two burner covers, and struck a match to the round wick, then did the same to the other burner. When the flame took hold and ran the circle of the wick, she flicked the match to put it out. As she tossed it into the stove tray with the rest of the dead matches, Kate felt her first contractions…it was just at that very moment that a snake reared

A small kerosene stove was used for heating laundry water or food.

its head up alongside the burner cover and whipped its tongue out. Startled, she let the burner cover drop back down, slammed the door shut, and stood rooted to the spot, shocked at what she had seen. Not really believing it, she cautiously opened the door again, and the snake swung toward her and hissed. She jumped back, let the door snap shut again, and stared at the little stove.

"What's wrong, Mom?" Billy asked as he walked by her with another bucket of water for kitchen use.

"There's a snake in there," Kate said, pointing.

"In the stove?" Billy asked. He set down the bucket and looked at her.

"In the stove."

"A *what*, Mama?" Evvie asked, pausing in the sorting of laundry.

"A snake...in the stove. He stuck his head up alongside the burner," Kate repeated. "It could be a rattler."

Billy snorted, bent over, and slowly opened the door a crack and then wider and wider, peering into the depths of it. He looked back at her. "I don't see a snake, Mom. Do you Evvie?"

With great hesitation, Evvie edged over and, careful not to touch any part of the stove, glanced in and shook her head. "I don't see a snake, either, Mama." She eased back, just in case there might actually be a snake in there.

"Well, I know a snake when I see one," exclaimed Kate. "It's probably in the drawer below the burners," she pointed.

Billy yanked open the shallow drawer and jumped back, then he grinned sheepishly at Kate and Evvie. "It didn't really scare me," he said. He grabbed the snake behind its head and pulled it out. "It's just a little ol' garden snake," he chuckled, and swung it around close to Evvie. He sniggered when she screamed, so he waved it in front of her again, a wicked gleam in his eye.

"Billy," Kate looked straight at him and shook a finger, "don't you do anything funny with that snake." She pointed to the screen door and commanded, "You take that thing out of here right now. I *mean* it." She tried to keep a straight face as he poked the snake at her, grinning. She could see he was having a great time but stood her ground and kept pointing to the door, faking a stern face. She knew Evvie was cowering behind her the whole time.

He held the snake as if to kiss it and said, "Poor little snake. You wouldn't hurt a flea, would you? These two females scared you, I bet. I'll just take you out to the garden away from these scaredy-cats. You can hide from them and eat bugs out there. These two just might hurt you if I don't." He haw-hawed and stroked the snake's head.

"That snake had better not be in the garden when I pick green beans, or I'll chop him into little pieces with the hoe," Evvie yelled after him. Billy just laughed louder and longer.

"Miss Scaredy-cat! Wew, wew, wew. Me and this snake are *so scared*. Maybe I'll put him in a safer place, like your bed," he jeered, and then crowing like a young rooster, he made as if going toward her room.

Evvie screamed. Exasperated, Kate grabbed Billy's arm and turned him toward the screen door. "Out," she said and gave him a push through it.

"Mama, I'm *not* going into the garden if the snake is in it," Evvie declared.

"Oh, hush," Kate said, waving away Evvie's worry. "We have washing to do, so let's get busy." Just then, another labor pain spread across her lower back, and she knew she did, indeed, need to finish the wash as soon as possible.

She told Evvie to go into the kitchen to see to the twins and Timothy and to mix and boil starch for the shirts, blouses, and linens. As Evvie stepped up to the door into the kitchen, Kate said, "Evvie get the starch as smooth as pudding with no lumps." Making smooth starch was a tricky thing to do.

Evvie turned to face her, "Yes, I know, Mama. I've done it before."

"Yes, you have," Kate called after her, "but remember to slowly mix the powder with the cold water first so there won't be lumps when you bring it to a boil. The iron will catch on those bumpy spots and scorch the fabric," Kate continued. The birth was getting closer by the minute, starch or no starch.

"I know, Mama. I remember," Evvie said again, this time a little testy.

When Billy came back in, still grinning from the snake, Kate had him bucket the hot water from the copper kettle into the washing machine. When it was full, she stuffed white clothes in and shaved slabs of lye soap into the load. She urged Billy to get the gas engine cranked by tromping on the gas pedal. Though it was usually stubborn, today the machine immediately barked into life and the gyrator began swishing back and forth. Her contractions weren't regular or close together yet, but they were gradually getting stronger. She really must hurry.

With Billy turning the wringer, Kate fed the clothes through it into the rinse water. When Evvie came back from making the starch, she declared that it was absolutely as smooth as butter. With the three of them working, they had seven loads scrubbed, rinsed, and hung out in record time. Just as Evvie came in from hanging up the last load, Kate's knees bent with a serious contraction.

"Anything wrong, Mom?" Billy asked.

"The baby's coming."

He and Evvie gasped. "Mom, what can we do? We don't know anything about this stuff!"

"Should you sit down, Mama?" Evvie asked. "Or lay down? I'm scared!"

"First, Billy, you get this copper kettle full of water again. Then go get the car started. You know how to crank it and keep it running. Then you and Evvie take the children over to Grant's. Tell Betty to stop for Hannah on the way back here. All of you stay there until someone comes to get you. Hurry up, now." She turned the open-mouthed Billy to the door and motioned for Evvie to get the children into the car. As soon as she heard it start, she heaved a sigh of relief. Then her water broke and ran into her shoes.

To boil water for the delivery, she again struck a match to the burners of the little blue stove, laid out clean white rags, and covered the bed with several old but clean sheets and blankets. As she prepared to undress, she noticed the kitchen floor was covered with a sticky goo of some kind, probably from the twins making peanut butter and jelly sandwiches. Though the contractions were now close and breathtaking, she couldn't let the floor be sticky, so she grabbed the rag mop from a nail on the back porch, filled the mop bucket with water, and began sloshing it back and forth to clean up the mess.

Through a series of blinding contractions, she hurriedly finished and felt the baby's head pushing to be free. With the next contraction, she braced herself against the door frame and held her breath, resisting the impulse to push. Using the mop as a cane, she inched her way to the bedroom. When she realized she might be alone when the baby came, she tried not to panic. Though she had been through this several times before and knew she could do it, she was truly grateful to hear Betty and Hannah, the midwife, come through the front door and bustle into the bedroom.

Hannah took the mop and handed it to Betty, who huffed and puffed, scolding Kate. Did Kate think that she and Hannah didn't know how to mop a floor? When it became apparent that the baby was coming, Betty dropped the mop, and they both rushed to ease Kate onto the bed.

Kate moaned when the next contraction pushed the head out. Before she could draw a deep breath, another pushing contraction wracked her whole body and one of the baby's shoulders appeared. With encouragement from Betty and Hannah, Kate grabbed the bedstead and pushed again. Feeling as though her body would turn inside out, the other shoulder slid free and, with a final push, the baby was born.

"It's a boy!" Hannah announced as she held him high and patted his bottom. "Look at that red hair, just like Billy and his twin sisters!" she exclaimed. "Oh, he is just a darling." She gave the baby a kiss and laid him on Kate's stomach to cut the cord, then wrapped the squalling infant in a warm birthing blanket and tucked him in beside Kate.

"What's his name?" Betty asked as she wiped Kate's forehead.

"James Edward," Kate whispered, holding him close and smiling at the newborn's tiny face, all scrunched-up and red.

"That's a good family name," Hannah nodded. Betty agreed and then went on to say, "You have your babies so easy, Kate. Why, I was in labor for hours and hours with every one of mine. Hours, I tell you. And here, you just popped him out."

Kate took exception to that statement. She felt exhausted and drained, and she wished with all her heart that Jim was beside the bed holding their new son. Her mind flashed back to the time that he delivered Billy alone when neither Betty nor Hannah arrived in time. He had been upset when they didn't show up until after the birth, but using his experience in delivering calves, he had done a wonderful job helping Billy come into the world. For days afterward, Jim had held his first son, grinning and rocking him, leaving the house only to do the chores.

When another contraction gripped her, Kate's smile vanished and that memory faded.

"It's just the afterbirth," Hannah assured her.

"No, it's not!" Kate gritted. "Another baby is coming."

"What? No, no, no!" Betty exclaimed. "Another set of twins?"

Hannah looked and smiled. "There's the head, Betty." Though Betty had momentarily lost her composure, she pulled herself together, picked up a soft white cleaning cloth and birthing blanket, and laid both close at hand.

"It's a girl," Hannah proudly stated. "Dark hair, like you and Evvie," she said to Kate. She cut the cord, wrapped the blanket around the newborn, and placed another wailing baby beside Kate. "You've done a great job, Kate. Both of them are healthy. Now here comes the afterbirth." She disposed of it, placed a comforting hand on Kate's arm, then turned to Betty and said, "Let's clean this up and let Kate get some rest."

"What's her name?" Betty asked, looking down at the babies, softly touching their cheeks.

"It's Marguerite Marie, after my best friend in high school," Kate stated.

"That's quite a name for such a tiny girl," Betty commented.

"She'll be Meggie. James will be Jimmy." Kate replied, looking tenderly at both.

Hannah and Betty worked together, talking softly to each other. Though totally exhausted, Kate listened to the conversation. With her eyes closed, she heard them discuss the age-old miracle of giving birth and of women sharing that experience with each other.

Kate lay in the clean bed and smiled with satisfaction at the tiny ones. She and Jim had outdone themselves again. Longing for him, she took a deep breath, smoothed the babies' perfect hands and tiny fingers. She checked out their toes and ached for Jim to do the same. Tired, she drifted and listened to the murmur of Betty and Hannah as they went about their work. It was a comfort to know she could leave them in charge. For the next two weeks, she would have someone help her while she recovered. She knew that a lot of it would fall to Evvie, but Betty would be here most of the time. For Kate, those two weeks were the most nerve-wracking part of giving birth, because it was difficult to have someone else doing her work when she wanted to be doing it. On the ninth day, Betty would certainly be here to see that Kate lay perfectly still while her uterus went back into place. She sighed then and went to sleep. She had done enough work for this day.

When Kate was back on her feet, Betty insisted that Emma come and stay for a while to help out. Emma was such great help that Kate kept her for a month, paying both girls a dollar a week each. The three of them finally adjusted to a schedule of sorts in order to accomplish the day's work. Evvie basically cared for the newborns—formula, diapers, and bathing—while Emma helped in the kitchen, and with the housework and laundry. At night, they took turns with the babies, and the weeks went by in a flurry of activity. Knowing that she would be doing twice the work if Emma wasn't around, Evvie appreciated her help and companionship.

🦆 🦆 🦆

To keep from waking the babies, Kate clicked the alarm button on the clock before it went off. It was five o'clock in the morning and, out the window, she could see that dawn was waking up the first day of her wheat harvest.

The ripe wheat had been cut, bundled, and stacked ten days or so ago and now the harvest crew, consisting of neighbors, would drive their trucks into the back field east of the barn and begin the harvesting of her crops. Looking out toward the field, Kate saw a team of horses hauling the lumbering hulk of a threshing machine into it. The driver might come in for a brief cup of coffee and a biscuit or two with honey. If he did, she had it ready. If he didn't come in, the family would be more than willing to dispose of the fare.

When the rest of the crew arrived a little later, they would begin greasing, oiling, and gassing up the machinery. Harvest for her, then, would be in full swing. It would take a week to ten days to finish her fields. She would cook the noon meal—what the farm people called "dinner"—for about ten men. But, thank goodness, they would go

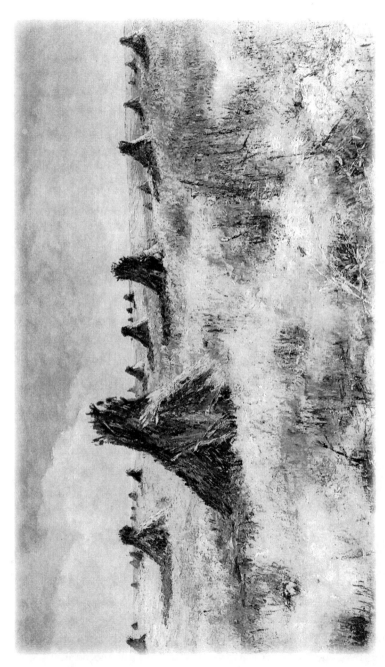

Shocks of grain were left to be threshed at a later date. Oil painting by Deacon Sharp, brother of author.

home for supper…most of the time. After they were finished with her wheat, the crew—which included Billy this year—would move on to the next farm.

She stood over the crib that the babies shared and smoothed back their wispy hair, careful not to wake them. At two months, they flourished, happy and fat on cow's milk formula, which was watered-down milk with a tablespoon or two of dark corn syrup, sorghum, or molasses. She kissed them gently then buttoned her housedress, tied her shoes, and went into the kitchen. She grabbed her apron from a nail and stirred the embers in the kitchen range firebox, then put kindling and wood on top. She measured coffee and water into the coffeepot and set it on the hottest part of the stove. Using the sourdough starter, she mixed up enough bread dough to make four loaves for the noon meal. She replenished the starter with flour and potato water and set it aside to work: bread for another day.

Billy shuffled in from his room, slit-eyed and scratching his head. He grinned sleepily at her and poured himself some coffee. "Mom," he said, looking in his cup and then into the coffeepot, "you forgot to put the eggshells in to settle the grounds. My cup's full of grounds."

"Oh…well, it's not hot yet, either," she said as she rolled out the biscuit dough. "The grounds will settle in the bottom of your cup, but here are some eggshells to throw into the coffeepot. If you go wake Evvie for me, by the time you get back, the coffee should be ready, and you can have some before you go out to milk. And tell Evvie to get Leah and Leslie up and see that they get dressed. She needs to dress and feed Timothy when he wakes up and do the same with the babies."

With a crooked grin, Billy poured the coffee back into the pot and threw the eggshells in, set his cup down, and sauntered into Evvie's room. "You get out of my room, Billy Boyd Robinson!" Evvie yelled. And stop telling me what to do!"

"Mom told me to come in and wake you up and tell you what to do, so I'm doing it," he said.

"You get out of here!" she shouted. Kate heard the bedroom door slam and was surprised that the noise didn't wake the little ones.

Billy came back, grinning like a Cheshire cat. He poured a cup of hot coffee and took a sip. "She didn't much like it that I did what you said, Mom, but I did it and it was fun. So…thanks!" he chuckled. He finished the cup, picked up the milk bucket from the back porch, and—whistling a lively tune—went out the back door.

Kate looked after him, shook her head, and turned the biscuit dough a half-quarter on the breadboard. She rolled it out and cut thick rounds, placing them on a cookie sheet, and popped it into the oven. She turned to the bread, kneaded it into a smooth, elastic-feeling mound, and gently tossed it into a large bowl, which she had greased with melted lard. She rubbed it around to coat the top, flipped it right-side up, covered the bowl with a damp cloth, and set it near the stove to raise.

Just as she had finished and was wiping her hands on her apron, she heard a car pull into the yard. Looking out, she saw Grant and Betty getting things from the back seat. As they approached with their arms loaded, she opened the door, and welcomed them in. Grant nodded, set the food where she indicated, and went back for more.

"I brought my special chocolate cake," Betty said without so much as a hello, "the one where you stir the soda into a cup of buttermilk

Crockery and other items were stored in a pantry or cellar for household use.

until it bubbles over into the dry ingredients. You mix that up and then you pour boiling water into the cup of cocoa until it's smooth and add that to the bowl. Then you beat the living daylights out of it. You know the one."

"Oh, yes," Kate responded, "the one Mother always made. But somehow it never seems to work out for me. I don't understand why. You must have the magic touch."

"It never fails for me. I don't know why it doesn't work for you," Betty said pointedly. Kate mentally rolled her eyes as Betty chattered on. "It always wins the prize at the county fair and beats even Martha Carver, who thinks she is the best cook *ever*." As she set the cake on the table, she motioned for Grant to set another cake beside it.

"I also brought my pineapple-upside-down cake with whipped cream. It's always such a favorite, too, no matter where I serve it. Oh," she exclaimed, "I guess these go into the pantry," and with that, she whisked one cake into the pantry and motioned for Grant to get the other.

He set down the food that he had brought in, picked up the cake, and grinned lopsidedly at Kate. Betty returned, still chattering. "Grant, be sure to put the whipping cream into the icebox," she ordered, then continued. "Grant is taking Billy to the field with him. He says that Billy is old enough to help grease and oil the machinery and drive a truck." Kate opened her mouth to agree, but only nodded when Betty's mouth kept moving. Grant walked to the door, motioning to Kate that he would help Billy with separating the milk and then come in for breakfast. Kate acknowledged his message as she arranged thick bacon slices in a large cast-iron skillet, pointing to the cream to be placed in the icebox. He nodded, picked it up, and left.

While Evvie bottled the babies' formula and helped Timothy into his high chair, she looked at Kate and made a pantomime of Betty talking. Kate nodded and turned the sizzling bacon, smiling secretly.

Betty, hands on hips, went on without hesitation, eyeing Grant as he went out. "Those men go out there in the field to scratch, spit, chew, smoke, cuss, and discuss. They talk endlessly about the thresher, the moisture, the price of wheat or barley or corn, who has the best crop, and the weather, and then more weather. It takes them an hour or more just to squirt a little bit of oil here and there, here and there. They pump and pump that grease gun to squirt that thick green goo into those

The cream separator was a device that isolated cream from milk.

little…what do you call those little holes? Oh, yes…'zirks.'That's it, zirks. Oh, dear," she sighed heavily. "Oh…the babies are starting to cry! And since you're cooking breakfast, shall I go get them?" Kate nodded and turned the bacon again. From the bedroom came cooing and baby talk from Betty. "I'll change them if you want me to," she called out.

"That's fine," Kate answered, dishing up biscuits, bacon, and eggs just as Leah and Leslie emerged from their room, sleepy-eyed and hungry. They climbed onto their stools and began eating.

Betty came back with a baby held football-style in each arm. She handed Jimmy to Evvie, who tested a bottle on her wrist for temperature and, satisfied, handed it to Betty, who went into the living room to sit in Jim's old rocker with Meggie. Evvie took a bottle and joined Betty to feed Jimmy in Kate's rocker.

Grant and Billy came back from the barn and set about separating and storing the milk. They washed their hands on the screened-in back porch and stepped inside for breakfast. Grant poured coffee for himself and Billy, put the coffeepot back on the range, and picked up the plate of hot biscuits. He motioned for Billy to take the bacon and eggs to the table. Kate joined them, knowing that Evvie and Betty would come as soon as the babies were fed. Kate placed a plate of food on Timothy's tray for his breakfast, which he ate with zest, making a mess.

After the meal was over and Grant left with Billy, Kate dipped a cup into the flour and spooned out lard from a large can for pie crusts. "I started the bread earlier," she told Betty. "Do you think five pies will be enough? Dried apple pies?"

"With my two cakes, I think five will be plenty. If any is left, we can serve it tomorrow. My kids are coming today, so there might not be any left at all," Betty said as she burped Meggie. She walked by Evvie and stopped to tickle Jimmy under the chin, getting a grin in response. "Wilma's bringing strawberry jam, tomato preserves, and pickles. She'll also bring along some fresh radishes and green onions." After she returned from placing sleepy Meggie into the crib, Betty said, "Let's get those chickens butchered. Did Billy lock them up last night?"

"Oh," Kate gasped, her rolling pin in midair, "he *did* lock them up, but I forgot to have him to put water on to heat this morning to pluck the feathers! What shall we do? With at least a dozen men coming, I have no meat to serve!"

"Well…" Betty thought, "let's leave the chickens until tomorrow, and we'll serve roast beef and potatoes today."

"Roast beef!" Kate exclaimed. "I don't have any beef roasting!"

"Oh," Betty said, "I forgot to tell you—Marjorie flagged us down this morning and said that she's bringing a big roast, and I think she said fresh tomatoes and green beans. Wilma's coming with her, and we can cook potatoes here."

Kate puffed a sigh of relief. "What lifesavers!" And then, "For pity sakes, when were you going to tell me all this? I declare, Betty! Where is your mind this morning?"

"I was going to tell you, but I just haven't had a chance."

Kate began rolling out a pie crust. "Leah and Leslie," she turned to the twins, who had just finished eating, "pick up these dishes, and then you two go out and let the chickens out of the chicken house and into the pen."

"Okay, Mommy," they said. They hurriedly placed the dishes into the dishpan and ran out, letting the screen door slam behind them.

With an irritated huff, Kate said, "How many times have I told those two not to let the screen door slam shut behind them? How many times?"

"I tell mine the same thing all the time, too!" Betty declared. She stepped up beside Kate and pulled enough dough from the bowl for a crust. "I just don't know how our old screen door hangs together." She began rolling the dough thin, casting sideways glances at Kate.

"What?" Kate asked. "Why do you keep looking at me like that?" She placed the thin crust into the pie pan, secured it up the sides, cut the excess dough even with the outside rim of the pan, and started rolling out the top crust.

"Well," Betty began hesitantly, "Victor's going to be helping with the harvest. He's with a different crew but, when he was at our house last night, he asked to help with your harvest. Grant told him that would be fine if the other crew didn't mind. He'll be here in a day or two to help."

"Victor? Jim's brother?" Kate said, looking at Betty. "I thought he went to jail years ago for assault and battery—on a *woman*. And she wasn't the only one!"

"He did, but he was released recently for good behavior. He's completely changed and such a nice guy, so polite and considerate."

Kate stopped rolling the crust and looked at Betty. "I'm not sure he should be working on my harvest."

Before she could continue, Betty interrupted. "In high school, before you married Jim, Victor was really sweet on you." She placed her crust in a pie tin. "He's handsome, and I hear he has a lot of money, too."

"How did he make so much money if he was in jail for years?" Kate asked.

"I don't know, but with money, looks, and a great personality, I think he's a really good catch."

Kate jerked, tearing a big hole in the top crust. "Betty! What're you saying? Are you suggesting that Victor take Jim's place?" She looked at her sister with her hands on her hips.

Taking more pie dough, Betty shrugged and, though her cheeks turned pink, she raised her eyebrows as if it could be a possibility. Outraged, Kate stated, "I am *not* interested in Jim's brother—or *any* man, for that matter. How can you even say such a thing! Jim's only been gone a few months, and here you are suggesting that I..." She left the sentence unfinished and glared at Betty, feeling an angry flush rushing into her cheeks.

"I only meant that you need someone on this place to help you with the farming, Kate. You *do* need somebody—and soon, you know. That's all I meant." Betty ducked her head and went back to rolling out the crust.

"Well, thank you very much, but I can manage. I will never marry again, so please don't bring this up anymore. Ever!" And with that, Kate turned back to the pies, wiping her face on her apron.

"Never? 'Never' is a long time, Kate," Betty replied loftily. "Life without a husband could get very lonely, I would imagine. And it's too hard for a woman to run a big farm like this by herself." She paused, took a deep breath, and went on. "Victor says he has come to court you and win your heart." She looked flustered—she was vigorously using the rolling pin to pound the crust flat—but she didn't back down.

Kate calmly set her pie aside and once again put her hands on her hips. She faced Betty squarely and said, "This conversation is over. I refuse to listen to any more of this. It is offensive to me. I am still in mourning, and it is unheard of for you to even mouth such a thing to me." Kate's eyes felt like fire as she glowered at her sister. "It's Grant's privilege to hire Victor for the crew, but that's *it*. Victor is just another hired hand as far as I'm concerned. And that's all! Let it go, Betty!"

"Those snapping dark eyes don't scare me, Kate Robinson, and I'll talk about Victor whenever I want to," Betty retorted. "Besides, if you're not interested, then why are you blushing?"

"Because I'm very upset with you, and you know my face gets red when I'm upset," she responded heatedly. She intended to say more but clamped her mouth shut when Billy and Grant walked in. She and Betty glanced at them and then glared back at each other in silence, arms crossed.

"We set the skimmed milk in the granary to soak grain for the chickens this evening," Grant informed them. "I figured we would have another cup of coffee before we went out to the field." Kate saw that he was curious about what was going on, but he casually poured two cups of coffee and nodded for Billy to sit at the table with him.

The tension was so thick it could have been cut with a knife. Kate said nothing but eyed the two at the table. When Grant looked a question at her, she raised an eyebrow and turned back to finishing the pies. Betty followed suit and silence prevailed. Knowing not to get into a battle between two women, Grant said something under his breath to Billy about the day's work. They quickly slurped the last drop of their coffee, pushed back their chairs, and went out the door, Grant's hand on Billy's shoulder.

Kate marched out the back door to the cellar for potatoes, brought them back, and started peeling. There was silence for several minutes until Betty tried to pick up the conversation where it left off, but Kate glared a warning at her.

"Betty, do *not* mention this to me again, do you understand?"

"Well, you have to admit that he's a good catch," Betty persisted, determined to have the last word. She rustled around, scraping food off breakfast plates and utensils. She washed and rinsed them in two big metal pans, which she had unhooked from the nails above the wooden washstand that Jim had built for that job.

Kate sighed, cut the potatoes, and placed them into a stockpot. She covered them with water to cook later and said, "Well, you can talk about Victor all you want as long as my name isn't in the same sentence."

Betty started to retort but Kate glared another warning at her. "As I said, not with my name in the same sentence." She picked up a finished pie and placed it in the oven. When she straightened, she was face to face with Betty, and they stood there staring at each other, as outraged as two teenaged girls. Unable to keep a straight face, Kate snickered and they burst into laughter.

Evvie and Emma came in from outside where they had picked strawberries. "What's so funny?" Evvie asked.

Wiping tears with their apron corners, Kate said, "I don't know, we just looked at each other and laughed." All morning long, as they worked together, they giggled, even when Marjorie and Wilma arrived with their contribution to the food table.

Twelve men came in from the fields directly at noon. They washed up on the porch and sat down at the laden table. After they had finished, the women and children ate, then the table was cleared. While the small children played and Evvie and Emma took care of the babies, the women washed the dishes and caught up on the neighborhood gossip.

By three o'clock, all was cleaned up, put away, and quiet. Marjorie and Wilma left, along with Betty and her children. The babies were asleep, Evvie was taking a nap, and Leslie and Leah were riding in the truck in the field, so Kate sat in her rocker for a while, thinking that this was going to be a long week. The men would work at least until dark, and perhaps later if the wheat didn't get too moist from the evening dew. She thought up the menu for tomorrow and made a mental note for Evvie to shut the chickens in after they went to roost.

▧ ▧ ▧

The next morning, when Billy came in for breakfast after milking, Kate had him fill the copper kettle with water and light the burners, just as if it were wash day. By the time Betty and Grant arrived and breakfast was over, the water for plucking the chickens was boiling. When Grant offered to cut off the chickens' heads, Kate thanked him

The kitchen range burned either wood or coal.

profusely. She couldn't do it without becoming nauseous and Jim or Billy had always done it in the past. Evvie tended to the babies and the twins went outside to watch Grant and Billy hang the chickens by one leg on the clothesline and slice off their heads. They thought it was great sport that the chickens flopped around headless and came in to tell Kate about it. Sickened by their tale, she sent them back out to play to get them from underfoot.

"Let's go get those chickens plucked and dressed out so we can get dinner going," Kate said to Betty. "Wilma is coming again, and Maxine will be with her today to help, but no children, except yours and mine. So, with potatoes, gravy, vegetables, bread, and dessert, I think six fryers will be enough." Betty agreed. They grabbed a couple of old shirts from the nails in the back room and went out the door to the killing fields, each carrying a bucket of hot water from the copper kettle.

As they dunked the fryers into the scalding water, Betty said, "Last night Victor came over again for supper and a visit. He sure is a nice guy. We sat on our porch and talked until almost ten. He's still sweet on you."

Kate heaved a deep sigh. "I thought we settled this yesterday, but maybe I didn't make myself clear enough. I am not interested in *any* man, and *especially* Victor. I didn't like him in high school, I've never liked him, and I never will like him. So, I don't want to hear about him anymore. The end!" She yanked the fryer out of the bucket and plucked a hot, wet feather. Flicking it from her finger, the entity smacked Betty on the right cheek, where it stuck.

Betty gasped, "Kate! You did that on purpose!"

Looking up, Kate said, "Oh, no...I'm *so* sorry," struggling mightily to keep from laughing. "Honestly, I didn't do it on purpose...really." She reached over and picked it off and then laughed. "But that's what you get for mentioning Victor again. Now watch and I'll show you what will happen to you if you say his name one more time." With eyebrows raised and a droll smile, she plucked the fryer thoroughly, washed it in clean water, and started scraping off pin feathers with a dull paring knife, tearing out big chunks of skin.

"You might leave some skin on that bird," Betty sniggered. "The poor things; they're all naked and defenseless—to say nothing of being dead." And then with a cocky grin, Betty took up a sharp knife and said, "This is what you will become if you *ignore* Victor." She sliced opened the chicken, tugged out the guts, and threw them in a bucket. "That's what you'll be—an eggless, empty shell of your former fertile self!"

Carrying the fun a little further, Kate studied the chicken in her hand. It was limp with its skin torn from the energetic scraping. "'Poor thing' is right," and laid it down. "But," she said, "this is what will happen to Victor if he even says one word to me about marriage." She took the chicken, placed it on the cleaning table, and crossed its legs. Snugging the wings against its sides, she bowed her head and intoned the words, "Dearly Beloved, we are gathered here today to pay our respects to Jim's brother, Victor Robinson, who died of an unfortunate accident with a dull paring knife. May he rest in pieces. Amen."

Betty looked at Kate and Kate stared back until their composure broke with a snort, and they burst simultaneously into a fit of giggles. The more they giggled, the funnier it became. As they tee-heed, they took turns posturing the naked chickens into all manner of ridiculous poses, and they laughed until their sides hurt and tears ran freely.

"Mama," Evvie called from the back door, "someone is here. It looks like Wilma and Maxine." Kate wiped her eyes on her shirttail. "I suppose we should get busy with the meal." They picked up the pans of chickens and went into the house, smothering their grins.

As the four women busied themselves with cooking, Billy came in with the news that the wheat was just right for threshing and, to save time, the men wanted the meal served in the field so they could keep working. Since everything was going right, they didn't want to stop.

They left food for Evvie and Emma, who would stay with the smaller kids and clean the kitchen. The women packed fried chickens into two large cookers; hot coffee was put into quart Mason jars, which were wrapped in sun-warmed gunny sacks. Fresh lemonade, with chipped ice from the block in the icebox, was poured into gallon jars wrapped in wet gunny sacks as insulation. There were piles of green onions, strawberries, fresh bread, pickles, butter and jam, creamed peas, potatoes with gravy in huge pans, and—of course—the hot pies, which were carefully placed on top of the other food, along with the chocolate cake baked by Marjorie. The fare was divided between two cars, one with Maxine and Betty, the other with Kate and Wilma.

Though Kate was aware that she wasn't exactly a good driver, she knew that she was better than Maxine, who was notoriously bad, or Betty, whose driving would scare God himself. Billy, with Leah and Leslie beside him, drove an empty truck, having unloaded the wheat in the granary. Maxine took the lead with Kate behind her and then Billy. The fact that Billy followed her made Kate extremely nervous, because he kept revving the truck's motor and trying to pass her on the wrong side. The rough narrow road wouldn't accommodate both vehicles side by side. When they reached the turnoff to the field, he pulled out and bumped his way ahead of her, throwing dust from the field and wheat chaff from the truck bed on them.

"Just wait until I get there!" Kate vowed to Wilma. "I'm going to skin him alive. He thinks he's smart because he can drive this year and is in the fields with the big guys."

"Oh, yes," Wilma replied. "When Keith got old enough to drive, the girls didn't have a chance, though they're older. Males, sometimes, are just too full of themselves." Just then they hit a furrow, which threw the chocolate cake that Marjorie had baked onto the floor between the seats.

"Oh, dear, what did that do to the cake?" Kate asked, keeping her eyes on the direction they were going but casting a sideways glance at Wilma.

"Well," Wilma chuckled, "it looks like the men may have to spoon it into their mouths and lick the frosting off the floor, but I think the kids won't mind doing just that if they want cake." Kate nodded and kept driving, bumping and pitching over furrows, hoping nothing else would take a dive onto the floorboards.

When they arrived at the scene, Kate saw that the action was in full swing: thresher, trucks, and tractor making a lot of noise, and the men—sweating and chewing tobacco, spitting and coughing from all the dust—were working together, performing their assigned tasks synchronously.

Kate pulled up behind Maxine, who had parked a safe distance from the smoke and smell and action. They got out, set up a couple of card tables, and began to unload. After the food was all arranged, the men took shifts coming in, filling their plates, wolfing down the meal, and gulping cold lemonade as they sat or leaned where they could find a place. While devouring the pies, which had miraculously survived the drive, they sipped the lukewarm coffee, watched the remainder of the crew work, and discussed the progress of the tractor, which was not running as it should. When they were finished, they relieved the next bunch to come in and eat.

After the last of the crew went back to work, the women and children sat on the quilts, which were brought for that purpose, and had their picnic. While the sun beat down on them, the women relaxed, gossiped, laughed, and settled arguments between the younger children. Afterward, the children ran wild, accompanied by barking dogs.

Maxine asked, "Where's the cake Marjorie sent?"

Kate looked sheepishly at her. "Well…you see…one of those bumps sent the cake to the floor, and there it is," she explained, pointing toward the automobile.

"I see," said Maxine. "Shall we let the children eat what they can of it?"

"I think that would be a great idea," Kate replied. So they handed out spoons and the children made a beeline for the car to eat all the cake that they wanted for a change. As a consequence, a couple of the mothers doctored the kids for stomachaches that evening. But while the children indulged in cake, the gossip went on among the women.

As Wilma scraped chicken bones and other morsels off plates for the dogs, she said, "When the crew was over at Bud Richards' place last week getting his wheat in, my husband came home one evening absolutely starved. When I asked him why, he said that he couldn't eat the meals Bobbi cooked for them. The meat was like leather, the gravy was really lumpy and thick, the potatoes were burned, biscuits like cardboard, and pies like glue. He said that though they tried, the crew didn't eat much of what was on the table."

"Now, that's bad cooking when these harvest hands won't eat what's placed before them," Betty remarked. "But Grant bragged on the chocolate cake Bobbi baked the next day. He said it was the best he had ever eaten. I just can't imagine that she could turn out a chocolate cake better than mine, especially when she can't cook a decent meal," she huffed. "He shouldn't have said that, because I just might not bake another cake for him, ever again. At least I told him that."

"I imagine you did tell Grant exactly that," Kate said and, smiling, she innocently turned her gaze toward the children, who were catching grasshoppers, riding in the trucks, and chewing the raw wheat into a nutty flavored gum-like substance. "Sounds just like you," she finished so quietly that Betty didn't hear, though the ladies near Kate heard and nodded their heads in agreement. They liked Betty, but they knew that she didn't like to be in second place.

Wilma teased, "Betty, I know you'll somehow get that recipe from Bobbi, and then you'll not be able to keep from baking it, just to see if yours is better. Hers actually did win the blue ribbon at last year's fair, you know."

"Because the judge was an old boyfriend of hers," Betty retorted.

After that remark, the women ribbed Betty a little bit for being jealous, but they didn't carry it too far for the sake of friendship. They soon began comparing recipes, babies, husbands, and quilting ideas, all the while packing up. When they arrived at Kate's house, they helped carry everything in and put the leftover food away in the ice box. They washed up the dishes, pots, and pans that were taken to the field and finished the cleaning before Maxine and Wilma left.

Kate and Betty, with help from Evvie and Emma, put dishes and pans away in short order. They sent Leah, Leslie, and Kenneth outside to play then, with a sigh of relief, they looked at each other and, Kate said, "Thank you, girls. Now, you two will just peek in at the babies, please, while Betty and I plan tomorrow's meal. I think they're asleep, so quietly take Timothy upstairs for his nap in Billy's room, and then do what you want." Evvie and Emma looked into Kate's bedroom, and when Evvie turned to Kate with her finger to her lips, signaling the little ones were sleeping, Kate nodded and waved them upstairs.

Kate sank into her rocker and motioned for Betty to sit in Jim's, hot coffee in their hands. They sighed again, sipped their coffee, and leaned their heads back for several moments, eyes closed, enjoying the quiet. Before long, though, Kate sat forward and said dryly, "Well, we know for sure that we don't have to worry about dumping Marjorie's chocolate cake tomorrow. I think it's Maxine and Dorothy's day, and neither of them takes cakes anyplace. And, hopefully, we won't be

The icebox held a block of ice that lasted about three days.

hauling all that food and those drinks to the field again, but we probably will."

"Yes, indeed, we probably will," Betty said with a prim English
accent as she leaned forward. She held her cup with two fingers and
daintily sipped, her pinky curling in a refined manner. They looked at
each other with prissy faces and chuckled at the silliness.

"Chicken it is again tomorrow," Kate stated, "and whatever goes
with fried chicken—perhaps tea, scones, and fancy cookies?" She puckered her mouth, wobbled her head in a persnickety manner, then dabbed
at the corners of her mouth with a kerchief pulled from her sleeve.

"Indeed," reiterated Betty, following suit. "But, in the meantime,
I must go home to see that my upstairs and downstairs maids have
their work finished so that I may come back tomorrow for the *fancy*
meal," she simpered and drained the last drop of coffee, her finger still
crooked. Handing her cup to Kate, she stood, smoothed her dress and,
with hips wobbling from side to side, sashayed primly to the stairs and
bellowed, "Emma, it is time to go home now." Kate held her breath,
but when the babies and Timothy slept on, she watched with amusement as Betty wiggled back, took her cup, and shimmied her way into
the kitchen to set her cup down. When she returned, her manner sent
them both into a fit of giggles.

The girls descended and looked befuddled at each other. "What's
so funny?" they asked. Kate and Betty shrugged and let the joke fly
away.

As Emma, who was just old enough for a driver's license, spun
out and erratically guided the car out of the driveway, Betty waved
back with a look of apprehension. In reference to Emma's driving, she
called out, "See you tomorrow, I hope."

"See you tomorrow," said Kate, waving back, hoping that Kenneth,
who was hanging out the window of the back seat, wouldn't fall out.
The car swerved a little when Emma waved back.

The next day was the same routine: the flour-coated chickens
fried in a large skillet of hot lard, hot fresh bread from the oven, potatoes, gravy, fresh green beans, and the women sweating over the hot
stove, wiping their brows with the corners of their aprons. It was
Maxine and Dorothy who came, bringing large pans of bread pudding for dessert.

Betty informed Kate that Victor would be with the crew today. "Oh, that's just dandy," Kate retorted, her stomach growing tight with the news. But she had no time to worry about it just then. Betty smiled sweetly back at her and raised her eyebrows suggestively, which Kate ignored.

Near noon, Kate said, "I hear them coming in. Thank goodness we can serve it up here today." The other women murmured agreement. "Leslie and Leah, you two take the water bucket that's out on the back porch, fill it with water, and put it back on the stand. Rinse out the wash basin, make sure there's a bar of soap beside it, and see to it that there's a fresh towel on the roller. No, no, no, do *not* argue with me! Just go do it! And hurry up: They're coming into the yard." She gave them a little push in the right direction, then returned to the job of scooping food into large bowls and putting chicken on platters.

By the time the men had washed up, the stretched-out table in the dining room was loaded with food, which included fresh radishes, cucumbers, and onions from Kate's garden.

As she hurried from the kitchen to the dining room and back, Kate knew that Victor kept his eyes on her, but she made it a point not to look at him. One time, though, when he caught her glance, he winked, and the bowl of green beans slipped from her hands onto the floor. Two of the closest men jumped up to help, but she waved them back to their meal.

"Oh, Kate!" exclaimed Maxine as she placed peach jam on the table. "Did you burn yourself?"

"I'm fine, and I'll clean this up. So be careful, don't step in it." And with that, she hurried to grab a rag from the back room. When she returned, Victor got up to help her. She glared at him, arms akimbo, and said sweetly, so as not to cause a scene, "Go back to your food, please, while it's hot. I don't need help." She blocked his way by standing firm. With a suggestive grin, he turned back to his plate and made some kind of comment to the guys nearest to him. They haw-hawed, nodded, and took up the task at hand—eating so they could get back to the field as quickly as possible.

While the men talked with full mouths, the women quickly replenished empty bowls and platters. When the harvesters declared they could eat no more, rich bread pudding with thick cream, a plate

of oatmeal cookies, and hot coffee were brought out. They somehow found room for it all. After they pushed away from the table
and thanked the women, they went outside for a hand-rolled smoke
before going back to the field. Since smoking wasn't allowed out in
the fields for danger of fire, it would be their only cigarette until
evening. Burning a wheat crop to the ground was a dreaded horror
of harvest time, whether by cigarette, vehicular backfire, or lightning.

As the smoke drifted lightly into the house, the image of Jim
standing out there in years past, smoking and going over the afternoon work with the men, flashed into Kate's mind. Knowing that he
wasn't there and never would be again, her gut twisted like a rope.
Overcome with emotion, she quickly walked into her bedroom to
gain control of her feelings. Salty tears ran for a minute or two,
and then she took several deep breaths, went back into the kitchen,
and proceeded with the clean-up alongside the other women. They
averted their eyes and kept on working, uncomfortable and at a loss
for the right words. She didn't know what to say either, so she just
started humming an old hymn as she worked. Soon Dorothy was
humming with her and Maxine was gossiping with Betty, and the
awkwardness disappeared.

She wiped her hands on her apron and stepped up to the screen
door again, where she could hear the plans for tomorrow and next
week's jobs. The men were estimating that Kate's fields should be finished in a couple of days, and then they would go on to the Jones
place, which was the farm just west of Kate's. They thought that the
harvest in this area would wind up in about another month. Knowing
that her wheat would be safely in the granaries in a few more days,
she breathed a sigh of relief. She said a little prayer, then, that all would
go well and that none of the men would get seriously injured during
harvest.

As she stood there listening, Victor's face appeared on the other
side of the screen door, startling her. She gasped when he whispered,
"Hi, Sweetie. How about a date?" Kate turned on her heels and joined
the women again, shaken and her heart skittering. The women evi-
dently hadn't noticed anything, for they went on with their work,
and soon the kitchen was cleaned up. Kate huffed a sigh of weariness
when Maxine and Dorothy left, and Betty wasn't far behind.

🐚 🐚 🐚

It seemed she had slept for only a minute when the alarm jarred her awake. She turned it off and buried her head under the pillow, glad the twins hadn't awakened. Then, bone weary, Kate moaned, threw back the covers, yawned, stretched, and slid from the bed. She tried desperately not to think about Jim and struggled to keep good thoughts in her mind. After dressing, she started yet another harvest day, which would be the same menu except for a pork roast, which was ready for the oven, and cherry pies, compliments of Dorothy, who had left them yesterday. Gertrude and Irene would be the help today.

Since it was the last couple of days in her fields, Kate knew the men would be working late in order to finish while the weather held. She would make pork sandwiches for them this evening at suppertime to tide them over until they finished.

As she shoved cornbread into the oven for breakfast, she heard Betty and Grant drive into the yard. She had sausage patties on to fry as they walked in. Betty had a secret, pleased look about her, which made Kate raise her eyebrows, wondering what her sister had up her sleeve today.

"Look who's here for breakfast, Kate," Betty said. She stood to the side, holding the screen door open with one hand and a bowl of potato salad in the other. Kate turned from her cooking just as Victor peeked in. Startled, one of the sausages Kate was turning missed the frying pan and landed on the stove top, sizzling. "It's Victor," Betty grinned, and slyly brushed by Kate to deposit the bowl in the icebox in the back room.

Holding a pan of cinnamon rolls, Grant followed her through the open screen door. He looked back and said, "Come on in, Victor. Kate always has a pot of her good coffee on the stove to go with these cinnamon rolls."

Kate felt the blood rush to her face. With shaking hands, she flipped the burning sausage back into the pan, turned the other sausages, and covered the pan with a lid. She glanced at Grant as he went by and could tell that he didn't know about Betty's mission to pair her up with Victor. She was profoundly grateful for that.

"Hello, Kate," Victor said as he stepped in, his wide grin cutting a devilish curve in his darkly tanned face. Like his brother, Victor stood six feet tall and was lean, strong, and self-confident. His blue eyes, which were lighter and colder than Jim's, pierced through Kate in a manner that frightened her to the core. She knew without a doubt that she had a battle on her hands. She barely nodded back and, with her knees wobbling, went on with the cooking.

Her face red, Kate placed the sausages on a plate and cracked eggs into the skillet, totally ignoring Victor until he sidled up to her and attempted to whisper something in her ear. She stepped aside, grabbed the coffeepot and took a cup from the cabinet, poured it full, then handed it to him. Grant came up, took the pot from her, and got cups for himself and for Billy, who had just joined them. While pouring the cups full, he looked at Kate with a puzzled expression. When she shrugged and went about her business, he turned away and said, "Victor, Billy, let's go sit down and enjoy this breakfast. Today is the last day here, I think. If not, tomorrow will be, and then we'll move on to the Jones place."

"Right," Victor said. He gently patted Kate's shoulder and whispered, "I'll see *you* later." He followed Grant and Billy to the table, sitting where he could watch her.

Incensed, Kate gritted her teeth and kept her mouth shut to prevent an embarrassing scene. She wished with all her heart that the floor would open up and swallow Victor whole. As she placed the eggs, sausages, and cornbread on the table, Grant gave her another questioning look. Was it because her face was red or because she was behaving differently?

Just then, Betty came out of the back room. "Kate, you and Victor should spend some time together and get acquainted again. It's been years, hasn't it?"

Kate flushed angrily and glanced at Grant. Finally realizing what was happening, Grant spoke to Betty in a stern voice that Kate had never heard him use toward anyone, let alone his wife. "Betty," he said, "I figure Kate can handle her own life. You could help her get this breakfast on the table, though. And I reckon Victor would like more coffee. So would I."

Betty opened her mouth for a scathing retort, but Grant stopped her with a look. She clamped it shut, turned on her heel to grab the coffeepot, and angrily sloshed the hot liquid into the men's cups, purposely running Grant's over. Kate knew that later that night, there would be one heated confrontation in the Grant Sloan home.

Kate silently thanked him, apologizing with her eyes. He shrugged and gave her a sideways grin. He knew that he'd get a tongue-lashing that evening, but right now he wore a sheepish grin and went back to the conversation going on around him. In the hubbub of children and adult noise, Betty said very little, sulking at Grant's rebuff. Kate nodded to herself; she was up for a tongue-lashing, too. From the time they were little kids, Betty had been good at scolding. But dealing with her temper seemed a snap compared to dealing with Victor. *That* was downright scary to Kate. Victor continued to watch her every move, and since Betty liked him so well, Kate let her serve him.

Finally, with a last sip of coffee, Grant stood and said, "Victor, Billy—time to get to the field, help oil and fuel that beast of a machine, and get on with this day. The sun has had time to dry the wheat, and it looks like a fine time to get Kate's fields finished."

Victor finished his coffee while Billy made a sandwich with cornbread and a couple of sausages, took a swig of coffee, and swaggered out the door, so proud to be included with the men of the harvest crew. As Victor followed, he sidled over to Kate and touched her arm. "Goodbye till later," he whispered, and made for the door. The spot he had touched felt as though it were on fire, so she covered it with a cold, wet dish rag. As he went through the door, Victor began to sing, "K-K-K-Katy, beautiful Katy, you're the only g-g-g-girl that I adore. When the m-m-m-moon shines over the c-c-c-cow shed, I'll be waiting at the k-k-k-kitchen door." He closed the screen door, still singing until she could no longer hear the words. Betty giggled.

"I told you," she said. "He really is sweet on you." She looked Kate straight in the face, challenging her.

Kate took a big breath, counted to ten, and thought, *Well, I guess I won't get a tongue-lashing after all.* She said evenly, "Betty, I don't want to be mad at you, because you're my sister and hopefully my friend as well. So, please, I beg of you: I want this nonsense to stop. I am too tired, too old, have too many children, and—though Jim has passed on—I still love him. I have no room in my heart for anything else—just my children, my late husband, and this farm. I can see that you still grieve for Jim, too, so you ought to realize that I miss him so very much."

When Betty opened her mouth, Kate interrupted sharply. "No, let me finish. Once again, I don't like Victor. He is repulsive to me—always has been and always will be. So please, let it go. *Please*," Kate pleaded.

Somewhat chagrined, Betty nodded. "I'm sorry, Kate, but I'm just worried about how you'll manage this farm by yourself."

"Somehow, I'll get it done," Kate assured her.

Just then, Evvie came in and handed Meggie to Betty, who took the baby, cradled her, and sat down to feed her, while Evvie fed Jimmy. Kate finished up the breakfast dishes, her tears slipping into the soapy dishwater, a terrible pain and longing for Jim deep in her heart.

As soon as breakfast was cleaned up, Gertrude and Irene pulled into the yard and the flurry of getting the cooking going for the noon meal eased much of her sadness. Work proved a healing balm, it seemed. They took the meal to the field again and, thank goodness, Victor was in town at the elevator unloading wheat when they arrived. When he returned, he had to load up again, so one of the men took a plate of food to him and he ate while he waited for the truck to fill.

Since conditions were right to continue working, the crew sent Billy in to tell Kate that the crew would come in to eat after dark. By the time they finally came in, everybody was bone tired—except Victor. While wolfing down the pork sandwiches, he tried to banter with the guys, but they were too weary to respond. As he talked, he watched Kate, seeking to catch her eye to no avail. He teased Evvie and Betty as they served up the meal, guffawing so loudly at his own stories that the men started looking at him in a strange way. But Kate could see that Billy hung onto Victor's every word. After all, according to Victor, he was a man of the world and had seen many wonders, some of which he was telling now. Kate, knowing that Victor had spent a good deal of his life in jail, kept her mind on her job, scurrying around to keep the platters full. In the general hubbub, no one seemed to notice her silence except maybe Grant, who shot an occasional look her way. She shook her head and went on working. With a slight frown, Grant would look at Victor and then at her. With eyebrows raised, she shrugged and went into the kitchen, taking dirty plates with her, where she started dumping scraps into the bucket for the chickens.

Grant soon came into the kitchen. "Anything wrong, Kate?" She shook her head and continued working. "Well, we didn't quite finish your last field today, but I figure we should be done by mid-afternoon tomorrow. We had too many problems with the machinery, but I reckon we have it all fixed now, so we'll move on tomorrow, late in the afternoon." She nodded to him and he left.

At last, the work of the day ended and everyone went home, including Betty and Grant. Leah and Leslie begged to be allowed to bed down on the screened-in porch on old blankets they had found in the upstairs closet. The youngsters jabbered for a while, then they dozed off, leaving her in the solitude of the kitchen. Billy, Evvie, and Timothy were in their own beds, the babies in their crib.

As the quiet settled around her, she remembered that she had ironing from the bushel basket of clothing that Evvie had sprinkled down a couple of days ago. She needed a dress for tomorrow, so she stirred up the fire in the kitchen range, placed the sadirons on the top, and moved the heavy skillet toward the back of the stove; she usually left it there overnight for it to season properly. Tomorrow, she needed to remind Evvie to iron the remainder of the clothes to keep them from souring in the summer heat. She would just iron a dress for herself now, and one each for Leah and Leslie. That was all she was going to tackle before she went to bed. Thank goodness harvest was nearly over on her place, and then it wouldn't be necessary for her to get up at four. Even the days when she went to help with cooking at the neighbor's, she would have the luxury of sleeping until six in the morning. She heaved a sigh of relief with that thought.

Such a load of work Evvie has carried this summer, Kate thought as she shoved more corncobs into the stove. Evvie had taken care of the twin babies, watched Leah and Leslie, washed many of the dishes, carried water, weeded the garden, brought in wood and coal for the cookstove, swept and mopped floors, and made beds—the many numerous, seemingly menial tasks. All of it was hard work for a fourteen year old—a beautiful, lovely girl with thick hair that hung in a shiny, shimmering fall to her tiny waist. It was as black as Kate's once had been. She had inherited Jim's height, as had Billy, which gave her a willowy frame and gave Billy lankiness that, strangely, emanated strength. Evvie and Billy had more than done their share this summer, and she would certainly like to reward them somehow.

While she waited for the irons to heat, she sat in Jim's rocker and sipped the last of the lemonade, which by now was weak, warm, and acidic from sitting around since supper. She pondered what she could do for them. With a sigh of regret she knew that, for the present, things would stay much as they were. She needed their help and would for a span of time. All she could do was perhaps see to it that they had new shoes and clothes for school in the fall and a home with her, where they had her respect as a necessary and integral part of the family and the farm.

When the irons became hot, she hooked one with the wooden handle that locked onto the top of it. She shook out a dress and pulled it over the end of the ironing board. With her mind on Evvie and Billy, she somehow didn't know Victor was there until he grabbed her, pinning her arms to her sides. Her heart took a dive. *He must have sneaked in through an open window or the front door,* she thought. And he reeked of homemade corn whiskey, which she knew he had gotten from Old Jocko at his run-down place just over the pasture hill. The half-crazy, goat-raising old hermit, with cancer covering the whole side of his face, made the strongest booze in the county and sold it freely to anyone with enough cash to satisfy his wants. He was an ornery old coot, and her children were afraid to venture too close because he had threatened them with a gun more than once.

"Alone at last," Victor slurred against her neck, his hand over her mouth. "K-K-K-Katy, beautiful Katy," he sang softly in her ear. Using all her strength, she struggled to twist loose, but he held her fast against him. He nibbled on her ear and mouthed, "You're a lot of woman, Kate; too much woman for my brother. At least I always thought that and told him so before he married you." Disgust, panic, and then anger surged up and through her, and she stamped on his foot. He laughed. "Come on, Kate, relax and let's enjoy ourselves." He ran his roughened hands down her thigh.

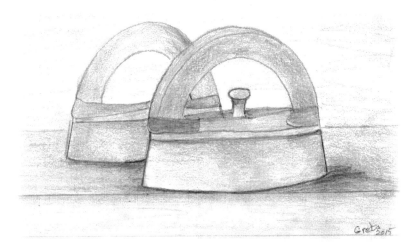

Sadirons were heated on the kitchen range.

The adrenaline boiled up and over and, with every ounce of energy, she elbowed him in the stomach. "Ooof!" he huffed. She could tell that it had knocked the wind from him, but he still held onto her. When he could draw a breath, he wheezed and chuckled, "I like a feisty woman, Kate, and with you, this promises to be more than just interesting." He staggered a little, squeezing her tighter.

She realized then that she couldn't overpower him so she leaned back, as though she was yielding to him. At the same time, she tightened her grip on the hot sadiron that she had picked up before he grabbed her.

"That's it, Kate. Just relax and we'll have a lot of fun. I knew all the time that it was really me you liked and wanted, not my dear brother." Pulling at her dress, he bent to kiss her neck. In one desperate move, she shoved the iron hard against his leg and held it there, listening to the sizzle. With satisfaction, she smelled burning flesh and knew she had done some serious damage.

"Damn!" he roared, jumping back and releasing her to grab at his leg. He tore at the fabric that was ironed to his skin. Kate held the sadiron out, levered the catch, and dropped it on his foot. "Son of a bitch!" he bellowed, hopping on the other foot.

Shocked from his attack, trembling, and breathless, she was further violated by his cursing—she had come from a generation where real men didn't utter those words in the presence of women. But she didn't dwell on that: She had to prepare for when he came at her again. Keeping a wary eye on him, she backed up to the stove and reached behind her for the heavy cast-iron skillet.

"Damn you, Kate," he snarled. "You'll pay for this in a big way." He advanced toward her like a mountain lion—stealthy and extremely dangerous, eyes glittering. She waited, knowing she must knock him senseless and drag him out before the children woke and became involved in the situation. She adjusted her hold on the skillet to get ready.

"You hurt me, Kate. Now I'm going to hurt you. I'm going to take you, right here and right now." His voice was tight with pain. "You'll marry me out of shame for what happens here tonight. Then I'll not only have you, but all of my brother's precious assets that *he* inherited instead of me."

She stood her ground and hissed, "Get out of here!"

"No chance of that…not while I'm this close to getting it all."

He pounced and she swung the heavy skillet with all the strength she had in her body, catching him across the nose. Blood spurted and Victor went down on one knee and then the other. To make sure he stayed down, she hauled the pan up and let him have it again. He toppled face down on the floor in a rag-like heap. She stood over him with the skillet, prepared to hit him again at any further sign of movement.

"Mom!" Billy exclaimed, standing in the doorway, his face rumpled with sleep. "What're you doing? I heard lots of noise down here and came to see what was going on." He knelt down and shook Victor's shoulder. "Uncle Victor, are you all right?" He looked up at her. "What have you done, Mom? He's bleeding!" At Billy's touch, Victor moaned and stirred a little.

Trying to gain control of her shaking body, Kate commanded, "Billy, don't ask questions: Do exactly as I say. I'll explain later. Before he comes to, you have to help me get him onto the porch, and do it before the rest of the house wakes up. I'll take his arms, you take his legs, and we'll drag him out."

Shaking his head, Billy opened his mouth to refuse, but Kate interrupted. "No! Don't say anything or ask me anything. There's no time to lose. He's coming to, and we've got to get him out of here!"

"I'm not going to help you, Mom. You hurt him. Why? He's helped us a lot. Out in the fields, he treated me like an adult." He gave her a stony look.

"Never mind! I'll do it myself. Go on back to bed. I'll take care of this," she snapped. While Billy stubbornly stood and watched, she grabbed Victor's ankles and pulled, but she couldn't move him more than an inch at a time. Then Victor groaned and rolled onto his back, trying to sit up. Panicked and terrified, Kate cast a black look at her son. "Billy, you get over here and help me—*now!*"

As he unfolded his arms and reluctantly moved to obey his mother, Billy's stubborn expression turned to one of defiance. He glared at her but did as he was told. With a series of strong heaves, they yanked Victor onto the porch, where they released him. "Now, go back in before he wakes up," she ordered, and she pushed him through the door in front of her. She closed and locked it, then leaned against it, panting, her knees like hot liquid.

"Mom, we can't leave him out there, bleeding like he is," Billy objected, facing her. "He's moaning and he's hurt. Why did you hurt him like that?" he demanded.

"We *can* leave him and we're *going* to leave him out there. I told you I would explain later."

"I don't want to hear what you have to say, Mom. Uncle Victor doesn't deserve to be treated this way." Billy tried to open the door, but she wouldn't move.

"You're not going out there! Just go on up to bed. We'll talk later, I said."

"Well, I just might call the sheriff and tell him what you've done," Billy threatened.

"That's a good idea," Kate agreed, facing him squarely. "You just do that, and then the sheriff can pick up a very drunk Victor off our porch and let him sleep it off overnight in jail. I wonder how Victor will explain all his bruises to the sheriff!" She yanked several old rags from the rag bag in the bottom of the cabinet and scrubbed viciously at the blood on the floor, getting most of it off while Billy stood there watching, trying to form a waspish answer that would save Victor. When the words didn't come, he glared at her, marched up to his room, and slammed the door, making Kate flinch. She thought that would surely rouse the children, but it didn't.

Taking a deep breath, she placed her ear against the door. She could hear Victor move and then use swear words that she had seldom heard before; words that sizzled in her brain, down into her nervous system, and then into her stomach. They were so awful and dark that she felt soiled just by their being mouthed.

Though she knew the door was strong enough to keep out a charging grizzly bear, it seemed flimsy to her, far too weak to keep Victor from bursting through. As she leaned against it once again, she looked for a weapon, fighting to keep her rising hysteria from overcoming her. She knew the gun in her bedroom was too far away, so she reached down from where she had dropped the iron skillet and picked it up. Listening at the door, she heard Victor, still cursing and shuffling, and she gritted her teeth with fright. When her heart had almost exploded with fear, she heard him slither down the steps. "I *will* be back," he said in a raspy voice, still calling her vile names. When she could no longer hear footsteps, she began to relax, hoping that Billy hadn't heard what Victor had called her.

Exhausted and still trembling, Kate made her way to the stove and put the skillet back on it. She picked up the coffeepot but found that she hadn't the strength to take a cup down from the hooks in the cabinet. Swishing the coffee around in the pot, she realized there wasn't enough anyway, so she plopped into the nearest chair.

Billy came back down the stairs and insolently leaned against the door frame, arms crossed, eyes fixed on her.

"What now?" Kate asked as she turned her eyes toward him. When he didn't move, she said, "Come in and sit down, if you want to talk." But he continued to regard her with contempt, so she said, "Well, all right, then. That's just fine with me. You can stand there all night if you want." She was tired: tired of Billy's stubbornness, tired of the all the work, tired of the heat, tired of the harvest, tired of missing Jim, and just plain tired of it all. "I'm going to bed," and with that, she stood.

"Mom," he blocked the doorway, "why did you do that to Uncle Victor?"

Kate took a deep breath, "Sit down and I'll tell you." He sat this time and she began.

At one point, he interrupted. "Mom, I just don't believe that. Uncle Victor in jail? He wouldn't hurt anybody. He treated me like an adult. He was and is my friend. Why are you making this up?"

"Have I ever lied to you, Billy?" Kate retorted. "Have I?"

"Well," Billy said, looking at her defiantly, "not till now, anyway."

Exasperated, she studied him for a minute and said, "Then why would I tell you such an awful lie about Victor?"

"I don't know why," he said, and scraping his chair back, he got up and went upstairs. He slammed his bedroom door again; still, no one woke.

She wanted to go up after him, make him open and shut the door quietly, and remind him that there were others in the house that were sleeping, but she hadn't the strength to move. She was astounded and thankful that the family had slept through all the commotion. With a heavy sob, she laid her head on her arms on the table and cried until there were no more tears. Not only had Victor attacked her, but he had also attacked and damaged Billy's trust in her.

The realization flashed through her mind, then, that Victor had been uncommonly nice to Billy during the harvest and that Billy, with the loss of his father, had responded fully to that kindness. It was no wonder then that Billy was so terribly shocked and distrustful of what he had seen and of her explanation. She knew then that, like Billy, no one else in the family or those helping with the harvest would believe her. If she said anything, she would be attacking an icon, for Victor had been pleasant and engaging with the harvest crew and all. This was not only her burden, but now it had become Billy's, too.

Wearily, she found an old rag, dipped it into water, and scrubbed at some of the blood she had missed. When she sat back down at the table, she stayed there for a long time, head on her arms, listening to the outside noises with keen ears. She was fearful of Victor's return and was trying to drum up enough courage to go to bed. Along about two in the morning, she stood up, blew out the lamp that had burned low, plodded to her room, and crawled into bed. There was no sleep, though, as she was jittery and nervous, thinking that every little sound was Victor climbing in through her window.

Several times during the night, she heard Billy tossing, moaning, and crying out. She went to check on him, but he was sound asleep. She wished she could sleep, as well, and returned to her bed, alone in her nightmare. Toward first light, she dozed a little, but it was a fidgety and tiring sleep, dream-filled with Victor's lecherous face sliding and slipping under her eyelids.

"Kate, you look awful," Betty said the next morning as they began the last day of the harvest. "Are you sick?"

"No. I just didn't sleep."

"Well, it's a good thing this is the last day for your fields. You need rest."

"I know," Kate answered as she poured milk into the biscuit mix, keeping her eyes averted.

"I think you should stay home tomorrow. Don't help at Maxine's," Betty advised. "I'll take your place."

"No, I'll go," Kate replied. "Maxine helped me, so I'll help her."

"All right," Betty said reluctantly. And then, "Victor left last night. I found a note on the table saying that he remembered he had something important to attend to in Kansas City." When Kate didn't respond, she went on. "I imagine he'll be back in a day or two, though, to help with the neighbors' harvests."

"I doubt he'll be back. I suspect harvest was just too much work for him."

"Why do you say that, Kate?" Betty asked. "He took time from his other crew to help here because we're family, and to see about you. He didn't collect any money, so why say that about him?"

Kate didn't respond to that but said, "If you remember, he always had such big, impossible dreams, and I have a feeling this harvest wasn't one of them. He was always out for big money made easily—which he didn't find in jail, by the way—and when he couldn't find it here, he left," Kate replied, shoving the biscuits into the oven.

"But he's not that person now. He turned his life completely around while he was in jail," Betty said. Kate didn't answer. She could see it would be of no use.

Betty's eyebrows went up. "Do you know something that I don't know?"

"You know what I know," Kate hedged when she saw Billy standing in the door, listening to the exchange. She glared at him to keep his silence. He poured himself a cup of coffee, slapped bacon and a fried egg onto a slice of bread, and left in a huff.

"Huh," Betty said. "Why does he have such a burr under his tail?"

"He didn't sleep last night, either. He's working too hard, as are all of us, but he's still just a young boy who thinks he's a man." Kate dished up eggs and sausage for the children and Grant as she spoke.

She wondered if she could get through the day without dissolving into hysterics or if she could stand to hear about Victor being such a great guy without blurting out the truth about him. She just wanted to be through with it all.

As it turned out, the workload permitted little time for thoughts or feelings, but Kate couldn't concentrate on her cooking: She burned the potatoes and the rolls and cut her thumb, which almost made her faint. In its thick bandage, the thumb was a further hindrance to her abilities as a cook. She couldn't fault Betty or the other women for looking questioningly at her but, since she couldn't bring herself to talk about it, she kept the secret to herself.

Due to machinery breakdown, it took the whole day to finish Kate's field, so when the day's work was finally done, she lay in her bed, too tired to sleep but thankful the harvest crew would be moving on. She would be going to the Joneses tomorrow and help with the meals, but it wasn't on her land. *When I come back home,* Kate thought, *I'll have a chance to become a mother again—take care of the children and see how much the babies have progressed.* As she lay awake, her thoughts turned to Jim and a pain cut through her. In the background, she'd heard Billy's bed creaking, creaking, creaking. Eventually, she went to his room and lightly touched his shoulder. He reared up with a wide-eyed look at her. "What?" he demanded.

Uninvited, she sat on the edge of his bed, careful not to get too close. "Billy," she began hesitantly, "I know you think that I lied to you about Victor, but I didn't. I have never lied to you, or anybody. I want to establish a solid trust between all of us, and the way to do that is to be truthful and keep my word." She waited, but when Billy only grunted, she went on. "What happened last night was terrible, but Victor's gone, and I'd like for you to try to forget this. I hope you can remember that Victor was good to you and liked you. I don't know what came over him, except that he was drinking, and that can be a real problem for some people. It makes them mean and hateful. So, think of him as your good uncle, and forget the rest."

Billy sucked in an uneven breath and relaxed a little, but said nothing. It was difficult for her to know how he really felt, but he didn't seem to mind that she was there, so she stayed with him until he went to sleep. It was too hot for the covers he had wrapped around himself, so she peeled them back, leaving just the thread-worn sheet over him. He was young, and Victor's betrayal would eventually recede into the recesses of his mind. But would she ever forget the assault? Right now, that seemed impossible, but she hoped that someday she could. She didn't want to carry that burden around. Returning to her bed, she grabbed Jim's pillow—his smell still lingering among the feathers—wrapped her arms around it, and repeated Psalm 23 until she, too, shifted into a deep sleep.

Harvest was soon over for the whole neighborhood. The rest of the summer went by in a flurry of gardening, canning, sewing school clothes, remaking Evvie's dresses for Leah and Leslie, and caring for the babies. After the sale of the wheat that fall, Kate hired a neighbor to plow the fields and plant winter wheat. She paid the property taxes, which included three years' of back taxes, and other outstanding bills. Feeling good that she had more than enough money to see them through until the next harvest, she purchased dresses for herself, Leah, Leslie, and Evvie, new pants for Billy, and winter coats for Timothy and the babies.

She invested a portion of the remaining cash in thirty Rambouillet ewes plus a ram, to be delivered in about a week. With the pastures and recently planted winter wheat that was growing thick and lush, she had enough pasture. Come next spring, the sale of wool and the lambs would give her more than enough money to pay off the bank note on the farm, which was due in April. Even then, she would still have money for the coming year's expenses.

She and Evvie were canning apple butter the day the farmer pulled in with a large truckload of the sheep that she had purchased from him. The late October day had turned a little cool, so when she turned off the stove, the two of them threw sweaters over their shoulders, put jackets on the babies and Timothy, and hurried out to watch Billy guide the truck as it backed up to the chute. Leah and Leslie ran from making mud pies and watched in fascination.

With a smile, Kate and Billy counted the blatting, baaing sheep as they poured from the confines of the stock truck. Extremely uneasy and upset in their new home, the sheep scurried here and there in the corral, looking for an escape route. At Kate's direction, Billy fetched some oats kept for the milk cow and the horse and scattered the precious grain in the trough, and they settled down to eat.

"Best to keep them penned here in the corral and fed for a day or so, least till they git used to bein' here," the sheep man advised her. "I see you have a holdin' pasture right close ta the barn," he said, looking over the set-up. "That's good. You kin let 'em into that pasture, prolly tomorrow or the next day after they settle down. Keep an eye on 'em, though. Best to bring 'em into the corral at night for another week so's they don't git afright from a coyote or some other predator, like the neighbors' dogs." Looking at her name on the check, he hesitated and then pocketed it. As he began to write out the bill of sale, he said, "Say, ain't you the one whose man fell off the windmill and died this last spring?"

Kate swallowed hard, "Yes, I am. And these are my children." She introduced them around.

"Ma'am, I'm sure sorry about that," he said after shaking Billy's hand. "If ya need any help with these-here critters, here's my phone number. Good luck ta ya." He nodded, climbed into the cab, and left.

At the breakfast table two days later, Kate said, "It's a nice day with no sign of rain or a storm of any kind, and the wind is calm. So let's all go out and run the sheep into the small holding pasture and get them out of the corral onto grass. We can keep an eye on them— that means all of us, Leah and Leslie—and watch that they don't get out. After they've been there for a few days and get the grass chewed down, we'll turn them into the big pasture. There's enough grass there to hold them until we can put them on the wheat fields for the fall and winter months. Let's finish eating and we'll go out and see how we get along, moving the herd."

After placing the dishes on the washstand for later, Kate and Evvie put sweaters and caps on the babies and made sure Leah, Leslie, and Timothy had sweaters against the October chill. Billy took Timothy's hand and helped him toddle along, while Leah and Leslie skipped hand in hand. Because Timothy was too slow, Billy heaved him onto his shoulders and opened the gate to let the sheep out of the corral. Even Kate laughed when the sheep raced from one bunch of buffalo grass to the next, sampling only a bite here and there.

Mimicking the old sheep man who had brought the sheep, Billy said, "It's like they ain't never gonna git another bite ta eat." His lopsided grin was aimed directly at Kate. "I know, I know," he said, "I ain't never 'sposed to say 'ain't,' but I did." He drawled. He grinned widely at Kate again, then reached down and picked up Timothy, who clapped his hands at the sheep's antics.

Kate goodnaturedly shook her head, glad to see Billy happy. She opened her mouth then to caution Leah and Leslie, who took to chasing the ram, but she was too late. The ram, tired of the game, turned on the girls, lowered his head, and charged. Screaming, both girls hightailed it for the corral fence and scrambled up. The ram aimed for them but butted the fence instead, and the impact stunned him. He stepped back and shook his head with what Kate thought was probably a good solid headache. Laughing, the twins taunted with a "nah-nah-nee-nah-nah," then scrambled down the other side when he shook the fence with another solid hit that nearly knocked them off. For the rest of the day, Billy and Evvie teased the twins for being such scaredy-cats. They tattled each time until Kate banned them to either carrying wood for the stove or to their room. It was cold enough outside that they chose their room, staying there until given permission to emerge.

After watching the sheep for a span of time and seeing that they grazed contently, Kate and Evvie returned to the house to finish the jam. Everyone had something to eat, the babies and Timothy were put down to nap, Leah and Leslie returned to their mud pies, and Billy stapled a fence wire in place.

Early in the morning, several days later, a light snow covered the ground, but it soon melted away in the drowsy haze of Indian summer. While Billy milked, Kate let the sheep into the big pasture and watched them to make sure they were fine. After cropping grass for a few minutes, the sheep became curiously restless, milling about and bleating. She scanned the outlying area, thinking that a coyote or dog might have spooked them, but she saw nothing. She stepped into the barn where Billy was just releasing the kickers from Bessie and said, "Something stirred up the sheep but I didn't see a thing, so I fed them more oats. It helped some, but let's keep a close eye on them today."

"There's no telling what spooked them. It doesn't take much, you know," Billy replied, untying the baling twine that attached Bessie's tail to the overhead rafter to keep her from swatting him with her tail. He hung up the kickers, released the stanchion, and hurried Bessie out of the barn. "That's probably all they wanted, was to be let out to move around in a bigger place where there's more grass. I'll turn Bessie out with them. Maybe that'll help."

"No, I will," Kate responded. "You go ahead and separate the milk; tell Evvie to start breakfast and to fry the cornmeal mush. The school bus will be here soon." As they stepped over the threshold, Billy pushed the door shut on its rollers, and she went to open the gate for the milk cow to join the sheep in the pasture.

Kate picked her way around the corral and noticed that the clear, warm day had taken on a sudden chill. Shivering, she pulled her sweater closer, opened the gate, and watched with amusement as Bessie plowed her way through the sheep, scattering them. The milk cow then raced across the pasture, her tail high like a flag as she kicked up her heels. The sheep, catching Bessie's mood, took off like the Devil himself was after them. *And well he might be*, Kate thought with a smile.

Standing there, she scanned the blue sky and saw a thin layer of dark clouds on the horizon. "Mmmm," she mused aloud, "looks like snow. Billy and I need to get the herd back into the corral before it hits. Evening will probably be soon enough, though," she told herself.

She went back into the barn to check the oat supply and noticed that Evvie had missed a nest of about a dozen eggs in the manger. It looked as though several had been there a while, so she picked them up one by one and shook each to feel or hear if it wobbled, rotten in its shell. If it did, she threw it out the window and placed the good eggs into a pouch made by pulling up a corner of her sweater. When she threw the last rotten egg out, a blast of wind rattled the door and shook the barn. Scurrying out, she noticed a white haze had obliterated the horizon and the air had gotten much colder.

Another gust picked up a blinding flurry of snow and swept it across the pastures. Quickly, she returned the eggs to the manger and started for the house to get Billy and Evvie to help get the sheep in. When she stepped out of the barn, she was wrapped in a white and furious world, a landscape that had become phantom-like. She rounded the corner of the barn and the full force of the wind nearly knocked her down, its frigidity piercing through her light sweater and housedress. She couldn't see past the length of her arm and cupped her hands around her eyes, searching for the shadow of the house. Because the storm blotted out everything familiar to her, she reached out for the barn's solid mass and felt assured when she touched its corner. She wondered if she could find her way to the house before the snow became too thick.

As she strained to see, she worried that Billy or Evvie would come looking for her. To prevent that from happening, she must reach the house quickly. She remembered how the mailman had left the security of his stalled car a year ago to find shelter from a prairie blizzard and was found a few days later, buried and frozen. She didn't want that to happen to her or the children.

Inching her way, she fumbled blindly over the rough ground, groping for the barbed wire fence that ran from the barn to the windmill and beyond. If she could make it to the windmill, she would only be a few yards from the house. She found the fence by walking into it, her sweater catching on a barb. By then, her fingers had become frozen nubs, and though she felt the barbs snag her flesh, there was no pain connected to the gashes; her hands were too cold.

Using the fence as a guideline, she inched along until she stubbed her toe on a rock and fell hard, hitting her head. Wobbling to her feet, she was so disoriented that she had lost all sense of direction. In her confusion, knowing she had to do something, she fought down the rising panic. Though the white wind whipped her into a pillar of ice, she must reach the house.

With extreme effort, she turned around several times, reaching for the fence, but she couldn't find it. Tears of frustration froze immediately on her face, and she had an overpowering desire just to give up and return to the barn, if she could find it. As she took another step, thinking it might be her last, she heard the ghostly clanging of the dinner bell over the roar of the wind. The bell hung on the porch of the house, and the idea that either Billy or Evvie thought to ring it lifted her heart and gave her courage. Stubbornly determined, she shuffled toward the sound. The wind slammed her with hard stinging nettles of snow and sucked the breath from her lungs. She covered her mouth with the corner of her sweater and began to run toward where she thought the bell was located, but she could see nothing. Falling to her knees, a gust of wind blew her back onto her haunches. It was futile.

"Ring the bell. Ring the bell," she whispered. Her head down, clothes frozen to her, she listened. And then, sifting through the howling wind came the pealing of the bell again, and Billy's call for her. "I'm coming!" she shouted, and stumbled to her feet. Steeling herself, she veered toward the bell and Billy's voice, sometimes crawling, sometimes trudging. With the last effort that she could manage, her knee hit the bottom step of the porch. Close at hand, Billy's call came again, his voice hoarse and cracking. "Billy, I'm here!" she cried out, but he didn't hear her, so she crawled up the steps and yanked his pants leg.

"Mom!" He dropped down beside her, then ran to the door and called for Evvie. Together, they helped her inside and into a chair by the kitchen range. They opened the oven door and propped her feet up on a board across it. At Kate's insistence, they wrapped her in Jim's old sheepskin-lined coat and then a blanket. After tenderly cleaning and swabbing Kate's torn hands with alcohol and iodine, Evvie wrapped them in strips of clean sheets. Billy and the twins brought her hot tea, hot milk-toast, and then precious hot chocolate until she couldn't swallow anything more. She let them fuss over her, though. It felt so good.

Timothy was right in the middle of it all, trying to help. Billy and Evvie let him do the simple things, such as making sure his mother's feet and legs stayed warm and covered, taking her cup when she finished, and handing her toast or crackers, even if she didn't want them. When they finally had Kate settled to their satisfaction, they pulled chairs close beside her and, though Billy and Evvie protested, Timothy climbed onto her lap, wanting to snuggle into the blanket with her. Kate opened Jim's coat and pulled him in. She held him close, all the while enjoying the scent of Jim in the coat. His tallness, his dark hair, his blue eyes, and his tough gentleness lingered in the fabric of that coat and in the fabric of her life.

"Jimmy and Meggie all right?" she asked.

"Warm and asleep, Mama," Evvie said.

Kate nodded and then dozed off, comforted by the closeness of her family and Timothy, who slept against her chest.

The storm blew and blew and the family, tied to the house with a rope, ventured out only for water from the well and to the toilet. The house became close and quarrels broke out. Kate kept them busy with cleaning their rooms, sorting out old and outgrown clothes, and bringing wood in off the porch, which Billy had hauled there as preparation for a winter that had come far too early.

Kate worried about the milk cow and the sheep, but for fear of losing him out there, she wouldn't let Billy brave the storm. The animals would have to survive as best they could. There were gullies in the pasture for them to find shelter in if they would or could.

During a lull on the second day, Grant rode his horse over, going through drifts that the horse could manage and around the rest. His concerns for her hands touched her deeply, and even more so when he expressed heartfelt gratitude that the storm hadn't taken any of them. She assured him that her hands were fine, just gouged from the wire and peeling from the mild frostbite, but she had suffered no long-term damage. The children interrupted each other, telling him how they had stayed in the house the whole time, playing games, sleeping, and eating. Billy, Evvie, and the older twins were glad to have a vacation from school, even though Kate had insisted—much to their anguish—that they study lessons each day while home. Kate let them

The heating stove was usually located in the living room.

talk for a while and then interrupted, "Grant, what about the sheep? And the milk cow?"

"Probably found shelter someplace," he replied evasively, and then—adding humor to ease the situation—he grinned. "They'll be hungry though when we find them." Kate saw clearly that he had no hope for the animals' survival. He stood up, cleared his throat, and said, "Billy, let's get busy and dig some paths to the outhouse, chicken house, and barn before I leave." Avoiding Kate's eyes or any more questions, he headed for the door but turned and said, "I'll let you know about your livestock tomorrow, Kate."

After Grant and Billy had cleared paths through six-foot drifts to the outbuildings, they found that all but three hens had frozen in the chicken house. Billy's white horse, Cotton, had somehow made her way to the lee side of the barn and, though cold, was still alive. Billy let her into the barn to feed and water her while Grant took the live chickens to the house to warm them. He hung the frozen ones from the rafters of the open porch to be cooked as needed. When they both came back into the house, they backed up to the stove with mugs of hot coffee in their hands to warm up before Grant was to ride home.

Grant, with his lop-sided grin, tried to lighten the situation again. "I don't suppose those frozen hens will lay anymore eggs for a while." He warmed up his and Billy's coffee and sat down at the table with Kate. "It's going to throw *them* off, too, you know," he said, nodding at the three hens huddled in a box behind the kitchen stove.

"I suppose you're right," Kate acknowledged with a little grin. Grant chuckled, a lovely sound filling the room on this frigid and dim October afternoon.

Grant looked at her over the rim of his coffee cup. "Food supply all right?"

Kate nodded. "For now, and I think so for the winter."

When Grant finished his coffee he stood, pushed his chair in, and said, "Best I get home, I reckon. Looks like another storm coming in." He shrugged into his heavy mackinaw and went out. Sliding her arms into Jim's coat, Kate followed, watching as Grant unwrapped the reins from the hitching rack that Jim had never taken down, though there hadn't been much use for it in a long time. *Those days are gone,* she mused.

"I'll check your livestock in the morning, Kate. Neighbors are getting together and going out to find each other's herds. Some are out there right now, checking. I'll be over as soon as I find out any-thing—sometime in the afternoon, I reckon." As he swung aboard Badger, he waved her back into the house, but she stayed out and watched him ride away just as the next storm was moving in. She worried that he would have problems getting home, but then she remembered how he and Billy had found her that day in the dust storm. They had returned her to home because the horses had known the way, so she knew that Badger would get Grant back to his family. As he faded into the thick snow, she ducked back into the house and suddenly felt very much alone.

By supper time the next day, Grant hadn't returned. She hoped that he had made it home safely yesterday in the storm that had blown in with a vengeance, and was still blowing. About midnight, the wind suddenly quit and silence fell heavily on Kate as she lay in her cold bed. She slid from under the covers and, scratching a hole in the thick frost on the glass, looked out beyond the nearly drifted-over window. Under the eyelash of the moon, nothing moved out there in that grim landscape. Bone-chilling cold seeped in around the window pane and under her nightgown. She shivered. She knew that her sheep had not survived, and neither had the milk cow. Shaking in cold despair, she looked out until her feet felt like chunks of ice, then she rummaged in Jim's sock drawer until she found his heavy wool boot socks and pulled them on. Finding his wool underwear, she put them on over her nightgown and crawled back into bed. It took a while for her to warm up, but when she did, she fell into a restless sleep.

When Grant rode in that next afternoon, Kate smothered a smile at the rigging he had fixed to prevent snow blindness. He had cut a piece of cardboard into a mask and painted it black with two slits for his eyes. He looked like a rascally raccoon, and she greeted him as such. She grew sober, though, when he didn't respond in kind. He swung off Badger, ran his hands down over the horse's haunches, and turned to face her as he took off his mask.

"Everybody all right?" he asked.

"We're fine, Grant," she paused, her heart in her throat, knowing he carried bad news about her livestock. "The sheep...and the milk cow. Are they...?"

"Let's go inside," he said. He tied Badger to the rail and walked over to her. She didn't move but looked him in the eye. He cleared his throat. "Kate, do you realize how lucky you were to make it in out of that storm? That's something to be grateful for." He looked at her bandaged hands, but she brushed his diversion aside.

"Where do you think they are? My sheep and Bessie?"

"I came to tell you, but can I come in?"

"Of course! You must be frozen." Quickly, she ushered him in and took his coat to hang up, offered a chair, and poured him a mug of steaming hot coffee. She sat down, her damaged hands wrapped around her coffee cup, and waited, Timothy on her lap.

"The neighbors and me," Grant began, "we went looking this morning for the livestock. Found most of them dead—smothered under drifts, bunched up. We found your sheep along your east fence, crowded into the corner, buried under three, four feet of snow. The breath of the live ones melted holes up through the snow, and that's how we located them; it was steaming out like smoke from a chimney. Only about nine ewes are left alive and the ram is with them. I don't know if those ten will make it after the exposure to the cold," he said. His halting voice cracked with emotion, but he went on, "We found Bessie close by, frozen."

While Grant talked, Billy came in and stood in front of the stove, listening. Kate propped her elbows on the table and dropped her forehead into her palms, too sad to respond. She heard Grant sip his coffee and say, "I'm real sorry, Kate. We'll get the live ones to you as soon as we can—before nightfall, I figure—so you can put them in the barn."

She nodded against her palms. Grant cleared his throat again and shifted in his chair, waiting for her to say something. Billy slapped his hand against his thigh, then grabbed his coat and went outside. Kate heard him chopping wood as hard and as fast as he could, which seemed to be his way lately of working off anger and frustration.

She took a deep breath, stood, and poured more coffee into their cups. "Well, I guess I knew all along, but I was hoping I was wrong." Despondency filled her. "It was hard to hear the words, though, because that made it real." She paused. "At least the windmill is still working," she finished lamely. Grant nodded but said nothing.

Carefully, she set the coffeepot back onto the stove and stood with her hand on the handle, thinking about dreams that evaporate when they shouldn't. The silence deepened. Evvie, who had been standing in the doorway with Leah and Leslie and hushing their questions, quietly took them into the living room, where she scattered blocks on the floor for them to arrange in alphabetical order.

Grant pushed his chair back and stepped over to where Jimmy and Meggie napped on a makeshift bed in the corner, covered heavily against the chill. "Beautiful babies, Kate—healthy, too." He glanced up at her. "Betty and I…well, we think that you need to either move into town or move in with us for the winter. There's just too much for you to take care of here by yourself—you and your family." He placed his hand gently on Jimmy's forehead.

"I can't do that, Grant," she replied. "I can't leave everything that Jim and I have fought and worked for. It would be like forgetting him. This is the life I know and the only life the children have known. We have enough food. We have warm clothing, shelter, fuel, and each other. It would be too costly in town, anyway, with rent and all, and I don't think it would work with all of us moving in with you."

He hooked his thumb into his belt and nodded, hesitating, head down, thinking. "Well, I reckon you're right…and you know we'll be around if you need us."

"Yes, you've always been around to help us." Tears welled up in her eyes. "Thank you for that—and I do appreciate your concern." She paused, then continued, "Someday, maybe next fall after the harvest, I can pay the bank what I owe them and have enough left to buy more sheep. But how can I get along without a milk cow? Do you think I can get one now at a decent price?"

"I'll bring one over," Grant replied. Waving away her protest, he continued, "She's yours for the milking and the feeding of her. When she freshens in the spring, you can give me that calf after it's weaned and the next calf the next year. Then we'll call it even."

"But you need a milk cow, don't you?" Kate argued.

"I have two and that's enough. I was thinking of selling the little Guernsey, anyway. She'll be just right for you." He held out his hand. "Deal?"

"It's a deal." She accepted his handshake. "Thank you, Grant."

"My pleasure," he nodded and retrieved his wool cap and coat. "We're not only neighbors, but family, too. We help each other out." She nodded and followed him out.

Badger nickered when Grant stepped out onto the porch. Kate, wrapped in Jim's old coat, stood at the rack once again and watched Grant settle himself into the saddle. He donned his makeshift mask, gave her a half salute, and turned Badger toward home. She waved as he rode away, a dark silhouette against the high snowbanks, outlined in winter's twilight.

That winter proved a hard one, the hardest that Kate had ever endured. With one blizzard after another howling across the frozen prairie, it was as if Mother Nature was having a temper tantrum of the worst kind. Kate's cellar was full of canned vegetables from the garden and fruit from the neighbor's trees. That, plus the rabbits and pheasants that Billy had bagged and the unlucky frozen chickens hanging from the rafters in the shed, would keep their table supplied with food. When they could make it into town, Kate sold cream to the creamery and traded butter, fresh bread, and cottage cheese for groceries at the general store. She took orders from the women in town for handmade quilts, embroidered dresser scarves and tea towels, initialed handkerchiefs, and crocheted doilies, delivering those wares to front doors. During the long winter, Evvie learned how to embroider beautifully as she and Kate sewed.

Just when Kate thought she and the children couldn't stand another snowstorm, spring arrived with a chinook wind that quickly melted the snow. The resulting moisture turned the winter wheat a lush green. She planted a large garden in late March and watched hungrily as the radishes, onions, and lettuce peeped through the soil. After a winter of canned food, fresh vegetables were what she and the family craved. Grateful that her family had made it through the winter and that the intense grief of Jim's passing was somewhat dulled, hope swelled in her breast. She was glad that she and her children were together on the farm.

SPRING
1933

The wind was soft and balmy at first, but it kept blowing until the soil dried into powder. Each day, more of it blew into the air, eventually leaving the crops with their roots exposed in elevated clumps, withering and turning yellow without moisture from the clouds that blew in from the west with the incessant prairie gales. Kate watched in despair.

Determined that her garden would survive, she kept it watered with a hose bought in town with creamery money and hooked up to the pipe in the well house. Though the garden struggled to survive, she and Evvie pulled a few new radishes and onions for the table.

It was when the green beans were blooming that hoards of locusts flew in on the wind, creating dark clouds that blotted out the sun. They landed and methodically chewed their way down the rows, eating the crops and the garden to the ground. The ravenous creatures were everywhere: in the house, barn, sheds, and chicken house. The chickens enjoyed the feast and ate until they couldn't eat any more. Kate hated stepping out of the house because of the crunch and the green goo that gathered on her shoes.

The greasy masses of grasshoppers made her and the children gag. Even Billy, who had a cast-iron stomach, retched at times. The grasshoppers chewed on their clothes and on the saddles and leather tack in the barn. They crawled on the walls and drowned in the stock tank and the well-house tank, which was the family's drinking water. At night, Kate could hear them chewing on anything and everything possible. She flipped them off her bed covers and knew the children did the same; Leah, Leslie, and Evvie shrieked, revolted at the nasty things. While they were sleeping, Kate covered the babies' crib and Timothy's bed completely with netting to keep the hoppers from chewing their eyelashes and crawling into their noses and ears. Kate and Evvie continually patched the holes in the netting. Grant brought over a load of poisonous sawdust that he, Billy, and Jack shoveled around the buildings and in the fields, which didn't help much. For every locust that died, it seemed another one or two took its place. Fighting to save the crops from the voracious creatures was useless. They were so thick in the fields that the rows seemed to move and shift along with their brown and green bodies as they devoured the grain. One evening Billy came in, white-faced and vomiting. They were crawling all over him, so Kate and Evvie scraped them off him in clumps. He shook for hours afterwards, declaring, "Mom, we gotta get out of here! There's not going to be anything left. None of us have had a decent sleep for weeks. How can we go on? I'd rather live in a nest of rattlesnakes!" There was an uproar as the rest of the family agreed wholeheartedly with him.

"We can't move, Billy," Kate said, trying to be reasonable. "We have no place to go and no money anyway. The hoppers came in and someday they'll go away."

"Yeah, when we're all dead," Billy stated. With that, Leah, Leslie, and Timothy began wailing in anguish as more of the insects crawled in under the door; Evvie wept silently in the corner.

But one day, when Kate went out to empty the slop jar into the outhouse, a strong wind came up, blew hard for three days, and took the majority of the locusts with it. Though the ground was covered with the disgusting things, most were dead. A few live ones still crawled around, devouring what they could find, but it was wonderful that the insects were nearly decimated. Kate and the children scooped them up from around the buildings and into piles, which were then saturated with gasoline and burned. She bought turkeys and more chickens to fatten on what remained of the locusts. The next day, she heard on the radio that there had been a locust invasion in the late 1870s that had brought massive destruction to the western states. Back then, seagulls had flown into Utah and devoured nearly all of the insects. That in itself was a marvel to Kate, and she wished it had happened here.

With her wheat crop destroyed, she was forced to sign a note for another season's farm supplies. When she came out of the bank, it scared her to see the farmers on the street corners, their faces gaunt and shoulders hunched. They stood together or hunkered here and there, sharing their misery. It scared her to see them sit, their hands opened and stretched across the loan desk in a plea of desperation, and in the grocery store, where they promised to pay as soon as they had the money. *How many will hang onto their dreams?* she wondered. How could she hold onto Jim's dream, which was her dream as well? It was only because of Jim's management and reputation that she had gotten the bank loan. He had faithfully paid it off every year, and the place was mortgage-free when he died, except for the delinquent taxes that she had paid. *Could she keep it all afloat in honor of him and his memory?* she asked herself.

With what little money she could spare, she ordered baby chickens with the idea of dressing out and selling the young roosters as fryers later in the summer and keeping the pullets for eggs. When the pullets began to lay, the fat older hens would be good roasters for her family and to sell in town. She also ordered turkey poults and a few geese, because they could and would range for themselves, keep the grasshopper population down, and there would be a good market for them during the winter holidays.

In the fall, she had saved enough money to hire a neighbor to work up the fields and plant winter wheat and barley. Timely rains brought the crops up, green and lush. She had kept the nine ewes, their lambs, and the ram through the summer, but she decided in the fall to sell them and rent the pastures to a banker, who wanted them to graze his cattle. The stipulation was that she could run her milk cow and Billy's horse on the same pastures. With the rent money, she paid most of her loan by the end of the year and all of her taxes. She salted away the remainder of the money in the cellar in empty fruit jars hidden behind the canned goods.

With the coming of Thanksgiving and Christmas, Kate and the older children dressed out the turkeys and geese, but not without many a complaint from Leah and Leslie. Kate sold most of each flock to women in town and to the grocery store for the holiday feasts. By lamplight, she entered the amounts in her book of figures and estimated that if everything went according to plan, she had enough to get through until after the wheat harvest next summer. With a faint smile and a sigh of relief, she leaned back in her chair and nodded. Yes, they could make it, and they *would* make it. She rubbed her forehead, pushed back her hair, and felt good. Standing, she blew out the lamp and went to bed.

1934

It was another hard winter, but spring came early with plenty of moisture for the wheat to grow, and July brought a plentiful harvest. After the planting was done and things settled down, Kate let Betty talk her into having a dance in Kate's big barn in October. Though she still mourned deeply for Jim, Kate knew that she must set aside her feelings for a time and let her family and neighbors have some fun for a change, so she agreed. The children jumped up and down, danced around, and yelled with excitement. So it was that preparations began for the big barn dance.

The day before the dance, Kate woke at dawn and went out to the barn before the children were awake. She knew they would join her as soon as they had had breakfast. Later, Grant and Betty and their rambunctious children would come over to help with the cleaning. It would be a time of joy for all, but it would be work, too. But for this moment, Kate looked forward to being alone in the spacious three-story building. She carried a bucket of water, intending to slosh it onto the floor and start the clean-up process.

Setting the bucket on the ground, she put her shoulder to the heavy west barn door, wincing at the squeal of the rollers as she shoved it open. She reminded herself to have Billy oil them before the dance. She picked up the bucket, took three steps up, and walked onto the central floor, which spread out over an immense area. Standing there, she took in the earthy smell of the building. Looking up and to the right, her heart caught: There was the loft where she and Jim would sneak away from the children to make love in that dim little room. He had called it their "love hideaway." She knew it had become a haven for spiders and mice now and not for lovers. She shivered at the thought of all those creepy, crawly creatures in that dark room. She wondered if the cot was still there or if the children, who had played there, had torn it apart.

Under the barn's apex, on a small platform beneath the hay window in the north, pigeons cooed and nested. Sparrows chirped and flitted about the rafters, carrying worms to their noisy nestlings. As she stood and gazed around, light played through the slits between the wall boards. The sun poured through in bright stripes that turned floating dust into feathery diamonds, creating a magical fairyland of sparkles. She was taking all this in when a mouse scurried across her toe, startling her. She jumped back, sloshing water on her feet, and then smiled as the mouse turned and ran away, every bit as frightened as she. "Silly thing," she said, watching it quickly burrow under debris in a far corner, where her babies greeted her with thin squeaks.

Setting down the bucket, she tested the floor and found it as solid as the day Jim had laid it. She unhooked the broom from its place on the wall and began the enormous job of sweeping dust away. While she swept, she enjoyed the smell of livestock and the sweet fragrance of the hay in the mangers. Below this floor, Jim had installed a milking area with stanchions and mangers, a milking area also used by the hens for the laying and hatching of eggs. She chuckled as she thought of the many times that she had reached under a hen for eggs only to receive a severe pecking, or have it fly up and scare the living daylights out of her, and that one mad hen that had always chased her and the girls with loud clucking and ruffled feathers. *This old barn holds many memories*, she smiled to herself.

In her mind, she could see Jim as he had worked to build the partition that divided in half the area below to create an open space in which to shelter livestock from the elements. It was protection for the ewes when they lambed in the spring or for a heifer that needed watching while she calved. As Kate swept, she thought that perhaps she should try sheep again next fall. After last winter's losses, she hadn't the courage or the heart to try them this fall, but next year, she might be ready.

On the ground floor of the south end of the barn, Jim had built a garage containing three enclosed granaries plus his shop/garage area. Doors to the granaries opened on the north side of the south wall in

the garage area. A workbench ran the length of the south wall and Jim's tools hung above it. It was a place to repair whatever piece of machinery, truck, tractor, or car that needed fixing. Billy and Grant had used the area many times since Jim's death, with Grant teaching Billy the mechanics of agricultural machinery and other repair or construction jobs.

Although the garage was without a door and open all the time, Kate hadn't been able to bring herself to go into it since Jim's death. She knew Leah, and Leslie had no problem with it, because they spent a lot of time playing in the loft. The access to it was a wooden ladder on the south wall with a hole at the top that required a step over and onto the floor of the loft.

Across the full length of the barn's vaulted roof ran a track for moving hay from the loft to the north window and dropping it into a wagon or to livestock in the corral below. The children often seized the frazzled-knot of the rope, took a run off the loft, and sailed out as the roller swept the length of the barn. She recalled the time when Billy was seven and Jim discovered him up in the loft, rope in hand, ready to swing. After a severe scolding from his dad, Billy hadn't tried that trick again until he was older—not to her knowledge, anyway. Kate knew, though, that Billy and Jack still swung from that track above, trying to land on the high platform under the north window. She shook her head at the recklessness of them. But she and Jim had been reckless, too, starting their life with nothing but the open prairie beneath their feet and a dream.

"Mama, we came to help," Leah and Leslie, big helpers at their tender age of nearly seven and a half, hopped in. Kate handed the broom to Leslie, took another off a hook for Leah, and watched them sweep with unsurpassed zeal. Evvie appeared with Meggie holding her hand and Timothy behind her. Jimmy tottered along holding tight to Billy's hand.

Timothy, who had insisted on carrying the quart jar of drinking water, dumped its contents on the floor. He and Jimmy watched with glee as the water spread out and disappeared through the cracks. Meggie ran over to share the mystery of the seeping water. It was so much fun that Jimmy tried to dip the jar into Kate's bucket, but she took it and hung it on a nail, much to their dismay.

Just then, Grant and Betty pulled up, well supplied with brooms, several ten-gallon cream cans of water, bars of lye soap, and the excess energy of their children. With everyone pitching in, they swept, knocked down cobwebs, sloshed water across the floor, and scrubbed away with brooms. Even the little ones helped by gleefully pouring more water onto the floor and watching the workers sweep it around. At noon, they ate the picnic lunch that Betty had brought. While piling plates with sandwiches, macaroni salad, baked beans, and dessert from the makeshift table that Grant and the bigger boys had cobbled together from planks and sawhorses, they laughed, poked fun at each other, and discussed plans for the upcoming dance, sitting on whatever they could find. Afterward, they all went back to work.

By evening, the barn floor was clean and almost shiny looking. The children made and hung paper chains and streamers, then stood back to admire their decorative handiwork. Their happy faces touched Kate deeply. With a sense of shame and guilt, she realized it had been a long time since her children had had any kind of celebration in their lives. It was then that she resolved to loosen up, put her grief in a secret place, and try to create a happier life for all of them.

The next morning, four men brought over a piano and some folding chairs, which they had borrowed from their church. It took all of them to haul the piano in and set it at the north end of the barn. A little later, the pianist, guitar player, and fiddler showed up. They rehearsed for about an hour and, deciding they were ready for that night, waved goodbye to Kate and left.

That evening, after her bath, Kate went into her bedroom to dress for the dance while the children argued over who was next for the bath water. As she looked for her dress in the makeshift closet, Evvie came in and said, "Mama, I am going to heat my own bath water. I'm *not* taking a bath after the kids. I'm just *not*."

"That's all right," Kate replied, standing in her slip in front of the mirror. "I told you long ago you could do that, so do it."

At the door, Evvie turned and said, "Billy said I had to use their water! That's what he said, so I'm going to give him a piece of my mind and tell him I can have clean water if I want clean water!" She huffed and walked out with a determined step.

"These children," Kate sighed as she smoothed cold cream on her face. She took a soft rag and swiped at the cream to get most of it off, amazed at the amount of dirt that washing her face had missed. She struck a match and lit the kerosene lamp, replaced the chimney, and stuck the curling iron down into the flame, balancing its handles on the rim of the globe.

Opening her face powder container, she rubbed the worn puff into the loose scented powder and patted it onto her nose, across her cheeks, and smoothly down her neck. She replaced the puff, closed the lid, and pushed the container to the back of the dresser top. Leaning into the mirror, she inspected the results and nodded approval. She took up the rouge and, with a fake smile, bunched up her cheeks and reddened the apple of each, wondering if she had used too much and looked like a clown. Close examination proved she had not. *Just right,* she told herself.

Turning her attention to her hair, she puffed in exasperation. Her recent perm had frizzed into something resembling a steel wool pad. To gain some control, she planned to take the curling iron to it and create a smoother mass. Once upon a time, her hair had been shoulder length, black, and naturally curly. Now, it was gray, dry, and the only curly part was the unruly perm. *Maybe the soot from the curling iron will blacken it a little,* she mused as she retrieved it from the chimney to undertake the task. The iron sizzled as she tested it by a touch from her wet finger. She pulled up a hank of hair and wrapped it around the iron, ignoring the sound and smell of singed hair. Shaping tight curls, she reheated the iron each time it cooled. Her hair was still a mess when she finished the arduous task, but it was a little better, so she let the matter go, resigned to the style. She wet a few strays into place with her finger.

She found black silk hose in the top dresser drawer and slowly pulled them on, working the back seam absolutely straight as she fastened each to her garter belt. She hesitated, shook her head, and stripped them off. The hose, her only really good pair, were for church, and they would be snagged beyond repair from all the straw and splinters of wood in the barn. She crumpled them into a silk pouch and placed them next to the rose-scented sachet Jim had given her for her birthday three years ago. She held it to her nose: It still had some of the scent, which carried her back to that day.

At the time, he had said something silly to her like, "You are the rose of my heart, my Kate," and she had melted. *Ah, yes, those were the good days*, she sighed. She took a deep breath and closed the dresser drawer on that memory. But the memories would always come, and she would always love them. *But there's no time for that now*, she thought as she found her white anklets in a drawer under the hose.

After dusting herself with scented body powder, she wiggled into a voile dress, hoping the double back and front panels of her slip would block the thinness of the fabric. She could only imagine the talk if someone, especially a man, could see her outline through the dress. She thought back to the hubbub at church one Sunday when Maxine's dress had been a see-through. It had kept the telephone party lines sizzling for a month afterward.

She could hear Billy and Evvie arguing about the bath water and stuck her head out the door. "Billy, you get down to the stock tank for your bath," she scolded. "The two of you need to pay attention to what you should be doing and get it done! Now!"

She shut the bedroom door to finish dressing. The first time she had worn this flowered navy blue frock had been to another barn dance with Jim, three, maybe four, years ago. She had just finished dressing back then when he had walked into their bedroom in his summer union-suit underwear, the back flap half-buttoned. He was fresh from his bath and had called over his shoulder to Billy that the water was still warm enough for his bath. "I'm going to the stock tank for my bath, Dad. But Evvie can use the water that the twins and Timothy used."

"No, I'm heating water for myself. I don't want to take a bath in *used* water, Billy," Evvie replied. "You're always telling me what to do!"

"Then pour that bath water on the garden," Jim had called out the bedroom door, "and you help her with that tub, Billy," he ordered further.

"Yes, sir," Billy had answered, and that was the end of the argument, at least within their hearing range.

Jim had shut the door then and looked at Kate with a certain gleam in his eye. "Looks like you're going to a party. Mind if I go along?" He pulled her close.

Kate had leaned against him, his body cool and fresh through his thin underwear. He kissed her on the cheek, the neck, and on down the front of her dress, unbuttoning it as his kisses deepened. When she pulled away, his arms tightened. "The children," Kate whispered.

"What about them?" Jim murmured, involved in his intentions.

"They just might come in. And besides, you need to get yourself ready. People will be arriving anytime and things need to be attended to."

Jim sighed, released her, and shrugged into a clean blue shirt, which darkened the blueness of his eyes. "It's a bad situation when a man can't do what's a natural thing in his own bedroom just because there are a bunch of kids around," he grumbled.

He had guffawed when she replied with impishness, "Jim, perhaps you should be reminded that we have all these children because of the 'natural thing' in *this* man's bedroom." As she brushed by him to see that the children were getting ready at a reasonable rate, she pinched him.

"Ouch," he said, and then cocked a suggestive eyebrow at her.

Ah…if she only had that moment back, she would give him anything he wanted. It's sad to postpone happiness and desire. *How,* she wondered, *can I go to this dance without him? He won't be there to waltz me around the floor, his blue eyes happy and all for me.* Suddenly she wanted to call off the dance and the festivities, but it was too late. She couldn't disappoint the children and the neighbors. As the adage went, "The show must go on." No matter how much it hurt her to be there without Jim, she had to put her feelings aside. She took one last look in the mirror and opened the door.

From Leah and Leslie's bedroom, Kate heard Timothy singing a song that they had taught him:

> "It ain't gonna rain no more, no more.
> It ain't gonna rain no more.
> How in the heck am I gonna wash my neck
> If it ain't gonna rain no more?"

Kate smiled at his lisping rendition but was surprised that he carried the tune so well.

Just then, Billy shouted through the house, "Here they come, Mom! Uncle Grant, Aunt Betty, and another car following. Come on, I'm all ready and waiting for you at the door!"

"You can't just walk out the door," she informed him. "You've got to take some of this food to the barn with you, or take Jimmy or Meggie, or both, before you go."

"Oh, right," Billy replied, coming back in and letting the screen door slam behind him.

Kate winced and sighed at the loud thump. "How many times must I remind him of the screen door?" she said under her breath. "Forever, I guess," but she smiled when he went into the kitchen for something to carry.

There was a scurry of action upstairs as the girls finished their preparations and came thundering down. "We're all ready now," Evvie said at the bottom of the stairs. With a flourish, she presented the bunch as they descended in style, Leslie and Leah helping the younger twins and Timothy following. Surprised, Kate looked with pride at her spick-and-span brood.

"Evvie, you've done a wonderful job! You all look beautiful," she said, surprised and pleased as they paraded in front of her with self-satisfied smiles.

"What fun," Betty exclaimed as she walked in the door. "Several cars followed us and are parked at the barn. I told them to put the food on the plank table in there and cover it up with the clean sheets you laid out."

"Good," Kate replied. "Billy, you and Jack carry that ten-gallon can of water. If we need more, you can come back for the other one later. Grant, would you carry that five-gallon cream can of lemonade? Betty, take the large plate of sandwiches, and I'll carry the other one. Emma and my girls can see to the little ones, Timothy can carry the cake in the carrier, and Kenneth can take the jar of pickles." She looked around. "I think that's all we need for now. Someone can come back for the coffee and other stuff we've missed. Evvie, you see that Leah and Leslie stay clean until they get to the barn, if possible. Oh, wait...Leah and Leslie, you can take those blankets for the babies to sleep on. I think that's all."

"Let's go dance," smiled Betty, "and do a little do-si-do, swing your partner, and promenade."

Grant looked at his wife with a quizzical grin and said, "Let's do just that!"

It was dark by this time, so Kate turned the lamps down, placing one near the window to cast light for those trips back into the house to retrieve some forgotten item. Betty led the way out the door, holding it open for the convoy that followed.

When Kate stepped out onto the porch, she took a deep breath. She was awed by the beauty of the prairie night with children chattering, twittering, hurrying toward the barn, then backtracking and running circles around the slow-poke grown-ups. They appeared as gamboling ghosts, floating in moonbeams. Kate hoped with all her heart that the night would be one to remember through the years to come—for them and everyone else.

As they arrived at the west barn door, more cars drove up. Kate waved them in and they poured out of their cars, food in hand. They greeted her warmly, laughing, their eyes sparkling, and entered with her, ready to kick up their heels. Still recuperating from the financial problems caused by the loss of livestock in the blizzard and by the locusts destroying their crops, they were ready for some fun.

Inside, the lanterns—hung from wire hooks attached to the huge upright log posts supporting the rafters—diffused a yellow glow, leaving a soft darkness in the corners. Down at the north end, the fiddler and guitarist tuned their instruments to the piano once again, stretching or loosening the strings for pitch. When they were in tune to suit them, they softly played a practice piece.

Waiting for the music to begin in earnest, the dancers stood visiting and catching up on the latest neighborhood and national news. Finally one of the farmers called out, "Let's have some music here and get this thing started." The pianist hit a chord and the musicians struck up the tune "Old Dan Tucker" and the caller began calling the dancers to the floor. The men clapped each other on the back and picked a partner—which had better be their wife—and sashayed onto the floor, where they chose a place in the square and jigged around, waiting impatiently for the caller to start. The women, stepping in time to the music, tittered at the antics of their men.

The caller began to call out the dance patterns and the squares of four couples started twirling, swinging, and tapping the choreography of the square dance. The men stamped in rhythm, leading their partners through allemandes left and right, the stars formed by hands joined in the middle of the square, and promenades around the circle, changing partners at the end of each pattern of calls. Even Old Man Metzger yelled, "Hoo, hoo, hoo!" and kicked up his eighty-year-old heels with glee. His wife of seventy-five years giggled like a teenager, lengthened her step to match his, picked up the hem of her full skirt, and swished it back and forth as they made their way in the promenade around and back to their home station. Soon, the barn echoed with shouting and squealing as the men whirled their partners around and off the floor.

Kate watched the younger pairs, who were Billy's and Evvie's ages, bashfully seek each other out and awkwardly begin to dance. It wasn't long before they caught the spirit and joined in the shouting, their young faces alive with excitement. She watched Evvie, dancing with Dale Heffner, and Billy as he twirled Shirley Cox, a beautiful girl, as the caller spouted the moves. When Shirley smiled sweetly at Billy, he blushed and missed a step. Right then, Kate could see that he was smitten. *Ah yes*, she thought, *young love.*

Some of the smaller children danced on the outskirts, but most of them had sought out corners to play games such as Jacks or just cars and trucks. Others were outside playing Kick the Can, Hide and Seek, or Annie Over.

Kate took Timothy, Meggie, and Jimmy to an open play area against the outer wall where Carrie Nelson, better known as "Granny Nelson," would watch over them. Granny didn't dance because of crippling arthritis. Eventually, these small children would bed down on old quilts and blankets on the floor and sleep the night away, undisturbed by the noise.

Granny sat in her padded rocker and tapped her foot in time with the music. After speaking to her, Kate smoothed a quilt for Jimmy and Meggie and settled them on it, where they played with a barn set. Timothy, not quite ready to give in to sleep, was in another corner with kids his age.

"Shore wish I was young and spry again like you, Kate," she said. "Why, I used to be the best dancer in the county, I tell you. I would shore give them young fellers something to appreciate with my good dancing in those olden days. I reckon, though, that them days is over for me, but only 'cause of my rheumatism, you know."

Kate pulled up a chair beside her and sat down. "I don't feel young anymore, Granny. I haven't felt young since Jim died. It just took something out of me and left a big hole in my heart."

"Now, you listen to me, Kate. You need a man. Yes, you do," she vowed when Kate started to protest. "I buried three and the grief from the first one 'bout near kilt me, I loved him so. But I found another and when he died, I found another. I just couldn't stand the loneliness, that's all. A woman needs a man and a man really needs a woman. It's way too hard to go it on your own, 'specially on a farm. There's too much work, you'll die before your time, all worn out and lonesome-like. Start looking. Don't wait around and bury yourself on this-here farm of yours. Git out and do some stuff before you git old an' crippled up like me. Being old and crippled ain't no fun, believe me."

Kate didn't answer, but she knew in her heart that she couldn't love anyone but Jim. Granny stopped rocking and touched Kate's arm. "Now, you listen. Here comes that knock-dead handsome Johnny Vaughn to ask you to dance. Now, don't you turn him down. Git out thar and kick up you heels," she said, shaking her finger in Kate's face.

"I can't do that. Jim has been and always will be my partner," Kate replied, turning her head to watch Jimmy pushing a toy truck on the floor.

Granny huffed, "Jim cain't dance with you no more, Kate. I hate to be so blunt, but he ain't here. He's gone and he ain't comin' back. You're not even forty, are you? So don't you be actin' like an ol' maid," Granny scolded. When Johnny offered his hand to Kate, Granny said, "Of course she'll dance with you!" Irritated at Granny and embarrassed, Kate stood hesitantly. Granny gave her a tiny shove just as the caller started a new round.

In a sing-song manner the caller began:

"I wish I was a granger, a granger, a granger,
I wish I was a granger, for a granger I would be.
With a pitchfork on my shoulder, my shoulder, my shoulder,
With a pitchfork on my shoulder, a granger I would be.
Allemande left your corner, ladies,
Allemande right your own.

Swing your corner lady round,
And promenade to your home."

Kate soon found herself laughing as they all joined hands and circled left, then right, then left, and her corner swung her off her feet. She danced back to Johnny, and her heart lurched at the sight of him. When his dark eyes met hers, a shock—like a bolt of lightning—shot through her. She knew by the light in his face that he felt it, too. As his arm encircled her waist, the electricity was like static on the radio. He held her closer and she let him, astounded by her own response.

Granny Nelson was right, Johnny was drop-dead handsome and a great dancer, at that. He stood six feet tall and was lean, with black hair and eyes. He possessed a certain quietness and confidence that suggested a maturity gained through hard times. His jawline and face were strong and masculine, his expression kind and gentle. The rest of the night she danced every dance, most of them with Johnny. Each time they came together, the earth trembled and fell away from her. During the "Waltz of the Wind," he held her so close she could hardly breathe—and, again, she let him, feeling his heart thudding in his chest. Around midnight, when he brushed his lips against her forehead, she pulled away.

"I can't finish this dance with you. Please take me to the side," she said. She knew people would talk about the outrageous public intimacy between the two of them, and the prairie telegraph would be hot with the news tomorrow.

"Why?" he asked, and stopped dancing. He looked at her, perplexed.

"Well, for one thing…I'm still in love with Jim," she answered, mincing no words. She took a breath, "And for another…it's break time and I need to help get the food ready. Please, just take my hand and lead me off the floor. People are looking at us." She started off the floor by herself then, but he caught up and said, "I'll help you with the food."

"No need," she replied, "there are women already started with it. You go on and talk to the men."

"Well…all right, but after the break, save the first dance for me."

"I'll do that, Johnny." She smiled as she left, the tumult inside her very alive and scary. When the music started up again, he came looking for her and swept her onto the floor for another square dance. The crowd was just as lively as before with much laughter during the learning of new round dances and changing of partners.

When the musicians began the "Goodnight Waltz," Johnny caught her up and gently led her through the lovely waltz. When it was over, he took her arm and walked her off the floor, his dark eyes creating a rising desire within her.

"Kate," he said with his mouth near her ear, "my wife has been gone for five years and your Jim for over two years. We've got to keep on living." He paused. "I feel we have something between us here, so let's don't just throw it away like trash without finding out." He drew back and looked down at her, his manner not as smooth as before, his voice husky. "Just think about seeing me a few times before you decide," he suggested, still holding her arm. Though she tried to put more distance between them for appearance's sake, he gently held on and said, "I'm willing to wait for your answer. I know you feel the same way I do."

"I can't promise you anything," she replied, "but I'll consider what you've said."

Still looking at her, Johnny said, "How about I come over tomorrow, help you clean up this mess, and we talk? I'll bring my kids and we'll all have a good time together. It'll all be aboveboard so the neighbors won't gossip about it. How about it?"

"I need to think about that, too," she answered, hearing her mind saying no but her heart saying yes.

He tried to continue the discussion, but she shook her head and said, "People are getting ready to leave, and I need to say goodbye to them at the door." With that, Kate turned her back on him, went over to check on her children before seeing to the guests, and found that all but Billy and Evvie—who were outside running through a game of hide-and-seek—were sleeping soundly.

Johnny followed her and said rather loudly in front of Granny, "I'll come over tomorrow anyway and my kids will help clean this all up. Then we'll talk about me and my kids visiting you and your kids on occasion. How would that be? No expectations, no pressure—just get acquainted. I'll be over tomorrow afternoon, if you agree."

Kate straightened from checking the babies and Timothy and was looking up at Johnny to protest when Granny declared, "Why, I think that's downright neighborly of him, don't you, Kate?" She turned back to Johnny. "I'm thinkin' Kate would shore like some help, come tomorrow." Kate tried to protest, but Granny slowly stood and said, "Wouldn't you, Kate?"

Flabbergasted, Kate stammered, "Well, I guess so." And then, "Now, if you'll excuse me, I must go say goodbye to people leaving." As she moved away, she knew she appeared upset, but it was just a face: Secretly she was bubbling up inside with elation.

The musicians prepared to leave and couples stood around in bunches, talking, laughing, lingering—prolonging their departure and their time to play. Slowly, they gathered up their belongings and sleeping children. The men and older children carried the sleepers and guided the other small ones to the cars, snuggling them together in back seats. The women gathered the bowls and plates and remaining food and took it out. They returned for the tiny babies, who would sleep soundly while being held all the way home.

The eastern sky was showing first light as Kate stood at the door and accepted polite thanks from the men, who nodded and shook her hand. The women expressed warm and heartfelt thanks and promised to visit her soon. When the last ones left, she stood in the door and waved as they drove away, including Johnny. As he drove into the beginning of dawn, she felt as if she had been abandoned and deserted.

Sorry that the dance was over, she and the children blew out the lanterns and closed the doors on the silent barn. With a sigh of contentment, Kate led Timothy by the hand to the house as Evvie and Billy followed, each carrying a little one. Half asleep, Leah and Leslie stumbled along behind, whimpering and fussing. The children were soon settled in their beds and the house became quiet. As she turned down her covers, Kate wondered what Johnny would say tomorrow when she informed him that he shouldn't waste his time on her because she wasn't available and never would be; at least in her mind, at this time, that was true. With that final decision, she slipped under the quilt and drifted into a sound sleep.

Right after breakfast the next day, just as Kate and Evvie were cleaning up the dishes, the telephone rang three short rings and a long one, their party line call. As soon as Kate said hello, Betty gushed, "Oh, Kate, what a wonderful time everyone had last night. So much fun! I've been listening on this party line since early morning, and everyone is all abuzz—most of it about you and Johnny Vaughn. Has anyone called you?"

"No, not yet."

"Well, they probably will. What's going on between the two of you?"

"Nothing," Kate answered. "He's a really good dancer, and I liked dancing with him, that's all."

"I think it's more than that, from the looks of things," Betty said. When Kate didn't answer, Betty went on. "Anyway, we thought we'd come over and help you clean up the barn this afternoon."

"Oh!" Kate hesitated, wondering how to handle the situation since Johnny was coming, too. She knew that Betty wouldn't leave her in peace if she knew that.

"Anything wrong?" Betty asked when Kate didn't respond immediately.

"Well…no, but I have help coming this afternoon."

"Oh, well—good; we can all work together and get it done faster. Who is it?"

"Johnny Vaughn and his children," Kate said bluntly, knowing there was no keeping a secret from her older sister.

"Johnny!? Hmmm," she mused. "His farm is the old Kettle place, isn't it? Over west of your place, about ten miles? He bought that several years ago before his wife died, didn't he?"

"I don't know," Kate answered tersely, refusing to give more information than necessary. "He offered to help, and I accepted, that's all."

"I saw how he looked at you last night. What's going on?" Betty asked again.

"Nothing's going on. They're just going to help clean the barn," Kate answered, trying to keep the exasperation out of her voice. Since she'd heard several receivers being picked up as she and Betty talked, which meant the whole neighborhood was listening, she didn't want to say too much. She knew the gossip had already reached far and wide.

"Well, we'll be over this afternoon, anyway. Like I said, we'll get it all cleaned up faster, and we can talk freely without all the party line receivers being glued to uninvited ears." With that comment, several receivers clicked off.

"All right," Kate replied with a sigh, "I'll see you then. Goodbye," and she hung up.

◈ ◈ ◈

After the noon meal, with the little ones down for their nap, she and the rest of her family headed for the barn. Leah and Leslie were excited and raring to go, but due to the lack of sleep, Billy and Evvie were more subdued. Betty and Grant arrived just as Billy rolled back the barn door. They had made a good deal of progress when Johnny came driving up with his offspring—Jerome, Amanda, and Tilly—in the back of his rather clankety-old farm pickup. Kate's children dropped their brooms, mops, and buckets and ran out to greet them. Her heart skipped a beat when he stepped in and said, "Afternoon, Kate. Looks like you already have some good help. We can go home if you don't need us," he offered with a quizzical look that asked what was going on.

"Oh, no—stay! I'm glad you're here. This is a big mess, and your help will be appreciated," she replied, steadying her trembling by leaning on the broom. "You know my sister, Betty, of course, and her husband, Grant, and their children," she said, and faced him with nothing more intelligent to say.

"Nice to meet you, Johnny," Betty said as she and Grant stepped up to greet him. "Of course we know you, though we live several miles from your farm." Betty gave Kate a sideways grin, one eyebrow raised as Johnny and Grant shook hands. "Handsome," she mouthed silently.

Kate said nothing; words couldn't find a path around her heart, which was in her mouth. *And my life is complicated enough*, she thought, *without fitting a man and his three children into it.*

Johnny broke the awkwardness by stepping to the door and calling to the children. "Hey, you bunch of wild Indians, get in here and help out! Then you can talk and play games. Come on, now," and he waved them all in.

"Johnny, these are Grant and Betty's children," Kate said after the children had all come in. "Emma, eighteen; Jack, seventeen; and Kenneth, who's eight years old," she added, pointing them out.

Johnny nodded. "These are my kids: Jerome, Tilly, and Amanda. Jerome just turned sixteen, Tilly's thirteen, and Amanda's eight. Shake hands with Betty and Grant and Kate," he told them.

Since introductions seemed to be in order, Kate said, "Well, these are my children, Johnny: Billy's eighteen, Evvie's sixteen, Leah and Leslie are seven, nearly eight. My little ones are taking naps right now: Timothy, who is three, almost four, and the twins, Jimmy and Meggie, two and a half." With all the introductions in order, the children picked up cleaning paraphernalia and began working, though they did more talking than actual work, Kate noticed.

Evvie soon went to the house and brought back Timothy and the little twins. They, along with Leah and Leslie, picked up trash and threw it into an empty fifty-five gallon barrel, which was used in the garage for that purpose. The grown-ups worked side by side discussing the dance last night, then the crops, livestock, and neighbors, over and above the children's rambunctious chatter. Johnny didn't touch or make any moves toward Kate; he treated her like a good friend, so she relaxed and enjoyed the small talk. They laughed heartily together over the children's imitation of Old Man Metzger's enthusiasm for the music and his lopsided dancing. "Hoo! Hoo! Hoo!" they hollered as they danced crazily around the barn, whirling and stomping with each step. "Hoo! Hoo! Hoo!" the little ones joined in, and around and around they went, grown-ups watching and laughing until Grant shouted above their noise, "Okay! Let's finish up here so we can go home and get chores done before dark!"

"Us, too," Johnny said, though his children protested loudly. As Betty and Grant loaded everything up into their car, Betty said in an aside to Kate, "We'll go first so you and Johnny can be alone to say goodbye."

"Alone? Have you counted his and my kids?" Kate asked. "Have you counted his kids and my kids *together?*" Kate realized then that she had risen to the bait and been hooked. Irritated, she hurriedly added, "Besides, we don't need any special time to say goodbye. We're just friends."

"Of course," Betty replied. With a slight smile, she said, "Goodbye, dear. I'll talk to you tomorrow." She opened the car door and Grant started the engine.

"Thank you for all the help," Kate waved as they drove out of the yard.

As Johnny and his children waved goodbye to Grant's family, he said, "Come on, kids, let's go home, too." But his children mingled with Kate's for a while, stalling. Johnny lingered, too, walking around inside the barn looking for things that might've been missed in the cleanup. Kate watched from the door, wishing there was some way for them to stay a while longer.

Timothy came up to Kate, pulled on her skirt, and said, "Mommy, I'm hungry."

Kate looked around at the crew and saw that their faces said the same thing. She hesitated just a moment then looked at Johnny, who smiled and shrugged his shoulders, leaving the decision with her. "Well," she said, "we have food left over from the dance. Johnny, if you and your family would like to share it with us that would be fine. There's nearly a full moon tonight, and you could do chores by its light."

He nodded. "Guess so. Wouldn't be the first time we did chores by moonlight—nor the last, I'm thinking."

"Us either," Kate smiled, leading the way into the house, Johnny holding the door for her.

Excited and chattering like a bunch of magpies, the children quickly set up two card tables on the screened-in porch, found chairs enough, and carried food out for the evening meal. As Johnny helped Kate carry the lemonade and iced tea out, he was careful not to make contact with her in any way. She appreciated that, but then she began to wonder if his feelings had changed. Then she scoffed at herself for her inconsistencies: first "no, no, no" and then "yes, yes, yes," but she knew in her heart it was more "yes, yes, yes!"

After they were all seated, Johnny said, "This is really great, but when we get back home, I want no complaining about doing the chores in the dark. Agreed?"

"Agreed!" shouted his kids.

"And all of you, too," Kate warned hers with a stern look. They nodded.

When he and his kids bowed their heads to say grace, Johnny tenderly took Kate's hand, which sent a strong tingle up her arm. She stifled a gasp; her first impulse was to pull her hand away, but she left it there because it just felt right.

Timothy insisted on saying the prayer. When he finished mumbling whatever it was that he prayed, he said a very loud, "Amen," and began to reach for food. Kate gently held his hand down until, with their heads still bowed, Johnny and his children crossed themselves.

"What cha doin'?" Timothy asked, his eyes wide and questioning.

"Shush, Timothy," Kate said softly. "It's their way of finishing a prayer and saying amen. But now we can eat, so let's go ahead." As she started the potato salad around, she saw that her children were confused about the prayer ending, when Johnny and his family crossed themselves. Timothy eased the situation by asking point-blank. Tilly explained their Catholic religion as well as she could, and soon there was a discussion of religious differences among the older children, which opened up new areas for all.

But Kate, with a sinking heart, remembered something very important, something that she had totally forgotten: Johnny was Catholic, and Protestants didn't marry Catholics. Period. She looked at Johnny and saw that he knew her thoughts. His clear dark eyes turned a muddy brown and he excused himself, walked through the kitchen, and out the back door. Involved in their lively exchange, the children didn't notice him leaving, and never even looked when Kate followed. She found him leaning against the north side of the house out of sight of the children, smoking a hand-rolled cigarette.

"I guess," he said, "that you think there's no chance for you and me—if there ever was a chance—with me, a Catholic and you, a Protestant," he finished the miserable sentence.

"I don't know what to say to make it any better," Kate replied, standing a few feet in front of him. "That's just the way it is. It wouldn't work. Today, when you came, I was so glad to see you, but I was afraid, because I felt I had no more room in my life for you and your family. Then I began to think that, since it would be you and your children, it would be good to have more family. Now, because of our religious differences, I know that I can't have that," she paused, "but I want it desperately. It seems that what we want but can't have makes us want it even more. It's funny how things work out that way. I guess I'm babbling, so I'll just say that I'm sorry." She paused again. "Besides, I still love Jim. He has my heart, so where does that leave you? What am I talking about, anyway? We *are* friends, and we can still *be* friends, can't we?"

"Well, Kate, friendship is not what I had in mind. I was thinking marriage, if you really want to know. I think we need to see each other until we know whether that's possible; if it is, we can work this out."

"It wouldn't work," she interrupted, "and you know it wouldn't. I'd lose all my friends and you'd lose yours. We'd be ostracized. Then what?" she asked, opening her palms with that question. "And I don't want my children to be raised in the Catholic Church."

He reached out and pulled her close. "I don't know, and you don't know that it wouldn't work, and I want it to work so much, Kate. I haven't looked at a woman since my wife died, until you." He kissed her lightly on the forehead. She pulled loose and hurried into the kitchen, her heart hurting. She stood there, one hand braced on the table. When Johnny came through to collect his children, he stopped and looked her directly in the eyes. "We have something here, Kate. Don't throw it away."

She shook her head and said, "It's no good." He left her there and went to join the children.

When he reminded his family that there were chores to do and they needed to leave now, they protested loudly, but he insisted. Knowing they were going, Kate wiped her tears with her dress hem, pasted on a smile, and stepped in to say goodbye. Johnny turned at the door and repeated quietly, "Don't throw it away, Kate." He walked across the porch but hesitated, looking back at her, and then went on to his truck. Her children joined her on the porch and waved noisily to them, saying, "Goodnight! Goodnight! Come again soon." After which they scattered to do their assigned chores in the moonlight.

She watched Johnny's pickup truck until it became a part of the prairie night. Needing her own space, she went around the outside of the house and rested her head where Johnny had leaned. The acid pain ripped through her heart like a searing ember. Scalding tears eventually seeped away a portion of her deep regret, but they didn't ease much of the everlasting, always-present, stomach-twisting sorrow for Jim, and now for Johnny. She stood there, sobs racking her body. It wasn't long before she heard Leah and Leslie calling for her. Someone, it seemed, always needed something from her. With a sigh, she straightened and, making her way back into the house, wondered why she denied herself someone like Johnny, who desired to grant her every wish. She could have him as a dear partner by simply saying yes. But that was too big of a gamble right now. *I'm not ready*, she told herself, *to take on all the problems and changes that decision would create.*

She dabbed at her face, took a deep breath, and went to see what Leah and Leslie were fussing about. Their problem turned out to be nothing more than a difference of opinion as to whose turn it was to sleep with a certain doll and who it belonged to. Kate took the doll, stashed it away, and put the twins to work washing the dishes, both squalling at the unfairness of her decision. She didn't really care about their opinion of her. *Living in this world*, Kate thought to herself, *the two of them will come to recognize that life isn't fair, and now is as good a time as any to understand that.*

By the time Billy and Evvie came in from doing the chores, the twins had finished the dishes and were upstairs squabbling again. Kate called up for them to stop it and to get into bed. While she and Evvie made sure the little ones were tucked in, Billy said goodnight and climbed the stairs to his room. Evvie patted Timothy goodnight and closed the door behind her. She said goodnight to her mother, but then turned at the bottom of the stairs.

"Mom," she hesitated, then took a deep breath and went on, "I think you should marry Johnny. He's really nice. I know he likes you a lot; I think you like him, too. He would be a great dad."

Surprised that Evvie had grasped the situation so quickly, Kate answered, "Yes, I do like him, but marriage is serious, and it's just not as simple as that. There are other things going on—and I still love your dad, you know. Besides, Johnny hasn't asked me anyway—and I wouldn't say yes right now."

"I love Dad, too, but us kids—we *need* a dad. And I pick Johnny. You should pick him, too."

"But," Kate replied, "there are so many bumps in the road. The big bump is that Johnny and his family are Catholics."

"Well, what's wrong with that?" Evvie queried.

"It's just not done," Kate responded. "Catholics and Protestants do *not* marry, at least according to today's rules and my upbringing. And...we barely know each other."

"Mom, Johnny is a good man. What difference does it make if he goes to a different church? There are kids in school whose parents each go to different churches. I don't get it."

"Well, it's late and I'm tired," Kate interjected. "Let's go to bed. I'll seriously think about this."

"Okay," Evvie relented, "but remember: You just promised to think about it—*seriously* think about it. You just promised me that."

"I keep my promises, you know that. But saying I'll think about it doesn't mean that I'll decide to marry him. Do you understand? Besides, as I said before, he hasn't asked me."

Evvie nodded and heaved a sigh of resignation. Dejected, she opened the door to the stairs. Before she took the first step, she again turned and focused on Kate and said softly but audibly, "He *will* ask you, and you need to decide to say yes." She took one step up the stairs and said in a stage whisper, "If he asked me, I would marry him in a minute. Yes, I would."

"Evvie!" Kate scolded. But Evvie went on up and quietly closed her door, giggling.

It was a rough night for Kate. She was torn between continuing to be Jim's widow or to take the risky step of possibly becoming Johnny's wife. Was it fair to Johnny, or to her? At nearly forty, she was still young, and the thought of being alone for the rest of her life made her feel empty. Granny Nelson and Johnny were right: Jim was gone and so was Johnny's wife, Yvonne. *They can no longer be a comfort to us,* she thought, *nor a helpmate, partner, or anything to either one of us.* What about the children being pushed into one family? How was that going to work out? She had noticed how Billy looked at Amanda, who was near his age. Then there's Evvie and Jerome, who seemed to really like each other, too. She rolled and tossed until she looked at the bedside clock and saw that it was four thirty. Tired and dismayed, she sat up, threw her feet over the side, and then fell back. She pulled the covers over her and fell to sleep, only to be rudely awakened by the alarm at six for the day's work.

The piano player and helpers came early to move the piano back to his house. Billy and Evvie took down the few remaining scraps of crepe paper strips and a forgotten lantern, then picked up the box of toys in the corner of the barn and stored them in the upstairs closet in the house. Everybody was dragging and crabby so—with the usual chores, meals, and other duties—the day passed into a welcome bedtime.

When the children were all bedded down, Kate went out and stood under the prairie moon. The fall night was still, deep-breathing, and lovely, but somehow—under all that beauty—the land was still wild, like a horse that remained untamed, running with abandon and kicking things to pieces. She looked up at the man in the moon and whispered, "I will tame my share of this prairie, though." Then her thoughts turned to Johnny and how her emotions were like a wild horse, untamed and running with abandon. She longed deeply for Johnny to be here enjoying this beautiful night with her, enclosed in his arms.

🦢 🦢 🦢

On a weekend late in October, the crowing of the rooster welcomed a beautiful dawn. It was Saturday, and with the chores done, Kate decided they would have a picnic at noon. She told the children to go out and make a place under the trees in the pasture down by the creek. Meanwhile, she and Evvie would make up cheese-and-lettuce sandwiches for lunch. After they finished packing the sandwiches, Kate was sweeping the kitchen floor free of bread crumbs when Billy came charging in carrying Jimmy, who was whimpering strangely. Leah, Leslie, and Timothy followed behind, crying. Billy said, "Mom, he's been bitten by a rattler! I don't know what to do!"

Kate dropped the broom and grabbed Jimmy. When he saw his mother, he began to scream, clinging to her neck so tightly that she had to loosen his choke hold. Billy, his face white and scared, showed her the two-holed bite on the boy's leg, which was already swollen.

"Evvie, call the doctor," she commanded. "Billy, get the car started. Evvie, after you call the doctor, get a chunk of ice and wrap it in a cloth big enough to tie around this leg. Leah, you and Leslie get one of your dad's ties for a tourniquet. Hurry! All of you!" She took another look at the swelling leg and then saw that Billy stood and stared. "Go, Billy! Go start the car! Where's that snake?"

Billy's glazed eyes focused on her and then he jerked as if coming awake. "Yes, yes, I'll go start the car! I killed the snake," he said as he ran to the door. While Evvie talked to the doctor, the twins came with the tie and Kate snugged it up around Jimmy's chubby little leg, hoping to stop the poison from going further.

"The doctor said for you to bring him right in to the hospital and he would meet you there, but to hurry," Evvie yawped as she made for the back room and the icebox. "He also said that you could make an incision and suck some of the poison out before it got too far into the bloodstream." She handed Kate the ice stuffed in an old sock.

"Oh, yes," Kate remembered. "Make a cut and suck the poison out. Get that snake kit from the left-hand corner drawer of my dresser, Evvie."

Kate held her darling little boy, who had become strangely quiet and calm. She wondered if she could make herself cut him to extract the poison, but she realized that she had to do it: As small as he was, the toxin was rapidly surging into his bloodstream. Totally panicked by that thought, she threw the door open and raced out with Jimmy in her arms to find Billy desperately cranking the car engine, which refused to start. Her only hope lay in the fact that they could get to the doctor in time. Fearful that they wouldn't, she yelled at Billy to start the old truck, but after a couple more cranks, the car started and, with Billy driving, they swerved out of the drive. Then the car died.

Kate looked angrily at Billy, "What did you do? Why did it stop?"

At that moment, Evvie caught up to them and opened the car door. "Here's the kit, Mom," she panted. "I thought you wanted it, so I ran to catch up to you before you left."

"I *do* want it." Kate grabbed it from Evvie, then she turned back to Billy. "What did you do to the car? Get it started!"

"I didn't do anything to it. It just stopped!" Billy replied. Casting a glare at her, he vaulted out and grabbed the crank from under the seat. He was hopelessly cranking when Johnny drove in.

Kate jumped out with Jimmy in her arms and, with the kit in her hand, piled into Johnny's car. "He's been bitten by a rattler! Get to the hospital!"

Johnny barreled down the road at an insane speed as Kate flung open the kit, made a deep cut in Jimmy's leg, and placed the suction cup over the bite. She began squeezing the bulb, blood running into her lap. The car careened over bumps and washboards that threw them around like rocks in a bucket. Though it took determination to keep the pump on the wound, she kept squeezing until it was full, then poured the contents out the window and repeated the procedure. Driving recklessly, they made it into town in twenty minutes, but Jimmy was having convulsions by that time. Inside the hospital, the Sisters spirited Jimmy away into the recesses of the building. When Kate and Johnny tried to follow, the Sister at the desk informed them that they had to wait and turned them toward the waiting room. And so…they waited, waited, and waited, both of them pacing.

Over an hour passed before Doctor Jensen appeared at the door and looked at them, shaking his head. "We did everything we knew to do, but we couldn't save him. He was so little that the poison went right into the bloodstream. I am so sorry." Kate screamed and fell to her knees, sobbing. The doctor and Johnny picked her up and set her on the couch. "I can give her a sedative and keep her here, or you can take her home and get someone to stay with her—at least for tonight. What do you think?"

"I want to go home to my children!" Kate cried out. Pulling herself together with a terrible effort, she steadied her voice and said, "They are there alone and scared. I need to go home. I want to go and take Jimmy home—take my baby with me!" Her voice climbed in volume with every word.

"That's fine, you can go home," the doctor replied, "but I can't release Jimmy yet. Johnny will take you home, but Jimmy stays here with me."

"Why?" she wailed, and more tears began to flow.

"Kate," the doctor said evenly, "you know he's no longer alive, and I have papers to fill out. Johnny can come back for Jimmy tomorrow so you can bury him in the family plot. I'll give you a shot now before you go, and also some pills for sleeping. Please, get someone in to help you for a while, Kate."

She nodded absently and sat up straighter. Johnny sat beside her, holding tightly to her hand, caressing it with his thumb. "I don't want to leave my baby here alone," she argued. "He'll be scared."

"Wait here," the doctor said, looking at Johnny. "I'll come back in a few minutes with the medicine. I'll give her a shot and after that you go to the nurses' station and take care of arrangements there. The Sister will help you. One of the Sisters will come sit with Kate while you do that."

Johnny nodded, tears running down his face.

On the way home, they were both quiet. Since she was drugged from the sedative, there wasn't much point in talking. "I'll stay with you tonight," Johnny finally said, his voice rough with emotion. "My kids are big enough to stay by themselves."

"No," Kate slurred, "call Betty. Your family will be frightened. Go home. Be with them."

Johnny protested but when she insisted, he relented, "All right, I'll call Betty as soon as you're settled in bed." She nodded, her head lolling.

Arriving at her home, Johnny went in first by himself and told Kate's children that Jimmy had not survived the snake bite. "Billy, come help me get you mother into the house; Evvie, get her bed ready, but first call your Aunt Betty and ask her to come over." Shocked, the children stood, dumfounded, not moving. "Come on, now," Johnny said gently. "We have to take care of your mother and get her to bed. Her heart is broken, and so are yours, but we have to help her. You younger children—get her nightgown laid out and some water for her to drink, and maybe something warm for her feet. She's shivering right now. So come on, let's get her to bed where she can sleep and rest. I'll tell you all about it after we get her comfortable. Evvie, make sure you call your Aunt Betty to come and stay the night." Numb, the children slowly went into motion and did as he told them.

When Johnny and Billy took Kate in, Leah and Leslie had a glass of water ready for her, which Kate refused. Evvie had found her nightgown and laid it out, then put a hot water bottle at the foot of the bed. Johnny and Billy helped Kate into the bedroom. He gave instructions for Evvie to undress her mother, get her nightgown on her, and put her into bed. Then he went out, shutting the door behind him.

Not used to seeing her mother naked, Evvie timidly undressed her and slid the nightgown over Kate's shoulders, then helped her get under the covers. Evvie's hot tears rolled off her chin and splashed onto Kate's face.

"Don't cry," Kate whispered, raising her arm to touch her daughter's cheek. "Little Jimmy is all right and will come home tomorrow from the hospital. The doctor said we can get him tomorrow." Evvie nodded, covered her mother with another quilt, then pulled up a chair and sat down, where she held onto Kate's cold hand. Through the fog from the shot the doctor had given her, Kate whispered a request for hot tea just as Johnny opened the door a crack and asked Evvie if it was all right to come in.

"Yes, it is," Evvie replied, standing. "I'm worried. Mama looks really tired, Johnny, and so sick. Will she be all right?" she asked as he came to stand beside her.

"Yes, she will, but all of you will need to help her. She hasn't had an easy time of it since your dad died, but she's toughed it out because she loves you kids and loves this farm." He bent down and smoothed back Kate's hair, then said, "I heard her ask for hot tea. So could you do that for her?" Kate saw him take Evvie's hand and lead her to the door, then he came back to sit with her.

After Kate finished the tea that Evvie had brought, Johnny called her back and took her aside. Quietly he said, "We'll make some plans tomorrow for Jimmy. Go ahead, take her cup; I'll be out in a minute. I just want to stay here with her for a while." Evvie nodded and left them alone.

Johnny took Kate's hand and held it to his lips. "I'm so sorry, sweetheart," he whispered, leaning to kiss her forehead. "Just sleep now." He brushed another kiss across her cheek and left, leaving the door open to hear if she called.

But Kate wasn't asleep and, from a hollow distance, she heard her family gather round the kitchen table and Johnny's voice as he began to tell them what had happened at the hospital. Kate wanted to hear so she got up, woozy and disoriented, and wobbled across the room. She leaned weakly against the door jam, where no one noticed her listening. With Evvie, Billy, and the twins seated, Johnny told them what the doctor had said and asked them how it came about that Jimmy had been bitten by the rattler.

Billy said, "Well, Mom told us we could have a picnic if I would take the younger kids outside to find a place for it down by the crick, while she and Evvie got the lunch ready. So I did. I put Meggie and Jimmy in the wagon with Timothy and pulled them around, with Leah and Leslie beside me. We looked at several places down there before we finally settled on a spot under a tree in the corner of the pasture. It's where the windmill pumps water for the stock tank, about a mile from the house, I guess. It's a nice shady spot under that tree, close to the crick. While I was tramping some of the taller weeds and grass down, Jimmy said, 'Look what I found, Biddie.' He can't say 'Billy,' it always comes out 'Biddie.' About that time, Leah yelled, and then Leslie screamed, 'No! No! No! Drop it!' So I looked around, and there he was, holding a snake up by its tail!"

Billy stopped, looking uncertain. "At first I thought it was a bull snake," he went on, "but then it rattled and made a strike at him. It missed, and that scared him, so he dropped it. Then he laughed because he thought it was funny, I guess. Before I could get to him, he bent over to pick it up again, with Leah and Leslie still screaming at him. The snake was coiled up by that time, so when Jimmy reached for it, it struck him on the leg. I ran over, stomped on its head a few times to kill it. I grabbed up Jimmy and told the other kids to follow me. I ran as fast as I could to the house." He paused, his voice shaking. "About halfway to the house, Jimmy started jerking a little. I guess the poison went through him pretty fast." Billy cleared his throat and went on, his whole body shaking. "By the time we got to the house, he was kinda limp and moaning. I handed him to Mom, and the rest you know, I guess," he finished, his voice cracking. Johnny nodded and looked down at the table, running his fingers through his hair. "My little brother is dead because I wasn't watching him close enough!" Billy blurted.

Johnny pushed his chair back and went over to Billy, placing a hand on his shoulder. "It isn't your fault, son. Some things just happen, and nobody can prevent them from happening." He gave his red bandana to Billy to wipe the tears away." They all were crying, including Johnny, who turned his head away.

Johnny cleared his throat and, just as he opened his mouth to speak, Kate wobbled into the room. "So that's what happened to my baby, is it Billy?" she slurred. "You caused my Jimmy to die of a snake bite because you weren't paying attention." Leaning on the back of Evvie's chair, Kate's words came out haltingly, the medicine still having its effect. She could see that it was as if she had slapped him hard, but she was so incensed that she didn't care. She really wanted to hit him and stepped in his direction.

Johnny rushed over and grabbed her arm, restraining her. "Kate, be careful what you say to these children of yours. It wasn't Billy's fault, so choose your words wisely," he advised in a quiet but stern voice.

Taken aback by his attitude, Kate glared at him. "Go home, Johnny. Go home and leave us alone!" Johnny stepped back. Her children looked at her in astonishment, their mouths open, eyes wide in shock and embarrassment.

"Mom," Evvie said, "he's here helping us take care of you."

"I don't need…" she began, but vertigo overcame her. When she grabbed for the chair back again, Johnny steadied her, gesturing for Evvie to help him get her back into bed. In her whirling mind, Kate could hear Billy's anguished sobs, but she didn't care. *He deserves to be sobbing*, she thought. *He killed my baby.*

When they came back into the kitchen from the bedroom, Johnny said, "Billy, come home with me for now. Evvie, fix something for you kids to eat. Leah and Leslie, you get these little ones ready for bed and put Meggie in your bed so she won't be alone. Evvie, you take Timothy to bed with you." That said, he gave them all a hug and told Billy to get his things together so they could leave.

"I'm staying here," Billy said. "I have chores and stuff to do."

Johnny hesitated. "Well, with your mother's mind like it is now, I think you should go with me. Jerome can do your chores until you come back, when your mother's mind clears a bit. So, come on with me."

"Nope, I'm staying here and do my work," Billy answered, arms crossed.

"Well…I don't think that's a good idea, but I guess you're old enough to decide for yourself. If you change your mind, you're welcome at my house, you know. I'll wait here until Betty comes." He had no more than said that when Betty bustled in and took over.

At that point, Kate slipped into a deep sleep.

To Kate, the next few days were like a dark, swampy, sinkhole that threatened to swallow her completely. She had no desire to even try to fight against its pulling hold on her. It was just too difficult to live, or even move, anymore. When little Jimmy was lowered into the grave right next to his dad, Kate—though unsteady and still in a drug-induced state of mind—was right there. She couldn't look at Billy for the loathing she carried toward him that came in inundating waves of agony and despair.

Grant and Betty, seeing the situation, convinced Billy to go home with them, leaving Jack to take Billy's place for chores. Though they tried to reason with her, Kate laid in her bed day after day, unable to move, eat, or even think. She wanted to die and be rid of the world. When the children came in to see her, she didn't acknowledge them at all. They came out crying and eventually quit going in except for Meggie, who climbed into bed with her, and Kate held her close.

The neighbor ladies gave Betty breaks by taking turns staying with Kate. They tried to reach Kate's mind with small talk, embroidery, quilting squares, and crocheting, but Kate was as dead as Jimmy—dead to everything. She couldn't remember how to do any of it, anyway. And she didn't want to do all those trivial things that make up a housewife and mother's life. It was all too much effort.

Johnny came one time. She railed at him with an anger that nearly scorched the walls, accusing him of trying to take Jim's place in her life. "I don't want you to come here anymore! Go away!" she shrieked. Betty came in then and mouthed that he should wait for her in the living room. He nodded and left. "I don't want him here!" Kate cried out.

"He's gone, now," Betty said, patting and cooing to her until she calmed down.

But Johnny didn't wait, and when he didn't come back, Kate began to long for him. She realized then that he was the only person she really wanted in her room, and that made her even angrier. *I will never, ever need anyone again!* she told herself. *They die some horrible death, or go away and never come back and leave me to suffer alone.* She pulled the covers over her head and curled into a ball, weeping.

🐚 🐚 🐚

The doctor came out twice a week, deeply concerned about Kate's mind as well as her failing physical health. When she didn't respond to any medication and didn't improve in six weeks, he suggested to Grant and Betty that she should be institutionalized for treatment in a facility in Kansas City.

After he left, Betty went into Kate's room and said, "Doctor Jensen thinks you should go to Kansas City for treatment, Kate."

"No," Kate said in a flat voice. "I won't go. I don't want to live. Just leave me alone and let me die. Why won't you let me die?" she wailed.

"I can't let you die, Kate. You need to live for these children— *your* children!" Betty implored. "You must get well! Your family needs you." She paused. "If you don't agree to go, Grant and I will sign you in. Someone will come then and put you in restraints and take you away," she said.

"Fine," Kate retorted, "just put me away so you can get back to your life and not be here all the time, helping me out. You can have my kids, too. I don't care."

"Kate," Betty replied, "you know we'll do whatever it takes to help you get well, but you have to help yourself, too. Your family needs you, especially Billy. He's suffering, not only from Jimmy's death, but also from his dad's passing. He thinks you hate him."

"Well, I *do* hate him. It's his fault that Jimmy is dead. I held my baby's little shuddering body as it twisted horribly. I watched him die, just as I watched Jim and my other two babies die. Now you stand there and tell me to get up and get going. I don't want to! Do you understand? I do not want to live anymore!" Kate turned onto her side and let that black sucking hole pull her under again.

"I'm sorry you feel that way, Kate," Betty said, "but if you don't make the decision, we will. And if you still refuse to go, the sheriff and Doctor Jensen will take you." Before Kate could argue further, Betty went out and closed the door softly behind her.

🐚 🐚 🐚

It was difficult to do, but after several days of consideration, Grant and Betty agreed with the doctor. And on the day Kate was scheduled to go, they arrived with Jack to pick up Kate's children—everyone but Billy, who would stay at the farm with Jack to do chores. Betty stayed with Kate while Grant took Kate's kids to Grant's mother's place, where she would care for them while Betty and Grant were gone for the few days it would take to get Kate signed in and settled.

When Grant returned, Billy came in from doing some of the chores. When Jack asked what remained to be done, Billy sent him out to feed the horse. While all this went on, Kate sat at the kitchen table, listless and limp. Billy backed up and awkwardly leaned against the door frame. He looked at his mother and said, stone-faced, "Goodbye, Mom. I hope you get better so you can come back to us and love me again."

"Go away, Billy. I will *never* love you again. You let that snake bite and kill my little Jimmy, my *baby*," she hissed. "So just go away. I never want to see you again, ever!"

"Fine with me!" he lashed out. He marched into the back room and came back through the kitchen with a rifle in his hand. "I'll just take care of that problem for you. You will never, ever see me again! Then maybe you'll be happy!" He stomped out, slamming the door behind him, and they could hear him running away.

Betty gasped, "Grant, stop him! Stop him!" Grant wheeled and charged out the door. Betty turned on Kate. "How could you *say* such a thing to him? How *could* you?" Before Kate could answer, there came a bang of a shot that rattled the window panes.

"No! No!! Dear Lord, no!" Betty screamed. She whirled and ran out the door behind Grant.

Kate's mind snapped open. She jumped up and raced for the door, flinging it back, and shoved past Betty. Though she never knew how, she reached the barn before either of them and pushed the door aside. Desperately, she looked around and then spotted Billy in the dimness, where he lay sprawled on his stomach in the first stanchion, profusely bleeding. She shrieked and knelt beside him, gathering him in her arms. His shirt was covered in blood that seeped onto her dress and into her soul. "Billy, Billy. What have you done? What have you done?" She pulled him closer, wiping at his head with her hand. "Please don't die. *Please.*"

Grant knelt, edging in beside Kate to loosen her hold on Billy. "Kate, he's breathing. Let me see." He gently checked him over.

Unbuttoning Billy's shirt, Grant said, "It's just a shoulder wound, Kate. It went clear through and it'll heal in time. He just passed out, that's all. Let's get him to the house." He took the bandana from his back pocket and held it against the wound.

Billy opened his eyes and moaned. "I'm not dead, am I? I don't want to die. I just want Mom to like me, is all." When Grant helped him to stand, Billy began to sob.

Kate felt Betty tugging her to her feet. Grant put his arm around Billy and, bearing most of the weight, said, "You're going to be all right, son. We'll get this bandaged and things are going to be all right."

Just then, Jack came tearing around the side of the barn. "I heard a shot. What was it?" His face blanched when he saw Billy's blood.

"An accident," Grant said. "He was trying to shoot a skunk and tripped. Can't let a skunk get in the barn, I reckon," he explained, covering for Billy and Kate.

They gradually made their way back to the house. Betty pulled out a chair for Billy and soon had the wound bandaged as best she could. While Kate held Billy's shaking hand, Grant called Doctor Jensen. Jack sat down at the table and looked questioningly at everyone, but no one spoke.

"Doc is coming out," Grant said. "He'll treat the wound for infection and bandage it, and he wants to talk to you, Kate."

Kate nodded, saying nothing, still shaky from the medicine and from Billy's incident. She was deeply ashamed that she was the cause of his distress, and further ashamed that she had caused her family so much suffering. When they had needed her to be strong, she had entirely retreated from the world. She hadn't been there to guide them through the sadness of living hand in hand with death and sorrow, to live through tragedy with integrity and inspiration.

"Well," Betty stood up. "I'm going to make a pot of coffee. I think we all need it. Will you drink some, Kate?"

Kate nodded. "With a slice of bread and butter, please," she said, feeling hungry.

Betty smiled and said, "Yes, you do need to eat something and get some meat on those bones." She looked at the rest of the family. "Bread and butter—Jack, Billy?" When they nodded, she fixed a big plate of sliced bread with butter and jam and set it in the middle of the table.

In about an hour, there was a knock on the door. "Probably the doctor," Betty said as she opened it. Carrying his official black bag, Doctor Jensen stepped in, looked around at the gathering, and said, "I'd like some of that coffee and bread, too, Betty." While she prepared a plate for him, he eased the homemade bandage off Billy's shoulder and looked at the wound.

"Well, young man, I can sew this gash, and no one will ever know the difference. But I need to clean it out first and that will hurt. So are you tough enough for me to use my probe, needle, and thread and start cleaning and sewing?" Though his face blanched, Billy swallowed hard and nodded. "Oh, well, I forgot to tell you that I'll numb it first," Doctor Jensen chuckled. When he finished about a half-hour later, he said, "Okay, you're good as new. Now, I want you to come outside with me and tell me exactly how this happened." When Billy looked frightened, Doctor Jensen said, "It's just a talk between you and me, outside where the adults can't be interrupting all the time with their version of the story. It's for my official file—strictly confidential. Come on, young man," he urged, clasping Billy's good shoulder and leading him out the door. Kate, Betty, and Grant looked at each other over the rims of their cups. Soon, Billy came back in with an open expression, asking for more coffee along with bread and jam. Doctor Jensen stuck his head in the door and called softly to Kate. Slowly, she stood and walked out to meet him on the bench under the locust tree.

"Sit down, Kate," he said, patting the bench beside him. After she situated herself there, he cleared his throat and said, "You realize that Billy narrowly escaped killing himself today." She nodded and he went on. "He has enough guilt over what happened to Jimmy without your condemnation, too. You know that it wasn't his fault, don't you?" She nodded again and he continued, "And yet you laid a burden on him that even *you* couldn't tolerate."

"I know," she answered, and felt her heart rend.

"Now it's up to you to see that you reassure him that this tragedy was *not* his fault and that you're sorry for blaming him."

"I know," she said again, trying to clear her head.

"Then stop wallowing in self pity, start eating, and get back to your work. You can't expect Grant and Betty to do that for you anymore. Work will be the best thing in the world to get yourself back on your feet. Get off the sleeping medicine and get yourself pulled together. You'll be surprised how quickly Billy will respond if you ask him for forgiveness—and if you forgive yourself. Tomorrow is a new day. I know that's a platitude, but it's true. Do you understand?"

"Yes, I do. I saw all that when I thought Billy had..." She couldn't say the awful words.

"All right," he said. "I'll check with you in a few days to see how things are going. Every day, you clean his wound; swab it with alcohol, apply iodine and the salve I left, and put on a clean dressing. Talk to him while you're doing that. Talk about his dad and Jimmy. He's still grieving for his dad, just as you are. Ease his emotional burden by talking to him. In doing that, he will begin to heal, emotionally and physically. And so will you and the rest of the family."

"Yes," she said, for she clearly saw how much she had let her children down because of her burden of hurt. She was proud that they had managed so well after their father had passed on. She needed their strength and they needed hers.

"Let me know if that wound begins looking red with puss in it, like it's angry."

"I will," Kate promised, "and thank you."

Doctor Jensen nodded, stood, and went into the house to retrieve his bag. He left Kate sitting under the tree, thinking.

Before long, Billy came out and sat with her, neither of them saying anything. Giving up the search for the right words, she finally began. "Billy, I hope you'll forgive me for the horrible things I said to you when Jimmy died. I know that I couldn't have stopped it from happening either, even if I had been there. It's a terrible loss, just like your dad, but we must go on and make something good of our lives. You're a wonderful, strong, caring son, and I want you to stay that way. As Doctor Jensen said, 'Tomorrow is a new day,' so let's start it afresh."

He draped his good arm across her shoulders, pulled her to him, then said, "Okay, Mom. We start a new day tomorrow." He smiled. Though his eyes still held deep sorrow and hurt, she could see that he was willing to forgive her, if she would accept him for who he was and had become. Then he sobered, "I'm sorry for what I did today. I'm glad I'm still alive, and I'm glad you're alive and that you're going to be you again. But I wish Dad and Jimmy were alive, too." His eyes welled up.

She nodded and clasped the hand that dangled off her shoulder. "I do, too," she said, "but we have tomorrow together."

"I know. Doc said the scar on my shoulder will remind me not to do stupid things again!"

"And me, too," Kate smiled. She marveled that he could seemingly recover so quickly from the ordeal. She wondered then just how much she really knew about this young man-son of hers. She had always taken him for granted. He was reliable, honest, sensitive, and cared deeply for all of them. She knew now, though, that he had a breaking point, as did she. She also knew that the horrible way she had treated him, almost losing him, would haunt her for the rest of her life.

"I think I'll go back in and have some more bread and butter," he said, taking his arm from around her shoulders. "Thanks, Mom, for what you said." He stood and walked briskly back into the house, imitating his dad.

Sitting there, thinking, she realized that Evvie also needed her as a mother and guide. At sixteen, Evvie had become a young woman. *I need to share myself with her,* Kate thought. *We should talk about the so-called secrets of womanhood, marriage, babies, and men, not just the work and duties of the house and family.* Kate knew it wouldn't be easy for her to talk freely about those things, especially sex. That subject just wasn't shared openly, and it was seldom spoken of in klatches of women. Her mother had never told her anything about body functions, and Kate had only known about such things through her peers. Then, after her marriage to Jim, it was the other married women who had educated her about babies and such things. She must make the effort to have those intimate talks with Evvie for her preparation and well-being as a woman, wife, and mother.

🐚 🐚 🐚

Grant and Betty protested when Kate explained that she would be all right and that they should go home to their family. Billy would take Jack home after they finished the chores; Jack offered to continue helping until Billy's shoulder healed.

"Thank you, Jack," Kate said. "I would appreciate that very much."
Grant agreed. "Okay, so Jack can go with us now and bring your
kids back here, Kate. He'll come over each day to help until Billy is
able to handle the chores alone. We'll telephone in a day or so to see
how you're doing," Grant stated, then the three of them left.

After they drove away, Kate looked at Billy and felt as though the
two of them had been on a long and lonely journey. In a way, she
supposed they had, for she had hated him from the day little Jimmy
was bitten by that rattlesnake. While waiting for the kids to return, she
made sandwiches for herself and Billy and engaged him in small talk
about the farm, the garden, and the livestock, and shared with him
her plans for the future. When he responded with such mature ideas
for it all, she was astounded, excited, and so proud of him. In what
seemed like a short time, but was probably just thirty or forty minutes, they heard Jack return with the rest of the family. Since they had
already eaten at Grant's and it was late, the kids got ready for bed and
she, feeling exhausted, would soon follow. Saying goodnight to Jack,
she hugged and kissed each of her children and tucked little Meggie
into her crib. When Meggie cried for her brother, Kate told her that
Jimmy had gone away to be with Daddy, and he wouldn't be back. To
comfort her, Kate decided to read a bedtime story. She sat Meggie on
her lap and began. When Leah and Leslie heard their mother reading
aloud, they rushed into the room to crowd close to her, Timothy right
behind them. He crawled up on Kate's lap with Meggie and listened,
wide-eyed.

Meggie woke in the night, calling out for Jimmy, so Kate put her
in bed with Leah, where she snuggled down, comfortable against her
sister. Timothy woke as well, and when he couldn't go back to sleep,
she tucked him in with Leslie. Back in her own room, Kate mused on
the fact that Meggie had known her father only by the family's rec-
ollections, but the memory of her brother was fresh in her mind. *As
young as Meggie is now,* Kate thought, *the memory of her brother will eventually fade.* But for Kate, the memories of losing Jimmy and then nearly
losing Billy would not fade quickly, if ever. *The important thing to focus
on now is that Billy is here safe and sound,* Kate realized as she slipped into
bed. Tomorrow was a new beginning, one she knew that—no matter
what happened—she was back where she belonged, and together she

and her family would enter the future. With that comforting thought, she dropped into a deep, restful sleep.

🖎 🖎 🖎

About two weeks later, she and Evvie were doing dishes and Evvie said, "Mama, I really miss Johnny. Leah and Leslie, and even Billy, have asked me about him and his kids. We *miss* them. Can't you call him or something?"

Kate looked at her, wondering how Evvie knew that she had had Johnny on her mind for the last few days. "I don't know if he'll want to see me after how awful I was to him," she replied.

"Well...I think you should try," Evvie answered. "You need to find out if he still loves you."

Kate hesitated then said, "I guess you're right." Several times that day, while the children were outside, she picked up the telephone with the intention of calling him, only to hang up before the operator asked for a number. By the end of the day, she was so exasperated with herself that she couldn't think straight so, after the children had gone to bed at almost nine thirty, she had the operator ring Johnny's number. The line was busy, so at a little after ten o'clock, she tried again, but the phone rang and rang. Disappointed, she started to hang up when he answered. Her heart skipped a beat. "Oh!" she said, her mind scrambling like a scared rabbit, frantically seeking words to say to him.

"Kate? Is that you, Kate?" His voice sounded sleepy and hopeful.

"Yes," she hesitated, wishing she hadn't called for fear he would hang up on her. "I hope I didn't wake you."

"Kate. Oh, Kate. I was asleep in my chair, but I can sleep anytime! It's so good to hear your voice. How are you doing? I've missed you so much."

"I'm doing all right," she answered, and then said, "I miss you, too. It's too late tonight, but since tomorrow is a Saturday, can you and your family come over in the morning and stay a while? The children have been asking for all of you. Please come."

"We'll be there about ten, with bells on."

"I just want to see you. I have a lot to tell you." She paused. "I'm not sure if I'm ready to be serious yet, but—as you suggested

earlier—let's spend some time together and see what happens. So we'll
see you in the morning, Johnny."

"Morning it is, then," he replied, chuckling softly. "Goodnight
now, and have a great sleep."

"I will. You, too, and goodnight," she replied and hung up, sighing
happily.

The following morning, Johnny and his family showed up close
to ten o'clock and Evvie ushered them into the house. They hugged
all around but, through the day, Johnny made no advances toward
Kate and she didn't encourage him in any way. Because of that, she
began to love him deeply as a true and trusted friend. She knew
he loved her with a deeper, more romantic love than she had for
him. She understood that he really wanted to marry her, but she also
knew that he accepted her friendship as it was, rather than lose her
completely.

Things continued to go well between Kate, Johnny, and their
children, and they spent as much time as possible together. On
Sundays, after Johnny and his children attended Mass and Kate's family went to their United Brethren Church, the two families enjoyed
the Sunday noon meal and afternoon together. Kate hadn't taken her
family to church since Jim had died, even though the pastor had been
to see her since then and had mentioned it again after the services for
Jimmy. But now that she had started again, she found solace in the
church and its message. But Betty couldn't let Kate and Johnny just
be friends. One morning, when Betty and Grant came over, she and
Kate were alone at the table when Betty asked, "Kate, why don't you
marry Johnny? What're you doing? Can't you see in those dark eyes
how much he loves you?"

"I can see it," Kate firmly replied, and said no more than that. Her
reticence sent Betty into a frenzy of curiosity. Kate smiled to herself;
she had always had that hold over Betty by not answering her sister's
burning, very nosey questions every time.

"Well, people are talking, you know. You're together just about
every Sunday and many other days, too, and that's grounds for all kinds
of rumors," Betty scolded.

"I don't care," Kate answered back. "Rumors are just that—*rumors*.
Johnny and I are dear friends, and that's all there is to it. People will go

on talking, so let them talk. I will go on living as I wish." She paused, then said, "I don't imagine *you* are talking, though, are you?" Her remark seemed lost on Betty, who looked as though she would pull her braids out with exasperation. It was obvious that Kate's lack of a decision drove Betty to distraction, and she queried Kate whenever they were together. It was of great satisfaction to Kate to keep everything private from her big sister, who loved to gossip.

As Betty opened her mouth to recount Kate's last statement, Grant walked in, looked around, and—guessing what was going on— he drawled, "Reckon we better go home, Betty. It's gettin' dark and it's chore time."

Kate smiled at him and nodded, silently thanking him. Though Kate knew that he was somewhat skeptical—and perhaps a tad jealous—of Johnny, he had never said anything about it to her or to anyone else that she knew of. Grant was a much-loved friend to her and gentleman enough to keep her faith in him as just that. There was a special place in her heart for him that went back to the days when he was courting Betty. At that time, Kate thought Grant was the most handsome, the kindest man ever and that Betty was just the luckiest woman alive when they married. If Kate had been older, she might have been the bride instead of Betty, but she was only fourteen to Betty's sixteen and Grant only had eyes for Betty. He had always treated Kate as his treasured younger sister. Kate felt that she actually saw him in a deeper way than Betty did. There was a sense of oneness between her and Grant, a oneness of old souls recognizing each other from another time.

As with recent years, the winter of 1934 was another hard one, with very little moisture and a constant frigid wind blowing every day. What little snow fell came mixed with dust that the wind picked up from the dry and powdery wheat fields. The wheat turned brown and was so sparse it couldn't hold the soil. Kate struggled to keep the family and house clean, but the brown snow-dust sifted into and onto everything. The family inhaled so much dust that they began to cough up brown mucous.

1935

Amid the wind and dust one day in February, Johnny and his family blew in. Delighted to be together on such a horrible day, they sat around the kitchen table playing gin rummy while the windows rattled and the dust continued to blow up and into the eastern sky and as high as the sun. In the middle of shuffling, Kate let the cards fall to the table and dropped her head into her palms. "I don't know if I can take much more of this wind, dust, and the devastation to the wheat crop."

"What do you mean 'wheat crop'?" Billy said. "There isn't one and won't be one this year. It's smothered with piles and piles of dust. I had to shovel it away from the barn door so I could get in. And one of the tractors is almost covered up with it."

"I know," Kate pined. "What are we going to do, Johnny?"

The children looked at him for an answer, alarmed at Kate's worry. Johnny gathered up the cards and began to shuffle and deal. He shook his head, preoccupied. After a moment, he answered, "I don't know, Kate. We're all in the same boat. Maybe the rains will come, and we can at least have a garden."

"But there are so many rabbits this year that a garden isn't even possible," Kate responded. "It's like the wind blew in rabbits instead of rain. Where did they come from? They're everywhere, and in large numbers."

"Kate, I..." he hesitated, and finished dealing. "I'm considering moving to Oregon. My sister lives there, and she says there are jobs available with the construction of dams on the Columbia River."

In unison, the children yelled, "No!" and then started babbling protests about Johnny and his family moving away and being separated from each other.

Kate sucked in her breath, her stomach turning over. He didn't look at her but picked up his cards and began arranging them in his hand. She gathered hers but didn't look at them. Meggie climbed onto her lap and picked up her mother's cards for her. Timothy, on Billy's knee, picked up his. When she thought she could trust herself to speak, she cleared her throat and asked, "Is anybody going to play?" She was so rattled and shocked that she couldn't keep the tremble from her voice, and that upset her even more. Why hadn't he said something before? He had to have been thinking about it for a while. He was always corresponding with his sister, and now he just dropped the bomb in her lap? She repeated, "Bid, anybody?"

"Mom!" Billy interrupted. "How can you think about this dumb card game when our friends are going to Oregon?" He threw his cards down, set Timothy on his feet, and stood.

"Wait a minute," Johnny said, placing his cards face down on the table in a neat pile. "I didn't say we were going; I said I was *thinking* about it."

Kate placed her cards on the table, too, her hand on top. Then she pushed back her chair, put Meggie down, and stood. She started to go outside but then remembered the wind and dust, so she sat down again, dejected and wilted. It seemed to her that her life was just one big heartache. *Where's the hope?* she wondered. She knew Johnny was looking at her, but she fiddled with the cards and wouldn't look up. Finally, with tears right behind her lids, she got up and went to her bedroom. She sat on her bed for a while, her heart on the floor, listening to Johnny trying to calm the children and explain to them his reasons for going. But they kept interrupting until, in exasperation, he said, "Okay, my kids, we're going home. We'll come back tomorrow. I need to talk to my sis again in order to make a decision." There was a real protest then, and she heard his chair scrape back. "No more talk today," he said. "Come on, we're going home," and he hustled them out the door.

She was upset and taken aback that he would go home without saying goodbye to her! He at least ought to have done that!

Someone tapped on her bedroom door. "I couldn't go without saying goodbye, Kate," Johnny said through the door. "I'll see you tomorrow. Call if you need anything." Before she could get to her feet, his footsteps receded and the outside door closed behind him. There was complete silence from her bunch until there was another tap on her door. Thinking it was Johnny again, her heart leapt like a deer over a tall fence.

"Yes?" she called hopefully.

"Mom," Billy said softly. "Come on out so we can talk to you about this. *Please.*"

She sighed, opened the door, and joined the others at the table. Bedlam broke out with them talking at the same time, the girls crying, and all looking to her for answers. She had none, and she told them so. "Tomorrow, when they come over, we will, hopefully, get answers—or at least *some* answers—and maybe we can talk them out of going away."

Betty called that evening. The wind and dust had picked up and visibility was down to nearly zero. "Grant thinks he can ride Badger over tomorrow if you need him. I told him only if the wind was down. Though I'm sure Badger could find the way, I don't want Grant out in that blinding dust. Are you doing all right over there? Do you need him?"

"Tell him to stay close to home. I don't want him out in it, either. Johnny brought his family here today to see if things are under control. He went home two, three hours ago. Tell Grant we're fine," Kate said, and then decided not to tell Betty that Johnny was considering moving to Oregon for a job. *It's definitely best not to say that over the party line,* she decided.

The next day, the wind and dust were so powerful and suffocating that there was no going out of the house, except to tend to the animals and go to the privy. When they did go out, they were guided by a rope tied from the house to each building, thick rags wrapped around their noses and mouths. Kate tried to call Johnny's home to tell him not to come but the lines were down, so she and the children spent a miserably dark day together with not even enough ambition to play cards or board games. It was a long day of talking quietly, as though the wind would hear them and somehow make their lives more miserable than it already had. Leah and Leslie questioned Kate repeatedly about Johnny and his family moving away. Each time she said, "I don't know. I don't know." Then they asked if he was coming over with his children, and she answered in the same manner, "I don't know, but probably not; it's too bad out there."

Toward evening, when Leah and Leslie came whining to her again concerning the subject, Kate turned on all of them and, emphasizing each word, repeated for what seemed like the hundredth time, "All of you, listen to me," and commanding their attention, she went on, "I... do...not...know! Do you understand? I...do...not...know! Now, you find something to do, or I'm going to send you to bed." They scattered to their separate rooms, Meggie going with Leah and Leslie, Timothy with Billy, and Evvie alone. Exhausted from being with them all day in the closeness of the walls, she went into the living room, picked up her crocheting and, in the dim light of the kerosene lamp, stitched on an afghan for an hour or more, glad to be alone. Before the wind finally quit, they were in the house for three miserable days with no telephone service, no one on the roads, and no Johnny and his family.

After the main roads had been partially cleared of banks of dirt, Johnny and his children drove into her yard in the late afternoon on the fourth day. While the kids were busy discussing missing school because of the storm, he took her aside and informed her that he was taking his family to Oregon to check out the job situation, and that they would leave as soon as possible. Her children overheard this and became terribly upset, but when he assured them they would be back before Easter, they settled down. After answering many questions, he then answered Kate's question with, yes, he had an old bachelor coming to stay at his place and take care of everything while he was gone. He kissed Kate tenderly on the cheek and took his family home early that day to get ready for the trip.

At supper time, the wind roared in again along with the dust, and the night was as dark as a black cat. The kerosene lamps did nothing to dispel the lack of light or the mood. Though Kate suggested a card game, there was nothing the children wanted to do. They milled around as though they were lost; finally, they all went to bed earlier than usual. With the windows tacked over with old sheets to keep the blowing dust at bay, what little light that might have seeped in through the coated panes was blocked. Since the house was dark and gloomy and outside was even worse, bed seemed like a good place to be. Carrying the lamp into her room, Kate slipped into bed and listened to the wind; it was dark outside, inside, and in her heart.

In the middle of the night, she woke with a start and sat up, listening. The silence wrapped around her like a shroud, close and heavy. Confused at first, she wondered what had wakened her. Then she realized that the wind no longer howled. She crept to the window and ripped back a corner of the sheet to look out on a desolate landscape of dust dunes. The scene reminded her of pictures in magazines about the Sahara Desert—surreal and spooky, as if she were in a different world. Quickly, she patted the sheet back into place and opted for bed, wishing that someone—Johnny, namely—was snuggled close...warm, alive, and comforting. She pulled the covers tight around her, curled into a fetal position, and eventually slipped off into sleep, where no wind entered her dreams of Johnny.

It was a hard goodbye when Johnny and his kids left the next week, but Kate and her children hung onto the promise that they would return before Easter. She knew that time would go slowly and it would seem interminably long before their return.

🐚 🐚 🐚

A few days later, when the sun came up on a beautiful February morning, she had no idea that it would be the last really nice day for several weeks. The frigid wind blew snow and fine dust nearly every day throughout that month. The children would lean into the maelstrom as they boarded the bus until, one day, Kate refused to send them to school anymore. She was afraid to let them ride the bus for fear that it would be caught in a dirty blizzard, so she taught them book lessons around the kitchen table. The whole family still coughed and spoke in raspy voices. She sent them to bed with wet towels over their faces while their bedroom windows were covered in brown sheets that once were white.

One day, when the sky had cleared a little bit, Grant and Betty came over and helped her catch up with shoveling snow-dirt and cleaning up the house, the males working outside and the females inside. They came often to help and visit and make plans for their farms. Sometimes, when she became so lonesome that she couldn't stand it, she had Billy start up the car and they all went to spend time with Betty's family. Every day, she looked out the window, hoping to see Johnny's car coming down the road. She wondered if he really would come back or if he would decide to stay in Oregon.

Then one dismal afternoon she looked out and there was his car, coming fast through the wind and dust. He had been gone for several weeks but, true to his word, he and his children had returned. When they walked onto the porch and greeted them with hugs and handshakes, the day brightened for Kate and the children. Johnny grabbed her, and the children danced around like crazy people. "Let's go inside," she said. And inside they went, where Kate made hot chocolate and coffee and put out freshly made doughnuts, which had been cooked to serve up with the children's lessons at the kitchen table. When Kate asked him about Oregon, he told her what a beautiful place it was, expounding on its greenness, tall trees, and the blessed rain.

Kate looked at him, half afraid and half wondering. "But you're not going out there, are you?"

He heaved a troubled sigh. "I have decided to move to Oregon, Kate. I have a job waiting for me, starting in May." With that, her children set up a terrible cry of protest and Kate's heart dropped to the floor. "I have to do it," he said. "There'll be no money coming in off my farm. I'll go out there, make a lot of money, come back in three or four years, and take up farming again." He stopped, looked around at the sad children, and then looked back at Kate. Hesitantly, he said, "Kate, will you marry me? Then we can all go. Come with me, Kate," he implored.

The children stopped mid-protest and waited for her reply, but she shook her head and answered, "I can't do that. This is my farm, and I must take care of it. People of my family and Jim's family are buried on this farm, in that graveyard." She pointed toward the cemetery. "I have lived in this area all my life. I can't just give the farm up and leave it to the elements."

"Kate," Johnny replied with strained patience, "you have no farm. What remains in the fields are piles of dust. The rest has blown as far away as New York City. There is no soil, no water, no rain, no nothing. Think about it! We can make a living out there."

"I can't. I just can't do that."

"Mom," Billy said, "please—just think about it, like Johnny said. There is nothing here but dust and wind." He made a wide sweep with his arms, indicating the farm. "We need to get out of here. We have nothing but broken-down dust fields. It's not a farm!"

"Mama," Evvie chimed in with tears in her voice. "Please." She paused and then spouted, "Well, if you decide not to go, then *I'm* going with Johnny." Her siblings all agreed with her.

"Don't be silly, Evvie—all of you—this is your home. We're staying here because your dad and I fought hard for this land, and I cannot leave it. So, Johnny, I must refuse your offer of marriage, though it appeals very much to me."

Abruptly, he pushed back his chair and said, "Okay, kids, let's go home. I won't ask you again to go with me, Kate, or to marry me, either. We'll be around for a while yet and we'd like to come over, if you don't mind. Maybe, before we leave, you'll change your mind." Kate shook her head but said nothing. Tight-lipped, he nodded and herded his protesting brood out the door.

I really can't blame him for being upset, she thought as she watched him drive away, *but I can't give up this land. Jim's buried here and my babies are buried here, and I just can't leave them.* She knew that Johnny would never come back to his farm, and soon there would be a painful, final goodbye between the families. *So be it,* she thought, feeling stubbornly righteous. Though her family kept badgering her to accept, she adamantly dug in her heels and refused.

The families continued to spend time together, and with Johnny and his family around, the time went by too quickly. She finally had to admit to herself that she loved Johnny and his kids, but she still didn't change her mind. True to his word, he didn't ask her again, and neither of them wavered from their decisions.

Warmer days came and, though wind and dust were frequent occurrences, the weather continued to improve. Kate gained a false sense of security then, feeling that everything would be all right. She could make it on her farm, even though the wheat fields were covered with dust to the point that the wheat couldn't grow through the suffocating dryness. The wind continued to blow, windmills trembling and tugging at their moorings as they vibrated in the constant, howling gale from the west. Though the churches prayed for rain, there came not a drop of moisture from the sky. The soil of the fields, their furrows often a mile in length, blew skyward, blotting the sun and darkening the sky.

緒 緒 緒

March twenty-third was Johnny's birthday. Kate planned an evening surprise party for him, asking Grant and Betty and their children over. The grown-ups would play pinochle while the children played outside games—*if* the wind didn't blow. If it *did* blow, they could play card games in the house. As soon as Betty and Grant walked in that evening, Leah said, "Aunt Betty, Johnny asked Mommy to marry him and she said no. Tell her to say yes. *Please* tell her to say yes."

Betty stopped so suddenly that Emma bumped into her. "Is this true?" Betty asked as Emma moved up beside her to listen. Betty raised her eyebrows and put her hand on her hip and, with a slight smirk, she repeated, "Is it true?"

Kate shrugged, "Well, yes it is."

"Is *what* true?" Grant asked as he stepped in the door. Betty turned to face him.

"Johnny asked Kate to marry him, and she said no." Not waiting for a response, she swung back to Kate. "And just when were you going to tell me?"

"Today," Kate stammered. "I was also going to tell you today that he asked me to go to Oregon with him. Here he comes now, so let's talk about this later." With that, Kate hurried to the door and ushered the Vaughn family in. Everybody shouted "surprise" and, with differences put aside for the evening, the birthday party was great fun.

Before it was over, though, while Betty and Kate were in the kitchen, serving up cake and homemade ice cream, Betty insisted that Kate tell her the details of Johnny's proposal and about the move to Oregon. "Kate," she said, after the situation had been explained, "I think not to marry him is a terrible mistake on your part. And you might consider moving to Oregon." Before Kate could reply, Betty went on. "Have you looked at those fields out there? Do you see any possibility of farming at all this year? Or even next year? I don't know how Grant and I are going to pull through at all, and here you have a chance to get out, and you won't do it!"

"I'm not going to leave and that's final. No more discussion, no more talk. So let it be, Betty."

"Well, it's the worst mistake you'll ever make, let me tell you," Betty stated as she dished up the cake and ice cream, then called the girls in to pass the brimming plates around to everyone.

"Mama," Leslie said, "you cut the cake, but you didn't put the candles on so Johnny could blow them out."

"Oh, my—you're right. Well, let's see," Kate hesitated, scrambling for a solution.

"I know!" Evvie exclaimed. "We can put a candle on each piece and Johnny can blow them all out while we sing 'Happy Birthday' to him." With that said, Evvie rummaged in the cabinets until she found a box of birthday candles.

The younger children readily agreed to place a candle on each piece of cake when Evvie asked them if they would like to do that. They sang loudly and slightly off-key, and Johnny good-naturedly puffed out the candles. It was a wonderful evening with very little wind, so the adults played cards and the children, outside, made up their own entertainment.

▧ ▧ ▧

The spring of 1935 continued to be so dry and windy that working in the fields or planting a garden wasn't plausible. The children attended school on a regular basis except on the worst days, and Kate and Evvie caught up on the sewing and mending that had accumulated. Evenings were spent playing cards, sometimes with Johnny and his family. It was a tedious spring and, with money so short, Kate worried how she could pay bills.

Johnny had rented his farmhouse to the same bachelor who had rented it earlier and planned to leave with his family in late April for Oregon. Before he could get on his way, however, the dust storm to end all dust storms ripped in with a fury on Palm Sunday, April 25. It was later referred to as "Black Sunday."

That morning, the children were still in bed when Kate woke up well before dawn. After dressing, she opened the door to a gorgeous sunrise—a dark-blue sky, birds singing, and a warm breeze. She walked out through the piles of dust that lined the paths and looked at the vast prairie with the pink and yellow horizon welcoming the sun. It was so beautiful that it took her breath away. She remembered why she loved this open land. It was wild with ugly moods, true, but open and free with a magnificent strength. It was like an untamed stallion with a gleaming coat—unpredictable, stubborn, and ruthless. She drew a deep breath and stood, lost in thought. Maybe there was a chance to save her farm after all.

As she stood there, soaking in the brightening sky, Billy joined her on his way to milk the cow. He stopped to gaze, too.

"Wow!" he said. "I haven't seen anything like this in a long time, Mom. Makes you feel good, doesn't it?"

"Yes, it certainly does make me feel good."

From the back door, Leslie and Leah shouted, "Mommy, we're hungry."

"I'll be right there," Kate called. With a sigh, she turned toward the house, promising herself that she and the children would go to church this fine morning—that is, if she could get them all gathered up, dressed, and ready in time, which she realized would be quite a feat.

Later, they were walking out the door all spiffed up and polished, when Johnny and his family drove in, ready to go to their church, too. There were too many for one car, so it was decided that Billy would drive Kate's vehicle with the older children while she and Johnny took the younger ones in his car. She and her children would be dropped off at their church, and then Johnny and his family would go on to the Catholic Church. After services, they would all convene in front of her church, go to her house, and partake of a fried-chicken Sunday dinner prepared earlier. That suited everyone.

There was a rabbit drive that day, but Johnny had decided that going to church was more important. Before they got into the cars, he said, "I just don't feel right about clubbing those rabbits to death. Even if there are far too many of them and they eat everything that grows, I just can't kill them with a stick as they're driven to me. I just can't do it."

"Me, either," stated Billy. "And it's awful to hear them scream like that. I just don't like it!"

"Gives me the willies," Jerome stated, "and nightmares. But they're everywhere—chomping, chomping, chomping."

"Yep, thousands of them, maybe even millions," Billy agreed.

🐚 🐚 🐚

Church lasted longer than Leah, Leslie, Timothy, and Meggie could, so Kate took them all outside to walk a block or two one way and then back the other direction. As the children skipped along beside her, Leah said, "Mommy, I really liked that one song we sang this morning."

"Oh? Which one was that?" Kate asked absently, her mind on how she was going to improve their finances and Johnny leaving for Oregon.

"That one about the cross-eyed bear; I think the bear's name is Gladly."

"Gladly?" Kate said.

"Well, you know—Gladly, the cross-eyed bear."

Kate stifled her laugh. "Oh, you mean, 'Gladly, the Cross I'd Bear'?"

"That's what I said, Gladly, the cross-eyed bear."

Before she could say anything, Leah said, "Not me. I like the one about bringing in the sheets...or maybe it's bringing in the sheep. That's the one I like. Which one do you like, Mommy?" she inquired.

Chuckling on the inside, serious on the outside, Kate said, "The word is *sheaves*, not sheets or sheep. 'Bringing in the Sheaves,'" she corrected with a smile. "I like them both."

"Really, Mommy?" Leah asked. "What *are* sheaves?"

Before Kate had formed an answer that Leah would understand, Leslie piped up.

"Both songs, Mommy?" she asked.

"Yes, I like both very much," Kate replied.

"Well, what are sheaves?" Leah asked again.

"Bundles of grain that are brought in at harvest time to feed farm animals," Kate answered.

"Oh," Leah responded. "I didn't know that."

"Well," said Timothy in his lispy manner, "I like the one about Andy. I don't know *who* Andy is, but I like singing about him."

"Andy?" Leah and Leslie snickered. "Who's Andy?"

"I told you, I don't know, but the song says, 'Andy walks with me, Andy talks with me, Andy tells me I am his own.'"

"Oh, yes," chorused Leah and Leslie together, "that's a good one, too."

Kate couldn't help chuckling a little this time. Amused at their muddling through the lyrics of the old hymns, she said nothing, as it would only confuse them further. But Timothy's favorite hymn about Andy stuck in her mind, and soon she was singing "In the Garden" under her breath.

"That's it. That's the song, Mommy!" exclaimed Timothy. He butchered the lyrics as he sang along, and Meggie bounced along beside Kate.

"Here we are at the park," Kate said. "All of you go play while we wait for Evvie and Billy to come out of church and for Johnny to come by for us. Go on, now." And they took off like a bunch of wild goats, running and jumping like crazy. She sat on a bench and watched them, smiling at their antics. Though she knew she would be upbraided by some in the congregation for taking them out of church this morning, she also knew those same ones would have been upset if she had kept her children squirming restlessly in the pew, jabbing each other and giggling slyly under their breath. If the church couldn't get a sitter for the children while the adults attended services upstairs, then she might keep them home until they were a little older. In the past, it had crossed her mind that perhaps she lost more religion than she gained while getting them ready and then keeping them quiet during the services. But they needed to be there, so maybe she would just let people grumble.

It was time for services to end, so she called to her children to return to the church building. It seemed like a long time before Billy and Evvie exited with the congregation, all shaking hands with the preacher and talking, visiting, catching up on the latest news. It wasn't long, though, before Johnny drove around the corner, and the two families situated themselves in the cars again.

On the way home, Kate noticed birds winging past the car en masse as rabbits and other small creatures careened across the prairie in several different directions, all at breakneck speeds. "What's going on?" Kate asked, glancing at Johnny as he tried to dodge the tangled migration.

"Don't know," he puzzled, "but something's sending them into a panic. Maybe it's the rabbit drive that's underway," he speculated. "All those people in cars tearing around on the roads have sent these critters into a running panic, maybe."

"But birds, too?" Kate said, perplexed. She looked back to see how Billy was driving through the mess and saw that he was having problems, too. He was swerving here and there, trying not to hit any creature in his path.

"Well, it's strange. Can't be a storm. The sky is clear and blue, no clouds, and no wind at all," Johnny said.

"Something's going to happen. Is it something like doomsday— the end of time, as the Bible promises?" Kate wondered.

"Don't think so, but we'll see." Johnny placated her. "Let's just get to your house as fast as possible." With that, he stepped on the gas, throwing a whirlwind of dust behind so when Kate looked back again, she could only see a faint image of her car behind them, like a mirage.

As they pulled up to her house, the sun was suddenly blotted out and the beautiful Palm Sunday became as dark as a deep winter night. "This is spooky," she told Johnny. As she got out of the car, she heard what she thought was booming thunder. Looking to the west, what she saw sucked the air from her lungs. A huge roller swept toward them across the flatness of the prairie.

"Johnny, look! Look!" she pointed.

"I've been watching it. It's coming hard and it's coming fast," Johnny stated. "Get these kids inside and I'll see to the others." He sprinted toward the other car. Kate grabbed Timothy from the backseat and gave him a push toward the house. Picking up Meggie, she said, "Leah and Leslie, you help Timothy. All of you run as fast as you can and see who can be the first to the door," she challenged them. Following close behind, she swatted Timothy on the bottom when he let go of Leah's hand and slowed down, crying that he could never win the race.

"Get going," Kate ordered, "or I'll give you harder swats that will make you run faster!" When he stopped right in front of her, she grabbed his hand and literally dragged him along.

Over the rising wind she heard Johnny shout, "You kids, get out of the car now and get into the house! You see that roller boiling toward us? Get inside as fast as you can or we'll never see you again— and I'm not kidding!"

Frightened, they did as ordered with no questions asked, deep fear gripping them all and powering their legs. They overtook Kate, buzzed by the others, and reached the house first, which upset the twins to no end, but when they turned to complain to her, Kate yelled, "You shut up and get into the house right this minute!" It shocked her to hear herself yell those two words; telling someone to "shut up" was not allowed in her house. But now she had said it to her own children.

"So, you never say 'shut up' in your family, huh?" Johnny shouted mischievously as he ran up alongside her. He picked up Timothy, took Kate's hand, and they fled toward the house. When inside, they counted heads and breathed a sigh of relief that all were there.

"Well," Kate said in an aside to Johnny, "once in a while I've been known to say 'shut up' when it suits the occasion."

"Yeah, I noticed," Johnny chuckled. Then the roller hit like a sideways bomb, loud and explosive outside and black as night inside. They stood transfixed, listening to the banshee of a wind howling at the doors and windows. The little children drew closer to their parents, seeking comfort and safety in the eerie dimness. Kate looked at Johnny with raised eyebrows, wondering if the preacher's sermon on the end of the world really was at hand. He looked back at her; though he hadn't heard the sermon, he knew her question and shook his head. She nodded and smiled at her foolishness.

Then she said, "Okay, it's really getting dark in here. Evvie and Tilly, go light the lamps, and then get the old sheets so Jerome and Billy can tack them up at the windows. After we eat, we'll play Monopoly or gin rummy."

Kate went to the window and looked out but could only see as far as the edge of the porch. The rest of the world had disappeared into an inky, black curtain of billowing dust. She shivered. Johnny joined her and pulled her close. "If it *is* the end, I'm glad that I'm here with you and that our families are together."

"Yes," Kate agreed with a smile. They turned to the children, who huddled around the kitchen table, eyes wide and fearful, silently waiting for the world to explode. The kerosene lamp in the middle of the table did nothing to dispel the gloom; it merely pooled light in the center, as did the other three lamps placed strategically around the room.

"Leah, Leslie, Amanda—you get the chicken, potato salad, butter, and jam out of the icebox. Evvie and Tilly, set the table. Timothy, get the pickles and onions. Jerome and Billy, when you get that last sheet up, find chairs enough for all of us. I'll cut the bread and you can carry it to the table, Meggie."

"You make a pretty good boss," Johnny stated with a twinkle in his eyes.

"Oh, sorry. I hope you don't mind that I included your children in my orders. I'm so used to using whatever help I have around that I didn't think twice about it."

"I'm glad you did. They seem to enjoy doing what you told them. I think you would make a great mother to them all. My kids really like you," he finished, kissing her on the temple.

"Well, mine like you, too, but as I said before, it just wouldn't work out because of our religious differences...and I'm not going to leave this farm to go to Oregon with you."

"If you really wanted this relationship to work out, it would, but you're stalling because you're afraid—afraid to free up your emotions and let go of Jim in order to love me, afraid to overlook our religious differences, afraid to start a new and different life with me. In my opinion, Kate, all that's just plain foolishness."

"Well, maybe it is, but I don't want to talk about it right now. The food is on the table and everybody is hungry," she replied.

"Okay, have it your way." He kissed her lightly on the cheek then said, "Sit down, everybody, and let's have a Palm Sunday fried-chicken-dinner-in-a-dust-storm-to-end-all-dust-storms. Tilly, you say the blessing, please." And the eternal wind raged and wailed, carrying dust into the east across the state of Kansas and beyond, while they ate and chatted, pretending that everything was all right.

Because of the sheets at the windows, the house became ever darker and the wind sounded fiendish, like a demonic power insanely attacking. As they sat around the table, playing dominos, a knock sounded at the front door. Startled, Kate pushed back her chair, but Johnny said, "No, I'll get it, Kate." All eyes followed him, watching as he opened the door against the wind and hanging onto it so it wouldn't whip it out of his hand. Standing there was Kate's neighbor, Ray Kleinsorge, with his back to the wind. He coughed and muddy tears ran down his face, which was coated with a powdery film of Kansas prime soil. "Ray," Johnny said, "what're you doing out in this? Come in. Come in."

"My wife," Ray choked, "in labor. Thought we could make it to the doctor, but her time is now—*right* now."

Kate jumped up. "Bring her in! We'll take care of it. I'll come and help you."

"No, Kate, you get things ready and I'll help him get her in here," Johnny said, rushing out with Ray and heaving the door shut behind them.

"Well," she said to all the children, "you can continue the game if you want, but the best thing for you to do is take lamps and go upstairs to read or just stay busy with something. Rosalie is going to have her baby in this house in my bedroom, and you'll probably hear some moaning, groaning, and such, but it's all right. It all goes with birthing." Without a word, they picked up lamps and scampered up the stairs, shutting the doors of their rooms. Kate hurriedly began gathering things for the birthing and, while she was fixing her bed with the old birthing sheets and a blanket, Evvie and Tilly came into the bedroom.

"We want to help, Mom," Evvie said. "We want to see this baby born. Please? We can help by getting things for you," she begged.

It was on Kate's lips to refuse, but just then the men brought Rosalie in and sat her on the edge of the bed. "Okay, girls, go to the bureau in that back room and get the rubber sheet, the bag of clean rags, a birthing blanket for the baby—one of the little, thin ones— then get my scissors. Cut some strong embroidery thread about twelve inches long and bring everything to me." She turned to Rosalie. "You picked a strange time to do this, Rosalie—one of the worst! If it's a boy, his name should be Dusty."

"It *is* the worst day ever," Rosalie responded, "and Dusty is a great name, but what if it's a girl?"

"Wendy. Definitely Wendy," Kate smiled.

"That's good, too," Rosalie gasped as a pain welled up. "I was afraid we wouldn't make it into town in time. Ray had gone out to the south forty and didn't hear the dinner bell when I rang it," she panted. "By the time he came in, the pains were about ten minutes apart. It was hard to see the road, the dust was so thick," she groaned, "and he ran off into the ditch a couple of times." She grabbed the pillow and bit down hard with another pain. When the contraction eased, she went on. "Getting stuck sure didn't help my condition any. My water broke as he spun tires trying to get the car out of the foot-deep dirt," she said in a strained whisper, her voice rising as she spoke the last two words.

"Hush, now," Kate said. "Save your strength for the job ahead." She turned to the two men. "You men go someplace and wait. There's coffee on the stove, cake on the counter, wind and dust outside. I'll let you know in a little while."

"Are you up for this, Kate?" Johnny asked quietly, stepping closer to her.

"Yes. I can handle it," she answered with more confidence than she actually felt. But she had been through the birthing process so many times herself that she knew what to expect. Purposely, but gently, she escorted the guys out the bedroom door, shut it, undressed Rosalie with soothing words, and eased her onto the bed.

The birth went quickly and relatively easily with no theatrics from Rosalie. When the baby boy slipped out, Kate smacked him once on his bottom and when he squalled, she laid him on his mother's stomach. After she had tied and cut the cord, she handed him to Evvie and Tilly, both about as white-faced as anyone could possibly get. "Be careful with him; he's slippery," she admonished. "Wipe him off with that clean cloth and then wrap him in the light, smaller blanket. Hold him up close to you for warmth," Kate instructed. "We'll hand him to his mother as soon as I'm finished cleaning up and making Rosalie comfortable."

The two girls recovered quickly and began making cooing sounds and baby talk to the newborn.

"He's so cute," Tilly said, over his squalling. "Look at all that black hair standing straight up."

"Oh, yes, he *is* really cute," replied Evvie, "but I'm not ever going through that to have a really cute baby. Ever!" she vowed. "I'm going to adopt, that's what I'm going to do."

"But the baby won't be yours," Tilly protested.

"Yes, it will. It'll be just like my own, and I won't have to have all those pains and stuff," Evvie responded adamantly.

Overhearing the conversation, Kate and Rosalie looked at each other and smiled knowingly. "I said the same thing when I was their age," Kate whispered to Rosalie.

"Me, too," Rosalie whispered back, nodding her head.

"Girls," Kate said, "give the baby boy to his mother and go tell his father that he has a healthy son."

Before they reached the door, though, Ray poked his head in and said, "I heard a baby cry. Is everything all right?"

"Right as rain," Kate said. "Come in."

"It's a boy!" exclaimed the girls. "And he's really cute."

"What did you expect? Look at his mother," beamed Ray. "Hey, Johnny," he called, "come in and look at this kid of mine."

Arriving at the bedside, Johnny said, "He *is* good looking, and the way he's bellering, he has lungs like you, so he must be as healthy and strong as a young bull."

"Yes, he is," stated Kate. "Now, Johnny and you girls, let's get out of here and let the mother and dad get acquainted with their new son."

As they sat down in the living room, Kate realized the dust storm still raged. Night had come down without any difference in the shade of light or darkness. "Well," she sighed, "there isn't any way that anyone can get to their homes in this blackout. Girls, let's get some supper on the table, and then we'll get beds changed so we can all sleep here."

She went into the kitchen with Tilly, Evvie, and Amanda behind her. Following, Johnny sidled up to Kate and whispered, "Does this mean that I get to sleep with you, Kate?"

She stopped in her tracks, looked him in the eye, and said, "No, it does *not*." Ignoring him, she started putting a meal together, his gentle chuckle irritating her. The two girls must have heard, for they giggled under their breath, and Kate's face flamed painfully hot and red. She sent them into the pantry for the dark chocolate cake that she had baked yesterday, with the rich fudge frosting. When they came out, Kate saw that, luckily, the cake was still whole in the cake pan, uncut and unnibbled. She was astonished that anything like that could happen in this house of voraciously hungry children. She went about the business of preparing melted cheese sandwiches and hot chocolate for them all.

"Sorry, Kate," Johnny apologized. "It just slipped out. I didn't mean to embarrass you. But I wish it were true, and so do you."

She turned to reprimand him and found herself openmouthed, the retort caught in her throat, because she *did* wish it. Her whole body flushed as though she had a fever. She turned away and cleared her throat; hands shaking, she cut more thick slices of bread, saying neither yea nor nay.

Johnny patted her shoulder and went into the living room with the little kids, who had been called downstairs after the baby's birth. They, of course, all went in to admire the new soul with much oohing and aahing. Billy and Jerome glanced into the bedroom and then came into the kitchen with Kate, wondering when they could eat.

🔖 🔖 🔖

Sorting out the beds later, Kate ended up in Evvie's bed, with Evvie and Tilly on the floor; Ray and Rosalie were in Kate's bed; Johnny was in Billy's bed with Billy and Jerome on the floor; and the rest of the children slept wherever there was a place for them. They loved it, like it was a big campout. When the hubbub settled down and sleep tiptoed through the house, Kate lay awake for a long time. The wind whistled and moaned around the windows with the dust sifting in wherever it found a crack. It was indigo dark, and an indigo feeling seeped up her spine as she listened to the desolate sound. It would be comforting to have a warm body sharing her bed, arms around her and holding her. She always seemed to be battling the wind and her emotions, but maybe it was just the weather itself that was after her soul.

Remembering the dust storm the day that Jim fell from the windmill, she shivered and turned over again, trying to dampen the thought that the wind really was a demon of sorts that wanted her very life and spirit. She lay there and wondered if it would eventually win the battle. But no, she told herself, she was an anchor on this farm. The soil held her solidly, and she held her family as securely as the windmill offered water. *It's the water, afterall, that holds it all together,* she thought. She turned onto her back to look through the blackness of the room and saw nothing, not even the windows. It really was like being in a black hole of moaning demons.

In Billy's room just down the hall, she heard Billy's bedsprings creak again and again. *He's not sleeping either,* she thought. In her mind's eye, she saw Johnny there and suddenly wished she could cuddle with him. Then she heard him get out of bed, his bare feet walking across the floor and his footsteps in the hall. He was coming to her. She gasped, her heart fluttering. Afraid the girls would hear, she quietly got up and, even more quietly, felt her way in the dark to the door, opening it a crack. Knowing full well it was Johnny, she whispered, "Who is it?" when he appeared just a breath away.

"It's me," Johnny whispered back. "I can't sleep, Kate, for thinking about you and me. I mean…I know you won't allow it, but I want to be close to you—especially on a night like this."

She stepped out and closed the door behind her. "Go back to bed, Johnny. It's just not a good idea, and you know it."

When he reached for her, she quickly drew back. "Johnny…go back to bed, please. My reputation is at stake here and I know you respect that. Besides, the children will know; the girls are in here, and I'm sure the boys have heard you. They'll know what's going on," she said, fighting her own rising passions.

"You're right. Just a goodnight kiss, then," and before she could resist, he touched her cheek with his cool lips then turned toward Billy's room, closing the door softly behind him.

For a moment, she leaned against the wall and wondered if Ray and Rosalie had heard, in spite of the fierceness of the wind and the cries of the newborn. A tremendous wave of relief washed over her; though it had been difficult, she had sent him away. It was the right thing to do, but she knew at that instant that she wanted to marry him, and she would tell him so tomorrow. She would deal with the farm and all that somehow. With that resolution in mind, she went back into Evvie's room and was sitting on the side of the bed, kicking off her slippers, when a soft voice floated up from the floor where the two girls lay.

"Was that Johnny at the door, Mom?" Evvie asked.

Startled, Kate answered, "Yes, it was." She adjusted the covers and slipped between the sheets, which were grainy with fine dust.

"My dad was at the door?" Tilly asked sleepily.

"Ah...well," Kate stammered. "Yes."

"He loves you, you know," Tilly stated.

"I know."

"Do you love him, Mom?" Evvie asked.

"I do."

"Then why don't you marry him?" Tilly asked.

"I think I will," Kate answered.

"You will? Good!" both girls exclaimed.

"But what about you and Jerome, Evvie? If I marry Johnny, you and Jerome will be brother and sister," Kate pointed out.

"That would be great," Evvie answered. "He'd be a good brother."

Befuddled, Kate said, "But...I thought he was a boyfriend of sorts."

"Oh, no, Mom; he's nice, but he's not my boyfriend. I sort of like Jackson Taylor, but he doesn't know I exist," Evvie sighed.

"Well, that's his loss," Kate said. Boy, had she ever been in a fog about Evvie's preferences.

"I like Jackson, too," Tilly interrupted, "but he only has eyes for Gloria Banks, the cute cheerleader."

"Gloria? I thought you and Billy really liked each other—a boy-friend-girlfriend thing." Kate puzzled through the situation, trying to recall Jackson Taylor and Gloria Banks and who their parents were. She would have to ask Johnny tomorrow—perhaps he knew.

"I like Billy like a brother," Tilly stated without hesitation. "Evvie and I would really like to be sisters, too, so you can marry my dad if you want to. I think you'd be a good mother to us kids. I really miss having a mother." There was a quaver in Tilly's voice as she said this.

Deeply touched, tears seeped across Kate's face and into her
ears. She swallowed hard and answered, "I would be honored to be
a mother to all of you." She paused, then said, "The first thing in the
morning, you two secretly tell Billy, Jerome, Amanda, and the twins,
then we'll gang up on Johnny and ask him to marry us! Won't he be
surprised! Now, hush—it's too late to talk. Let's go to sleep so we'll be
rested and beautiful in the morning," Kate teased. "Maybe we'll cook
a delicious breakfast and then pop the question."

"Oh, that's a great idea," Evvie and Tilly whispered excitedly. "He
will be surprised, won't he?"

"But," Evvie countered, "what about religion? Will that be okay?
And where will we live? Will we go to Oregon?"

"Johnny and I will work it all out," Kate assured them. "It's not
the church's business who I marry, whether he be green, purple, black,
Catholic, Jewish, Irish, or African. If people don't like it, that's just too
bad. Eventually, I think religion won't make a difference to our real
friends. We'll have to figure out what to do about our farms and moving. I don't want to leave: This is our home. But we'll work it all out,
somehow. Now, let's go to sleep."

Kate lay there, savoring the moment. Realizing how much she
loved Johnny, she felt proud that she was making a choice that would
not only make her happy, but her children as well. And with that, she
turned onto her side, adjusted her pillow, and—with her hand under
her head—she drifted off, listening to the girls whispering various
plans for the proposal. Their voices were like velvet against the grind-
ing dust speckling the windowpane. Sometime during the night, the
wind stopped.

Early the next morning, she walked through the house, fine dust
crunching under her shoes.

Everyone seemed asleep, but when she stepped into the kitchen,
the cooking range was going and Johnny was at the table, drinking
coffee and staring out the dusty window, his eyes seeing something
that Kate couldn't see. What he saw was not good, she could tell, for
he didn't hear or see her.

"Good morning, Johnny," she said. He jumped, slopping his coffee
across his knuckles and onto the table. "Oh, I'm sorry. I didn't mean to
startle you," and she grabbed the dishrag.

"Morning, Kate," he replied. He took it from her and absently swiped at the coffee mess.

Her stomach took a nose dive. Just when she had made up her mind to marry him, had he given up on her? In his mind, was he already in Oregon? "What's the matter?" she asked, dreading his answer.

"The baby has breathing problems," he said. Taking her hand, he gently held onto her. "I started up the stairs for you, but I heard you getting up. I knew you'd be down in a bit, so I waited for you here."

It's not me, then, she thought with relief. But then, *How selfish I am!* Feeling guilty but also deeply compassionate, she said, "No! Not the baby!"

Before she could say anything else, he went on. "I was up early and had just started the fire and coffee when Ray came out of the bedroom and said the baby was not breathing right. He said that he was going to wrap him in a blanket and take him into town to Doc Jensen. I called Jensen, but his wife said to take the baby to the hospital, because Doc was delivering a baby at the Machovich farm. So, I went back to the bedroom to tell them, and they were arguing about Rosalie not going. I came back out and poured myself a cup, and I've been waiting for Ray to come out with the baby."

Kate drew in a deep breath and nodded, feeling as though the world was too full of dreadful wounds. Softly she said, "I'll go in to Rosalie. You drive Ray and the baby to the hospital." She walked toward the bedroom just as Ray came out, the baby wrapped in a heavy blanket. "Need to go," he said. Johnny nodded, took another sip of coffee and grabbed his coat, opening the door for Ray. A wretched shriek came from the bedroom. "Bring back my baby! I want him here with me, not in the hospital so far away!" screamed Rosalie.

"Go on," Kate said to Ray. "You take him; I'll take care of this." But before she went in, Kate gently lifted the blanket and kissed the tiny face. She watched Ray and Johnny step over a huge mound of dust piled at the door, then she made her way to the bedroom to comfort Rosalie.

As she approached the door, all the children came piling down the stairs and asked who screamed. Kate put her finger to her lips and softly told them what had happened. Then she went in and left them to do as they were taught—take care of themselves and each other for a while. She could hear Evvie and Tilly softly sobbing and then the other girls crying.

It was a long day for all. With the phone lines down again because a truck had run into a pole, there was no way to communicate with Johnny or anyone.

When Kate and Rosalie were beside themselves with worry, Johnny and Ray returned in the evening with Doctor Jensen following. Kate met them on the porch, trying to shield Rosalie from any bad news. Johnny and Ray got out of the car looking worn and frazzled, Ray carrying the fussing baby.

"Oh!" Kate exclaimed. "The baby! He's crying! Is he going to be all right?"

"Doc says yes," Ray answered, grinning from ear to ear. Doctor Jensen nodded as he walked up. Johnny sat down at the kitchen table, where the rest of the family was eating their supper of fried potatoes and eggs. Ray and Doc entered the bedroom with the baby. Kate filled a plate for Johnny, but he pushed the food around with his fork. He took a tentative bite, which Kate knew tasted like cardboard: His exhaustion was deep.

She spoke, "Tell us what took so long and what happened at the hospital."

Johnny carefully placed his fork across his plate, adjusted it just at the right angle, and leaned back in his chair. Sighing, he said, "Well, it took us three hours to get the ten miles to town because of dirt that blocked the road in places. We had to get out and shovel some of it out of the way so we could go through, leaving the baby in the car by himself. That almost took Ray down, leaving that sick baby alone like that. When we got into the car one time after shoveling some more dirt, the baby wasn't breathing. Ray hugged him up tight, huge sobs racking his body. I grabbed that baby and started breathing into his mouth. I don't know why; it was just what I did. I did that to a calf one time and it worked, so I guess I thought it would work on a baby. Then I patted him on the back, and just kept up the breathing and patting, breathing and patting. Pretty soon, that tiny little critter sucked in a big gulp and started crying and breathing on his own. His face turned pink and he squirmed around, looking for milk. Can you believe that? Anyway, laughing like a fool, Ray wrapped him up again and, since we were so close to town, we went on to the hospital. Doc Jensen looked him over pretty good, said he was fine, and that we could take him home. Before we left, he had the Sisters give him some sugar water. That little guy was hungry and was he ever howling. After the Sisters fed him, they changed his diapers and clothes, and here he is, in that room in his mommy's arms." Johnny stopped and cleared his throat. "What a day!" He heaved another sigh. "Doc said that some babies are born with a membrane around their lungs and have problems breathing. I guess the baby's had dissipated a little but not enough, so when I blew into his mouth, the membrane broke completely, and he started howling." Johnny drew another deep breath. "I didn't know I was so smart," he cocked a grin that belied his feelings of profound gratitude.

"Johnny, what a wonderful thing you did! You saved that baby's life!" Kate exclaimed, her happiness tempered with a deep sadness that her little Jimmy had not gotten a second chance. But then she thought of how small it was of her to entertain such a thought. She was still hurt about her little boy's death, but Ray and Rosalie's baby boy had come to fill that empty space.

The children, meanwhile, all talked at the same time, excited and happy that things had turned out so well. Amanda timidly kissed her dad on the temple. When Tilly, Leah, and Leslie did the same, Evvie gave Kate a certain look as she planted a solid kiss on Johnny's cheek, much to Kate's surprise and Johnny's pleasure.

"Mama," Evvie stood back and said quietly, "what about our surprise that didn't happen this morning?" Tilly looked at Kate for an answer, too.

Kate responded, "Not today, girls, but maybe tomorrow. We'll discuss our surprise in the morning."

"What surprise?" Johnny inquired.

"It wouldn't be a surprise if we told you," Kate teased. The girls sent a pleading look at her and then at Johnny. Kate held firm. "Not today, girls. Tomorrow," she repeated. "We're all too tired."

"You're right," Johnny said. "I'm too tired for anything else today." The girls shrugged and, whispering under their breath, went upstairs.

Kate took hot coffee into the bedroom and asked if anything was needed. When she found that she could do nothing to add to the parents' happiness, she came out, poured coffee for Johnny and herself, and sat down.

"We had to wait a while at the hospital for Doc Jensen," Johnny recalled. "He was on a house call delivering another baby for Peggy Machovich. I think that makes about twelve for her, doesn't it?"

She nodded and said quietly, as though to herself, "I wonder how many more babies she can have before her body and mind give out completely?"

"Good question," Johnny said. And then, "When Doc asked Ray what the baby's name was for the birth certificate, I didn't know and neither did Ray. What *is* his name?"

"I'm not sure, but Rosalie and I talked about Dusty because of the dusty day he was born. If it had been a girl, Wendy, I think."

Johnny nodded, "Good names. Doc wanted to make sure Rosalie was okay, so he followed us out here. It took us a long time: The road grader had plowed through some of the drifts but didn't get all the way out here. Just plowed the main roads, I guess, and knocked over a telephone pole or two in the process." He put his elbows on the table and ran his hands through his dark, tousled hair, which Kate thought needed to be trimmed-up some. "And here we are," he said, his voice thick with weariness.

Kate's heart went out to him. She wanted to put her arms around him and hold him close. Instead, she reached over and placed her hand over his. He looked up at her with such love that her heart turned over. They sat like that for a while until she withdrew her hand. She thought about how the day had gone completely off of what she had planned. This morning, she and the children were going to ask him to marry her! *Now look*, she thought.

Doctor Jensen came out of the bedroom and asked for another cup of coffee. He sat at the table, accepting the piece of chocolate cake that Kate placed before him. "Is Rosalie all right?" she asked.

"Rosalie is mentally fine, but she's physically exhausted. She's going to need some help and rest for the next day or two, maybe more. I advised Ray not to take her home for a couple of days, Kate. I hope that's all right with you. She needs a woman's touch, and us guys—well, we don't do so good in that department, it seems," he smiled. "I'll come out again day after tomorrow and see how she is. She can probably go home by then."

"Of course, she can stay," Kate said.

"She can get up tomorrow," Doc stated.

"Tomorrow?" Kate gasped. "I had to stay in bed for what seemed an eternity! I got so tired of that bed, when all I wanted to do was get up and take care of things by myself."

"I know," he said, "but my idea is that women lose their strength and take a chance of blood clots if they stay in bed too long. So far, it's been a good theory. She has to take it easy for a week or so, but she'll get well faster by moving around. I better head for the office now. There's another woman due to deliver anytime and I need to check in. Thanks for the coffee and cake." He picked up his bag and went out the door.

"I'm going home now, Kate," Johnny said, "and take the family with me. The wind and dust have calmed down right now, so it's a good time."

"Yes, but come back tomorrow, if the weather permits. Let the girls stay tonight, though."

"Right," he said, and kissed her forehead. He stuck his head through the bedroom door. "I'm going home now, Ray and Rosalie. Be back tomorrow."

"Hey, Johnny, come in here. Rosie wants to see you."

Johnny went on in and Kate heard Rosalie heaping thanks and praise onto him for saving their son. She heard him answer quietly, saying he was glad the little tad was alive. Kate smiled and was still smiling when he came out, grinning.

"It's a good day," he said.

"Yes, it is," she answered. "I'll tell the girls they can stay the night here."

"Good," he said. "I told Jerome earlier that he'd be going home with me, so he's upstairs getting ready to leave." When Jerome came down, Johnny kissed Kate on the cheek and they left.

When Kate stepped into the bedroom to check on Ray and Rosalie, she heard Johnny's car start up and realized he hadn't been home for the last two days. She wondered about his chores, but then she remembered that he had the bachelor renter doing that for him. Holding the baby, she looked out the window and saw that the vehicle was leaving the yard, Jerome driving.

She stayed in the room for a while, just talking and holding the baby, whose name really was Dusty. She cooed to him, but her mind was on Johnny and how she, with his and her children, would propose marriage to him in the morning. Then she realized that with Rosalie here, the proposal would have to be put off for a couple more days. She sighed. Evvie and Tilly would be disappointed again. "Such a beautiful little guy," Kate said to Rosalie and Ray. "He's so lucky to be alive and to have such wonderful parents." Looking down at him in her arms, she chucked him under the chin. "Aren't you, Mr. Cute-Little-Dusty-Man?" His dark-blue eyes saw not her, but the world from which he had come just yesterday.

🖋 🖋 🖋

By nighttime, when all were in bed, she sat in her rocker, concerned because Johnny hadn't called to let her know that he and Jerome were home safely through the dust piles. She went to the telephone to call him and, just as she picked up the receiver, he called. He told her they had just arrived home and that the roads were nearly impossible to get through. He and Jerome would hopefully get back to her place tomorrow morning after chores.

During the night, the wind picked up again, sandblasting the windows with tiny particles of floury-fine dirt that slid down the glass. The blowing had abated by morning, but there was another six inches added to the three-foot piles already covering the fences, tractors, plows, and even the chicken house. The dust piled up where it found a foothold and stuck like an all-consuming, ravenous creature.

After the morning work was done and the children scattered here and there inside the house and out, Kate helped Rosalie to the table for breakfast. She drank coffee, ate toast, and held her baby boy close, covering him with kisses while Kate went about her work, humming aimlessly.

"Where's Ray?" Rosalie asked.

"He went home to see about things," Kate answered. "He'll be back later in the day."

"Oh."

"You can stay here until you feel like going home, Rosalie. Doctor Jensen said you could probably go after he checks you out tomorrow."

"Oh, good," Rosalie responded, then she paused and said softly. "I'd like to go back to bed now. I'm really tired, but I'm oh-so happy," and she kissed Dusty on the head and each of his tiny hands.

"All right, I'll help you. You have a right to be happy, and I'm happy for you, too."

"Where is everybody, anyway?" Rosalie asked as they made their way toward the bedroom.

"The girls are upstairs making beds and straightening rooms— Timothy and Meggie are with them—Billy is out doing chores. Johnny and Jerome will be here sometime soon, after their chores are done," Kate responded.

With the kitchen cleaned up, Kate stepped out to see for herself just what the wind had done. What she saw was staggering: Dust was piled as high as the windowsills now. It barricaded the barn door and, in her garden plot, it was layered like thick, worn-out brown blankets. In order to get the chores done, she saw that Billy had shoveled paths to the outbuildings, and she could hear him coughing from breathing in the silt. She ran her hand over her hair in desperation. What was she to do? How could she ever dig out from under this and have a farm?

With her jaw set, she looked at the landscape. It still reminded her of the Sahara Desert. *That's just what it is,* she thought—*a desert.* She stepped back into the house, deeply upset. Before she closed the door, she turned and gave a loud "yoo hoo" to Billy and waited for his answer. He needed to get back into the house before breathing anymore dust. He yelled back from the barn door, signaling that he had heard her.

In the kitchen, she pulled out a chair and sat down, elbows on the table and head in her hands. She fought to keep the depression from sinking in and overtaking her. As she sat in the midst of the death of her farm—the family's livelihood—a devastating thought slid into her head: How could she even think of marrying Johnny now and maybe going to Oregon? She was torn between him and bringing her land back to life. Her heart sank lower. "Oh, Johnny, Johnny," she whispered. "I guess I'll lose you, too." Her tears fell like rain—the rain that never seemed to fall onto this parched earth. *First Jim, then the two babies, then Jimmy, and now you, Johnny,* she thought. *If only my tears could water the burned-out soil. But you, Johnny, are alive and I must keep you somehow.* She sat, listening to the children come downstairs, but she didn't look at them until she heard one of the twins cough as if she were choking. Kate jumped up. "Which one of you is coughing like that?"

"Me, Mama," Leah answered. "I'm sorry. I've been coughing all morning and gagging up brown stuff that looks like wet dirt. I can't stop and I'm scared."

"Oh, my," Kate said, trying to remain calm. "Let's get a wet towel around your nose and mouth and some cough syrup and a pan for steam on the stove. I'll call Doctor Jensen and see what he thinks." She soaked a towel in water and rung it out. "Here's the towel," she said to Leah. "Now sit and rest while I make that call."

"Bring her in," Doctor Jensen said when Kate explained the situation. "Take her to the hospital, and the Sisters will get her under a steam blanket for the night. If she doesn't have pneumonia, with some rest and moisture to help her breathe, she should be okay in a day or two."

"I don't know if I can get to town," Kate said. "The roads..."

"The road graders are out, so I'll call the county and see that one grader gets out that way."

Kate sent Leah up to change clothes then went into her bedroom to put on a clean dress. When she told Rosalie what was going on, Rosalie got out of bed, threw on a robe, and said, "I'll watch the children while you're gone, so don't worry. I need to get up and do something anyway. When Doctor Jensen comes tomorrow, I think I'll be ready to go home."

"Well...if you're up to it," Kate said gratefully. "Even though Evvie and Tilly are capable of seeing to the little ones, it would be a comfort knowing you're here with them." As she talked, Kate rummaged through her closet for a dress. "Johnny and Jerome should be here before long, and Ray will be back sometime this afternoon." Hurriedly, she changed into her dress, tied her shoes, and checked her purse for money and found five dollars, which she decided was enough. "So make yourself at home. If you feel like eating, there are leftover biscuits and sausage in the icebox."

She told Rosalie goodbye and went out to see if Leah had changed to a clean dress, underwear, and socks. When Leah protested that she didn't want to go to the doctor, Kate gave her a stern look that quelled further argument. She called up to Evvie, who came out of the bedroom long enough to understand what was happening. Though Kate knew that Rosalie was still weak, it would do her good to be up and moving about, but Evvie and Tilly could take care of the house today.

Though the road had been graded, the way into town was a maze of dust in erratic piles, continuing to blow here and there. Kate had never been a good driver, and the zigzagging to miss those piles tested her ability to the maximum, which gave her a tremendous headache. It took two hours to get there, but she made it. When she pulled up in front of the hospital, she laid her head on the steering wheel to regain her self-control. To make things worse, Leah had whined and begged all the way in for Kate to take her back home. "I'm not sick, Mama," she had declared, coughing brown phlegm into a white, embroidered handkerchief.

"Well," Kate responded, "we're here and we're going to see about that cough. You have dust in your lungs, as you can see by what you're coughing up." She took Leah's arm and propelled her into the hospital where two Sisters waited. Kate followed along as they escorted Leah into a room, undressed her, and settled her into a bed.

Doctor Jensen came in, checked Leah over thoroughly, and listened to her lungs. "She's going to be fine, but I want her to stay here a day or two until she coughs up all that dust and can breathe better. It's not pneumonia, but it could become that if we don't catch it right now. So...relax Kate. Go to the kitchen and get a cup of coffee and something to eat. Tell them I sent you."

Kate called home to say she would stay the night and maybe the next one, if necessary. Rosalie said she would stay and go home with Ray the next day. She went on to say that since Betty was down with a cold, Johnny had offered to stay after she and little Dusty went home. With that, Kate went back to Leah and sat in a chair close by, sleeping fitfully and listening to Leah's ragged cough. The second night was much better: Surprisingly, she slept well then, as did Leah with very little coughing. Mid-morning the third day, Doctor Jensen said that Leah could go home. So they left after lunch with cough medicine in hand and instructions from the doctor. Leah would continue to clear her lungs, he said, but Kate was to call him at the slightest indication that Leah or any of the other children had the croupy, wet-dust-deep-down cough.

It was good to get out of the hospital. Driving toward home, Kate felt as though she had been somehow liberated. She pondered why she felt that way and decided it was because she was out in the open with fresh air. The day was clear with no wind, it was just her and Leah in the car, and Leah was on the mend. It took another two hours of skirting dusty drifts, and all the while Leah blabbed non-stop. Kate's head throbbed. Finally, Leah smiled with satisfaction. "Mom, I've been in the hospital. Nobody else has in our family! I've done something they haven't, haven't I?"

"Yes, you have," answered Kate. She didn't burst Leah's bubble by reminding her that Jimmy had been in the hospital, too. Leah was so proud of her experience and Kate let it go. She knew, though, that Leah would brag about it until the whole family and all her friends would get sick of hearing it. They would eventually avoid her, and then Leah would come complaining to her. "Leah," Kate began, "I think you might not dwell on that too long."

"Why not? *I've been in the hospital!*" she replied indignantly.

"Because people will get tired of listening to it."

"Why?" she demanded. "Not many kids my age have been in the hospital."

"All right," Kate sighed, knowing it wouldn't do any good. Leah being Leah, she would have to find out for herself the consequences of bragging.

While Leah continued, Kate's thoughts turned to the hospital bill and how she would pay it. It was just another problem that she'd worry through. The hard winter had used most of what she'd saved, and what she had earmarked for planting crops was nearly gone. But then she wondered if there would be any planting. There had been no rain to bring up the winter wheat, and with this dust and the rabbits, she questioned how plants of any kind could grow. Tomorrow, she'd check out the fields again, see what condition they were in. She had a feeling the sight wouldn't be a positive one. By the time they arrived home, Kate's feeling of being liberated had disappeared and her headache was blinding.

"Yay! We're home, Mommy!" Leah laughed. She piled out of the car before Kate had fully come to a stop and, before she could reprimand her, Leah sprinted to the house, threw open the door, and shouted, "Hey, everybody, I'm home from the hospital! I'm home and I didn't die, either!"

As Kate stepped into the house, the children were gathered around Leah, bombarding her with all kinds of questions. Leah answered them, sometimes correctly but, most times, exaggerated for dramatic effect. Kate shook her head and began putting away what few groceries she had bought in town.

Johnny walked his way around the gathering, took Kate in his arms, and whispered, "I am so glad you're here and that Leah is all right." He kissed her temple.

"Me, too," she said, and locked eyes with him. She kissed him on the cheek and pulled away, but held onto his hand. "I have something to ask you later," she said, "but not right now. When did Rosalie go home?" She changed the direction of the conversation.

"Yesterday—Doc was out and said she was fine, so Ray took her home. His mother is there to help," he answered. "Just what is it you want to ask me? I think I know," he replied, "but for now, supper is ready. We were just sitting down to hamburger gravy, potatoes, biscuits, and green beans. That's about all I know how to cook, and that was with Tilly and Evvie's help," he grinned. "They made the biscuits. Come on, everybody, let's eat!" he shouted to the kids. "I'm hungry."

"Me, too!" exclaimed Leah. "The food in the hospital was awful, not good like Mommy's." She piled her plate with potatoes and spooned an enormous amount of gravy across them, then slathered a biscuit with butter and jam.

"Hey," Billy protested, "save some for the rest us! You're not the only one at this table, you know. So pass that stuff around."

"But *I've* been in the hospital," Leah stated royally, her nose turned up. "I need food to recover."

"Big deal," Billy retorted. "Jerome and I have been here eating food that Evvie and Tilly cooked for the past two days. Now *that's* scary. So pass the stuff around and let the rest of us enjoy what Johnny cooked today."

Kate looked over the heads of the children and met Johnny's eyes. She raised one eyebrow and smiled a crooked smile. He nodded. It was good to sit down to a normal meal again.

After supper, Johnny came to her and said, "I hope whatever it was you were going to ask me can wait until tomorrow, because I need to go home. My milk cow looked and acted like she was going to calve today, so I better go check on her. I'll take my kids with me so you can have a quiet evening. I know you're tired, and we can catch up tomorrow."

Disappointed that once again she would have to wait to pop the question, she nodded then said, "That's fine. Tomorrow's another day, and I am pretty tired." He looked around and saw that the kids were involved in their own world and kissed her gently on the lips. The fire in her leaped up, but she returned his kiss with only a light one on his cheek and said, "Have a good rest tonight and we'll see each other tomorrow."

"Right." He lifted her chin with his finger but didn't kiss her because she drew back. "All right," he nodded. Then he said, "Hey, my kids, we're going home, so get ready." When they protested, he said, "We'll come back tomorrow. We *do* have our own home, you know, and we *do* have to take care of it."

"Well, if you two would get married, there would be only one place to take care of," Jerome stated.

"Go get in the car," Johnny ordered in mock sternness. He turned to Kate with a nod and a half-shrug. "True," he stated mischievously.

Flushing, Kate closed the door behind him and faced her family, who were looking sheepishly at her and nodding. "For your information," she said before any of them could open their mouths, "when they all come back tomorrow, we're going to propose marriage to Johnny. So don't give me any static about it. Whether you like it or not, that's my plan." She finished the statement with a superior air, expecting all kinds of comments, but what the kids said really warmed her heart.

"We think it's great!" they all clambered.

"That's what we wanted you to do," said Billy.

"Tilly will finally be my sister," said Evvie.

"And Amanda will be our sister, too." This came from Leah and Leslie.

"I like Amanda to sleep with me," Meggie lisped. "I don't feel tho lonethum then." Seeing how much Meggie missed her twin, Kate's heart twisted. She picked her up and held her close.

"I know, sweetheart. I'm glad you like Amanda," Kate said and kissed Meggie on the nose.

Billy put his arm around Kate's shoulders and said, "I'll have a twin brother now. Jerome and I are about the same age, and I think this is great, Mom. We never thought we would want another dad, but we've all agreed that Johnny would be a good one."

"Mama," Evvie looked seriously at her, "I hope someone will love me someday like Johnny loves you."

"Well," Kate said, her voice shaking with emotion, "I guess it's unanimous then. So I say that tomorrow is the day when we propose to Johnny, and we'll see what happens." They gathered around for hugs—even Billy, which was highly unusual, because they were not a hugging family.

It seemed that after the children reached school age, she and Jim stopped hugging them for some reason. Today though, she wrapped her arms around each one in turn and was surprised to find that she could easily tell them that she loved them. That was another thing that hadn't been done in the past, but she wouldn't leave the hugs and the love undone anymore. It was obvious that not only did the children want and need affection, but she did, too.

Kate hadn't told Betty about her plan to propose to Johnny, but if he said yes—which was a sure thing—then she would have them over and tell them in person instead of over the party line, though the neighbors would know soon enough through the prairie grapevine.

Before the sun came up the next morning, Kate was out of bed with a song in her heart, a song that radiated from her inner soul to her lips. She went about her routine humming "Indian Love Call." She had heard it on the radio as Nelson Eddy and Jeanette MacDonald blended their voices in the soaring notes. Johnny had said it was from the movie, *Rose Marie*. How he knew that, Kate didn't know, but it was a beautiful rhapsody. *Maybe I'll have it sung at our wedding*, she thought. *No, it's a little too operatic. "Let Me Call You Sweetheart" might be better.* But "I Love You Truly" was a traditional song nowadays for weddings, and it would suit them just fine. She'd heard Evvie and Tilly trying to harmonize together on it. She slipped her apron over her head, tied it, and put the coffeepot on, still humming "Indian Love Call" quietly.

She was pondering her choice of words to tell Betty about the plan when she heard a strange shuffling noise on the porch. Puzzled, she opened the door to see who was there so early in the morning, and there was Victor. Staggering and reeking of booze, he grinned at her like a Cheshire cat. Stunned, she wondered how he got there. Her first impulse was to step back, but then she stood her ground, solid as a rock; she didn't want to give him room to squeeze past her into the house.

"Victor," she gritted through her teeth. "What are you doing here? How did you get here?"

"Is that any way to greet your favorite brother-in-law?" he slurred, lurching against the door jam. He was disheveled and filthy.

She tried to slam the door, but he stuck his foot in and shoved it open, knocking her back against the table, where her foot caught on a chair. She fell then, hitting her head on the table leg. She saw stars. Dazed, she struggled to get her feet under her, but he was soon on her and had pinned her to the floor. "Remember the last time, Kate?" he slurred. "When you hit me and hauled me outside? I promised then to have you for my own! Remember that? *I do*." He began hitting her then, slamming his fists into her face. She tried to block the blows, but she could feel the blood begin to run.

Panicked, she felt for a weapon, making a swipe across the floor with her arm, but found nothing. He stopped hitting her and began to slide his hand up under her dress along her thigh, and she instinctively brought her knee up with all her might into his crotch. He screamed and fell off her, rolling on his side in agony. She was able then to scramble to her feet and stumble to the stove, where she again grabbed her trusty cast-iron skillet. Struggling back to where Victor was slowly raising up on one elbow, she hit him with as much strength as she could muster. He fell back, unconscious and bleeding.

Kate stood over him, panting, hoping he would move so she could hit him again, but he lay still. She wished with all her heart that he was dead, but she saw that he was still breathing. As she stood there, Billy and Evvie came rattling down the stairs and stopped in shock.

"Mom, we heard a loud noise!" Billy exclaimed. "Who is that?" he asked, kneeling. He turned Victor over. "Uncle Victor? Did you hit him with that skillet?"

Before she could answer, Evvie screamed, "Mama! Your face— you're bleeding! Your mouth...your eyes are puffed up. Did Uncle Victor hit you?" Kate nodded, shaken and dizzy. Sharp pains pulsed through her face and ribs. "Sit down, Mama," Evvie said, leading Kate to a chair. "I'll put ice on your face."

Billy jumped up from leaning over Victor and hurried to Kate, his expression one of horror.

"Don't just stand there, Billy," Evvie said. "Call Johnny and then call the sheriff and Doctor Jensen. And drag *him* out of here." She made a disgusted sweep of her hand, indicating Victor. "He stinks." Looking back at her mother, Evvie began weeping. "Mama, Mama— I'm so sorry." She poured warm water into the wash basin and gently sponged Kate's face, then went for ice from the icebox.

By this time, the pain in Kate's bludgeoned face had become unbearable, so she mumbled for two aspirin, which Evvie hurriedly gave her with a glass of water. "Please, a cup of coffee," Kate managed through the swelling, but when she got it she couldn't drink it because the heat hurt the open wounds on her mouth. She was able to sip a little at a time, though, and welcomed the strength in the dark, hot liquid.

Meanwhile, Billy hauled Victor's limp body out the door. Huffing with the weight of it, he dropped his uncle just beyond the porch and came back. Kate knew that he had to be remembering the night that the two of them had done the very same thing just a couple of years ago. Billy made the phone calls and then sat close to her at the table. "Johnny's coming right over, and Sheriff Johnson will be here soon," he said. "I'm sorry this happened again, Mom. I thought he would never come back, but I see now that I was wrong in thinking Uncle Victor was a good guy."

"What do you mean *again?*" Evvie asked. "This has happened before?" Billy nodded. "Why didn't I know?"

"Because Mom didn't want anyone to know, that's why," he replied testily. He then began to expound on his version of that night, when he and his mother had left Victor for dead on the porch only to have him stagger off muttering in the night, and how angry Billy had been at his mother for nearly killing Victor.

Kate leaned her head on the table. "Please," she moaned, "no more of that. Just help me to my rocker."

"Sorry, Mom," Billy apologized sheepishly. He took her arm and, with Evvie's arm around her waist, they helped Kate get to the rocker. Evvie grabbed a blanket off the couch and wrapped it around Kate, and when she and Billy went back into the kitchen for Kate's coffee, he started the tale once again. When Kate thought she couldn't stand another minute of the account, Johnny, wide-eyed, flew through the door, his family following.

"Where is she? Where is she?" Evvie stepped aside so he wouldn't run into her and pointed to the living room. When Johnny looked at Kate, he said, "Kate! Oh, Kate, my darling! Let me look at you!" He knelt in front of her and wept openly, his warm hands clasped around her cold, trembling ones. "Did anyone call the doctor or the sheriff?"

"I did," said Billy. "Sheriff Johnson is coming right out, but Doc's in surgery. The Sisters will get a message to him, though, and he'll be here in an hour or so." He hesitated, then asked, "Is Mom going to be all right?" By this time, all the kids were gathered close by.

"Let's just make her comfortable by getting her onto the couch and covered up. Get the hot water bottle on her feet, and warm that blanket in the oven for just a little while," Johnny ordered. "She's shivering with shock. Get some more ice, Evvie, for her face." When Kate was settled on the couch, Johnny asked, "Anything broken, Kate?"

Kate tried to shake her head but the effort was too painful. She mouthed the words, "don't know," closed her eyes, and hung onto Johnny's hand. She was so grateful that he was there with her. When the two aspirin took hold, the pain eased somewhat, and she dozed a little, trying to gain strength through Johnny's warm, strong hand.

She began to cry then in soft, racking sobs. Johnny pulled up a chair and murmured softly to her, just as she had done when her babies had cried out in pain.

She slept then—or she fainted, she never knew for sure—but when she woke, she was in her bed. The sheriff had picked up Victor, and Doctor Jensen was moving her arm, checking for broken bones. He examined every inch of her, causing a good deal of pain when he turned her over to look at the heavy bruise on her back. She gasped when he felt her sore ribs for broken bones. "Some bad bruises here," he said. When he felt her stomach, she gasped again. "Here, too, but nothing broken that I can tell, Kate." He swore under his breath while he worked. Through her misery, Kate understood that what he muttered was a disparagement against men who beat women. He mumbled something along the lines of "those kinds of men should be flogged until they can't stand up straight." She agreed with him wholeheartedly.

Doctor Jensen called Johnny and the children into the bedroom, where they gathered around her. "You all need to hear what I'm going to say—even you, Kate." He addressed Johnny but made sure by looking directly at each of them from time to time that they all understood that what he was saying concerned everyone. "Well, Johnny," he said, "she's very badly beaten, but with rest and tender care, she'll be as good as new in a month or so. A badly bruised rib or two will be painful for quite a while, so don't let her lift anything heavier than a coffee cup. Her intestines are bruised, too, but there's no internal bleeding that I can tell. Give her beef or chicken broth, pudding, and other easily digested food." He looked warningly at the family. "There are no big open sores, just split lips, so nothing to bandage. But the bruises are as painful as an open sore, so be careful when you help her. They will heal, but not without turning ugly looking with all kinds of colors, from black and blue to red, yellow, and green."

He sighed tiredly. "To keep her from contracting pneumonia or getting a blood clot, she needs to be up and about three or four times a day starting tomorrow. You girls will be in charge of giving her a bath about every other day or so. She will protest, because she won't want to expose her naked body to you, but you must insist. Though her lips are split open and sore, make sure she eats. The best food, as I said, is broth until she can chew. He didn't knock out any teeth, so that's good. Now, I'm going to leave, but I'll be back day after tomorrow to check on her. Oh, she can also have Jell-O, too—anything soft." With that, he picked up his bag and herded them all out of the bedroom. He didn't shut the door so, through the fog in her brain, Kate faintly heard his further instructions.

"I've given her a sleeping potion, so let her rest for now. When she's awake, make sure she gets hot or cold tea and water frequently. If she's sleeping, don't wake her up to eat or drink. Give her more of the sleeping medicine if she's in a lot of pain. Rest will do her more good than anything else until the pain eases." He shrugged into his suit coat and shook Johnny's hand. "Oh…no visitors for three days. Call me if you need me."

"I will. Thanks, Doc," Johnny replied. He opened the door for him to leave, then closed it. Turning to the family, he said, "You heard Doc Jensen, so we're going to work together to get her well. No whining, no fighting, no loud noises. If you go in there to see her, talk softly and maybe read to her. She's very badly hurt, so we'll take care of her—understand?" He looked at them one by one until he got an affirmative nod from each. "I'm going to call Betty now and tell her what's happened."

Betty came right over, but when Johnny insisted that he stay with Kate, she surprisingly relented, saying that she would be over every day to see her. Johnny suspected that Betty really wanted to make sure they were caring for her sister properly.

Under the influence of the sleeping potion, Kate dreamed that Victor was using a hammer on her head, and that she was in a dark room, crying, "No! No! Stop! Victor, stop!"

"Kate. It's me, Johnny," he whispered. "Wake up. It's only a dream. I'm right here beside you and everything's all right."

She couldn't stop the dream, though, or the pounding in her head. "Stop!" she continued to cry.

"Kate," he touched her hand gently, and she gasped and then fought, thinking it was Victor. "Kate," Johnny said firmly. "It's Johnny here, not Victor. It's all a nightmare."

She struggled to open her eyes and managed to see through the swollen eyelids. She saw against the lamplight that Johnny sat on a chair beside her bed. Her heart pounded like a drum, sweat streamed off of her, and she needed the chamber pot. The older children had heard the commotion and were pouring into the room, alarmed. Realizing they were there, the bedroom settled down around her and she knew where she was. I need the chamber pot, please," she whispered through her mangled lips.

"Right," Johnny said. "Girls, this is the job for you. Us guys will leave the room for a while. If you need help, let me know."

"We don't need help, Johnny," said Evvie. "We can do it."

When the coast was clear, Johnny went back in to ask Kate if she needed more medicine for her pain. She nodded yes and began to doze off a few minutes after he gave it to her, but she heard him tell the kids, "Go on to bed. I'll sit with her for a while. I'll come get you later, Evvie, to sit with her while I catch some shut-eye. Scoot, now. "

In just a little while, Kate was calling out in her sleep, crying and kicking. Though he held her hand, she didn't settle down but became increasingly agitated and vocal. He knew some of the problem was the medicine, but he became worried that all her floundering around would make her wounds worse. He walked to the other side of the bed, turned back the quilt, and crawled in beside her, then gently pulled her to him. Immediately, she calmed down and settled into a deep and restful sleep. He lay awake for a long time and then he, too, drifted off.

It was morning when Kate woke and wondered who was in bed with her. For a minute or two, she thought it was Jim and her heart filled with joy. Then reality set in, and she reasoned that it was probably Evvie beside her. But then Evvie and Tilly came in and stood by the bed.

"Mama," Evvie whispered under her breath.

Kate peered up at her, her head pounding like a kettle drum. "What?"

"I think you're going to have to marry Johnny for sure, now."

"Why?" Kate asked groggily.

"Well," Evvie paused for drama and cut a knowing glance at Tilly, "because he's in your bed. You two are sleeping together, and you know what that means." Still whispering in order not to wake Johnny, Evvie grinned teasingly, as did Tilly.

"What?" Kate croaked and turned her head slowly, reached out her arm, and felt a body beside her. Lifting her head painfully, she saw by the tuft of black hair above the covers that it was, indeed, Johnny who lay there. With a soft little *woof*, she sat up. Her head pounded with the effort and every muscle in her body raged in pain. She slid her feet out and into her slippers, and then whispered, "I think I need some coffee or hot tea, so you girls just help me get to the kitchen. And never you mind that Johnny is sleeping in my bed, you hear?"

They nodded, looking at each other and then at Kate, index fingers to their lips. Smirking conspiratorially, they reached for Kate's robe, helped her into it and—with one on each side of her—the three of them silently slipped through the door. Johnny stirred and turned over, snoring softly.

Evvie and Tilly giggled together as they prepared hot tea for Kate, sharing their little secret with each other. Kate knew what they were saying and sighed: *Let them enjoy it,* she thought.

They gave the steaming tea to her in a fancy glass cup. She thanked them, hoping the hot liquid wouldn't sting her lips. She lifted the cup, took a sip, then asked, "Is there still some soup left? I need a pain pill, too."

"Oh, Mama," Evvie wailed, sobering instantly, "talking made your lips bleed. Here, let me get a clean rag to hold against them." She reached into a bottom drawer of the cabinet for a rag, wet it, and began patting Kate's bleeding lips.

"I'll do it," Kate said, flinching from Evvie's tender but rough touch. "There," she said when she had dabbed at the blood to Evvie's satisfaction. "I'll keep the rag here in case I need it again." She laid it on the oilcloth-covered table, picked up her cup, and took another stinging sip. "I would like some soup, though, if there is any."

It was difficult to ask for help. She had always been the helper, and the role reversal wasn't comfortable for her, but it was so much less painful if they did it. She swallowed her pride and carefully sipped her tea, watching. They were such good girls that tears welled in her eyes...or maybe the tears were there because she really was in terrible pain, physically and mentally. She hoped that Victor was hurt as badly as he hurt her. In fact, she hoped he was hurt so badly that he would be in terrible pain for the rest of his life. That's what she hoped.

The soup, which was mostly beef broth, was wonderful, and though it hurt to purse her lips, she swallowed it gratefully. As she lifted the last spoonful, she heard Johnny stirring in the bedroom. Knowing the girls would tease him and her, she prepared herself with appropriate comments that would be acceptable to all of them. She dreaded to think what would happen when the rest of the bunch woke and heard about it.

When he came out of the bedroom, though, he was smiling in such a big way that Kate leaned back in her chair and wondered what was up. She sat and tried to recall the night; she faintly remembered nightmares of Victor hitting her mercilessly and of her fighting him off. And then Johnny's voice had come out of the nightmare, his warm body was next to hers, and then morning had come with Evvie and Tilly beside her bed.

Johnny poured himself a cup of coffee and sat in the chair next to Kate, the girls casting looks from the corners of their eyes. "Kate," he said, "I guess these two found us in a compromising situation this morning, and so I have something to say to you." Kate nodded and waited, silently giving him permission to go on. "Since you are now a compromised woman, I want to make you an honest one and save your impeccable reputation." He paused, carefully took her hand, and asked, "Will you marry me?" Her heart skipped a beat because she and the children had planned to ask him the day before.

Though it was somewhat painful to do, she nodded her head. The girls cheered so loudly that the rest of the household tumbled down the stairs, wanting to know what was going on. When Tilly and Evvie told them the news, the roof came off the house and the kids started dancing, singing, and laughing.

"I guess it's a go," Johnny said. He kissed his fingertips and transferred that kiss gently to her cheek. "Let's get the preacher out here today and get this done," he chuckled with joy.

She shook her head no, but he insisted. She held up her finger and used her other hand to wet her dry lips with the damp rag. "You might consider a marriage license first," she garbled, and pointed to her face. "I look awful and feel awful."

"I don't care how you look. I know how beautiful you are under all those nasty wounds," he replied. "So I'll go get the license and talk to your pastor or the priest, and let's just do it, Kate. Let's just do it!"

"All right," she whispered, "let's do it, but what about our farms and our churches?"

"I have a plan," Johnny said. "We can merge our acreage and, with our big family, I think we can handle it all. What do you think? At least we can give it a try. We'll settle about the churches later."

"Thank you," she breathed.

🦋 🦋 🦋

In the three days required for a marriage license, Johnny accomplished everything that legally needed to be done and Kate pushed herself to get better. She wanted to be able to stand up straight for the ceremony, which her pastor agreed to perform in her home.

Evvie, Tilly, Leslie, Leah, and Amanda spent that time decorating the living room by hanging red-and-white crepe paper stringers, fashioning red paper roses, and baking a white cake covered with a seven-minute white frosting topped with coconut and red rose decorations. They went to town with Johnny and, with his money, purchased Kate a white dress with tiny red flowers and red trim from the most expensive store in town, which was a first for all of them. Although the dress was not what Kate would have chosen for herself—she was much more conservative about her outfits—it fit perfectly and the high neckline and long sleeves covered the angry bruises on her arms and neck. She had to admit, too, that it looked really good on her, and her black church hose and shoes were okay with it all.

Kate enjoyed watching the children in their activities. The girls practiced singing "I Love You Truly" until Kate became tired of it. On the day of the wedding, Tilly and Evvie began early in the morning to help her bathe, curl her hair, and apply make-up. At ten o'clock—with Grant, Betty, Granny Nelson, and the children from the three families combined—Billy and Jerome walked her from her bedroom into the living room, where the preacher waited. As they began the short march, the girls sang their practiced song like angels—which, of course, Kate thought they resembled, all dressed up in their Sunday best.

As Billy and Jerome placed Kate's hands in Johnny's, his smile beamed like a room full of candles. It almost embarrassed her, but she managed to smile a tiny smile through her cracked lips. When he gently kissed her to seal their promises, the wind swept in like a huffing giant, bringing a cloud of brown dust with it. The pair looked at each other, shrugged their shoulders, and smiled. They realized that they had a long, rough row to hoe, but they had each other, their children, and two farms: Somehow they would make it. Johnny and the boys would work both farms, which totaled one-and-a-half sections. Eventually, when the sons married, they could have a share of the two prairie farms. Johnny liked Pastor Dan so well that, at the Pastor's invitation, he and his children became members of Kate's church.

Four weeks later, when Kate's wounds had nearly healed, the neighbors and friends honored her and Johnny with a shivaree, a party to celebrate their marriage. They all brought loads of food and, while the children played outside, the adults played pinochle with three tables of four players each. The two partners who won a round of four hands at one table advanced to the next table. After a certain amount of time, the partners who won the most games won a prize; the table that lost received what was called the "booby prize," a white elephant of sorts.

During the evening a neighbor, Harold, remarked to Kate that he expected her to have another baby in about nine months. She laughed, picked up a fork, and playfully tossed it at him. Much to her chagrin, it stuck in the back of his head like an arrow in a tree, wobbled momentarily, and fell to the floor. The laughter throughout the room drowned out her abject apologies. Midnight came quickly and everybody left in a good mood, congratulating them and wishing them well. When all the guests were gone and the children in bed, Kate stepped into Johnny's arms and said, "Together, we will be all right."

"Yep," he replied. "Together, we'll be just fine." He gave her a solid kiss and said, "Let's go for a walk in the moonlight. The stars are shining and I think Mother Nature has decided that she's done with throwing temper tantrums for the time being. Tonight's the night to walk around this farm, so let's do it." Kate pinned a shawl around her shoulders, Johnny took her hand, and they went out into a still, soft prairie night. They ignored the smell of dust covering the somber land

and the odor of dried vegetation. Instead, they admired the stars. They stood on that open prairie looking up, looking beyond themselves into the depths of a promising future for them, their children, and the land that held them together—like anchors in the wind.

About the Author

Greta Sharp Hemstrom was born in a farmhouse north of Colby, Kansas, in 1932. She grew up in the area, fourth in a family of nine children. After her own children left home, she acquired an associate's degree in Liberal Arts in 1989 from Mesa College (now Colorado Mesa University), Grand Junction, Colorado. Ms. Hemstrom is a musician and a writer and dabbles in oil painting. Her first book published in 2008—*Slates, Chalk, and Inkwells*—is a history of area schools. She wrote biographical articles about local pioneers for the *Olathe Messenger*, a newspaper published in Olathe, Colorado, and many of her poems have been accepted for publication in *Geodes*, a quarterly poetry newsletter produced in Montrose, Colorado. Ms. Hemstrom's second book, *Anchor in the Wind*, is a historical novel and her first work of fiction. She and her husband live in Montrose, Colorado.

CPSIA information can be obtained
at www.ICGtesting.com
Printed in the USA
FSOW02n0820130915
10933FS